Praise for …

THE LOST LOVES OF THE BIBLE SERIES

CHOSEN

"An exciting novel from a talented new author."

Karen Kingsbury, best-selling
author of the Redemption series

"A story that is sure to be a classic! Exciting, dramatic, and filled with truth. A great read from the first page!"

Brock and Bodie Thoene, best-selling authors of
the Zion Covenant Series and the A. D. Chronicles

"This book defies normal boundaries … a truly astonishing first novel."

T. Davis Bunn, best-selling author of *Gold of Kings*

"*Chosen* is a richly detailed retelling of Queen Esther's story. A gem of a read."

Carol Umberger, author of the
award-winning Scottish Crown Series

"Ginger sweeps the sands of time from this figure of ancient history, giving her voice once again—and what a compelling voice it is! To revisit this ancient story is to gain a vision for the contemporary world."

Siri Mitchell, author of *Kissing Adrien* and *Chateau of Echoes*

DESIRED

"Everyone who likes historical fiction will enjoy *Desired*. Vivid and compelling—I loved it!"

India Edghill, author of
Wisdom's Daughter and *Delilah: A Novel*

"To be a woman in the ancient world was a fearsome thing. In this sweeping story of the clash of pagan and God-fearing cultures, Garrett takes us into the lives and hearts of three women who loved Samson, and in the process, she shows us the longing for freedom and purpose in our own hearts as well."

T. L. Higley, author of *Pompeii: City on Fire*

"In *Desired,* novelist Ginger Garrett takes readers on a journey of Samson's life as seen through the eyes of the women who loved him, giving a fresh look at this often confusing hero of Scripture. You will never see Samson quite the same way again.

Jill Eileen Smith, best-selling author
of The Wives of King David series

REIGN

REIGN
The Chronicles of Queen
Jezebel

GINGER GARRETT

1968

David C Cook
transforming lives together

REIGN
Published by David C Cook
4050 Lee Vance View
Colorado Springs, CO 80918 U.S.A.

David C Cook Distribution Canada
55 Woodslee Avenue, Paris, Ontario, Canada N3L 3E5

David C Cook U.K., Kingsway Communications
Eastbourne, East Sussex BN23 6NT, England

The graphic circle C logo is a registered trademark of David C Cook.

The website addresses recommended throughout this book are offered as a
resource to you. These websites are not intended in any way to be or imply an
endorsement on the part of David C Cook, nor do we vouch for their content.

This story is a work of fiction. Characters and events are the product of the author's
imagination. Any resemblance to any person, living or dead, is coincidental.

Scripture quotations are taken or adapted from the Holy Bible, New
International Version®, NIV®. Copyright © 1973, 1984 by Biblica, Inc™.
Used by permission of Zondervan. All rights reserved worldwide. www.
zondervan.com; and from *THE MESSAGE*. Copyright © by Eugene H.
Peterson 1993, 2002. Used by permission of NavPress Publishing Group.

LCCN 2013933124
ISBN 978-1-4347-6596-3
eISBN 978-1-4347-0514-3

© 2013 Ginger Garrett
The author is represented by MacGregor Literary

The Team: Terry Behimer, Nicci Hubert, Amy
Konyndyk, Caitlyn Carlson, Karen Athen
Cover Design: DogEared Design, Kirk DouPonce
Cover Photo: iStockPhoto

Printed in the United States of America
First Edition 2013

1 2 3 4 5 6 7 8 9 10

022813

You who hesitate, cast aside all illusions.

Abba Kovner, "A First Attempt to Tell"

Sacrifice of the Beloved
886 B.C.

Jezebel held her sister by the shoulders at the edge of the fire pit. Priests surrounded her, dancing and calling to the goddess, their red robes stirring the dust, raising a filthy veil around them.

Jezebel's feet slipped near the edge, but she caught herself. The swift movement jerked her sister's limp head up, and Temereh opened her eyes. Jezebel stared at her reflection in the glazed orbs. Temereh's pupils were now huge and black, fully dilated, the last muscles in her body that seemed able to work. Temereh was her identical twin. Together, they would have turned twelve years old in another month.

"What do you see?" Jezebel whispered against her will. She had to know. The sorcerer who had sold her the paralytic drug she had given her sister said that victims often saw the goddess Asherah just before death. The old man meant it as a word of comfort, seeing how distraught Jezebel was. He did not know that Jezebel's grief was not for her sister, not for what had to be done. Not at all. Jezebel grieved instead for herself, for those years when she had been at the mercy of her sister.

The rising white smoke from the fire, burning bright far below, stung Jezebel's eyes, making them water. She blinked hard to scare the tears away; Temereh must not think Jezebel wept for her death.

A confusing stench rose with the smoke, the foul tang of burning hair and sweet roasting meat. Jezebel's heart beat faster.

Temereh's face darkened into hatred, and her lips trembled. She made an odd gurgling noise, trying to spit in Jezebel's face. Her mouth did not work. Jezebel watched, fascinated, then looked around to see if anyone else had noticed. No one else had drugged their sacrifices, though, so they were busy holding flailing children and dragging them to the edge. It still hurt that no one noticed her, not even now. But every family had to sacrifice one child, the most beloved one.

No adult moved to stop Jezebel or save her sister. All were consumed by their own sorrows. Jezebel hated them for that. No one would save Temereh or the other children being sacrificed. No one would stop Jezebel. Jezebel wanted this done, wanted Temereh to die. Temereh deserved to die, because she was the beloved child. But Jezebel wanted to be rescued from the burden of killing her.

Temereh's eyes filled with the old familiar disdain. If Temerah saw the goddess (and Jezebel doubted she would), the miserable liar would keep it from her sister.

Sparks flew upward from a burning tunic as another child was tossed into the pit. Bright orange and yellow flames burst through the roiling white cloud. Heat boiled the skin under Jezebel's fingernails.

It hurt.

Jezebel let her sister go.

Temereh's face never lost its mask of hate as she fell. She didn't scream, though. That was an insult to Jezebel, but then she remembered the drug. Temereh couldn't have screamed. Jezebel sighed in disappointment.

Jezebel looked around as adults stumbled past her, their faces red and swollen from heat and tears. No one congratulated her. From the temple above them, Jezebel heard her father's loud wail. He knew Temereh was dead. He was already mad with grief after their mother's murder. And now, to lose his beloved daughter, to face life with only Jezebel at his side? She was a poor reflection of the child he loved, like a bronze mirror darkened by fire.

Jezebel knew how bitter tonight was for her father, a cruel demand from Baal and Asherah, the god and goddess he served as the highest priest in the Phoenician empire. Her father was powerful, but he wasn't strong. Not strong enough to do this, the ultimate sacrifice required by the god and goddess. She had to be strong for him, even if he didn't love her. Someday he might, if he saw how strong she could be.

Years of abuse at Temereh's hands had given Jezebel that strength. Jezebel had stopped loving her sister long ago, and she learned the hard truth that to feel nothing was to be capable of anything.

The next week, Jezebel followed the priests as they set out to bury the bones from the fire pit. The sacrifice of the beloved was the most honorable sacrifice Baal and Asherah ever demanded, done only in times of great peril and uncertainty. But bones did not burn. Bones never burned. They could only be buried. She knew that from scavenging the trash heaps. She often found bones from the kitchens during her searches late at night, when she was hungry and dared not disturb anyone to care for her needs. Bones were not like the other kinds of trash.

If bones were not buried well, predators came. Six years ago, when Jezebel was five, she had rummaged along the beach where a group of sailors had held a bonfire before departing. No one watched over Jezebel; no one cared for her. She had no gifts, not like Temereh. In the womb, Temereh had sucked everything good from Jezebel and kept it for herself. Jezebel knew that whatever good she found in this world would be by accident, or wit. And the sailors had left good meat on the bones. Jezebel judged the carcass to be a leopard, because of the feline skull lying upright in the sand nearby. She had run her hand through the silky gray ash at the edge of the pit, selecting a delicate bone with plenty of meat and sinew left near the top ridge. She had just sat on her haunches to eat when a snub-nosed hyena with a torn ear wandered onto the beach. Its glittering eyes went to the bone she held, and it began to giggle. It wandered toward her, eyes sweeping side to side as it giggled softly. Jezebel dropped the bone and ran, but the hyena leaped the last distance between them and bit her, hard, on the calf. The bite took months to heal, and Jezebel never forgot the lesson. Bones had to be buried deep, or bad things came.

Now Jezebel was relieved to see the priests go deep inside a cave, dig a pit, and use plenty of dirt, with big rocks placed on top. Sometimes, she knew, they threw bones in the caves and did not bury them, especially if hungry children watched. So this burial was good, she thought. And these bones were useless to anyone, she told herself. There was no meat left.

She wished her legs would stop shaking. The king was dead, but Jezebel had given Baal and Asherah exactly what they had demanded. She had proven herself worthy.

I

Spring, Four Years Later
882 B.C.

Ahab

A lonely howl broke through the muffled noises, the grunts and clatter as twenty men ate their dinner. Prince Ahab looked up from his bowl, over the heads of the men sitting opposite him around the fire. In the distance he saw its eyes, caught in the moon's light, watching him. It was only a feral dog.

Ahab couldn't eat anyway. He set the metal bowl down between his legs with a grunt. Obadiah, his father's administrator, was sitting on his left and glanced down at the bowl, then quickly away. Obadiah had planned just enough rations to get them into Phoenicia tomorrow, but he had counted on every man in the party having an appetite. Neither Obadiah nor Ahab ate much, though. Neither had wanted to go on this trip, and neither had to put their feelings into words. They had known each other since boyhood, and Ahab knew Obadiah dreaded the trip just as much as he did. Ahab wondered if this was what it felt like to be a prisoner of war, forced to march to a

frightening, foreign destination. He wondered what she was thinking tonight, his intended bride; did she feel the same?

Tired of himself and this dread, Ahab picked up the bowl and
walked into the darkness. The dog stood its ground, baring teeth as
hair rose along its back. Ahab set the bowl down and backed away,
startled when a litter of puppies burst from the undergrowth and
rushed to the bowl before their mother. The dog's luminous eyes met
Ahab's. They were too thin, those little ones. They had needed that
meal badly. He hadn't known she had starving puppies to feed. It
frightened him. Even if he did something good, it might have unex-
pected impact. Obeying his father was honorable, but who knew
what might come from it.

It's what the old prophet Elijah had warned him about.

Obadiah stood and walked out to Ahab. Obadiah hadn't touched
his own dinner either and, seeing the dogs, turned on his heel, coming back with his food seconds later. He seemed shocked to see the
stark outline of ribs along the puppies' bodies. Obadiah knew only
about life's cruelty from the many scrolls he read and the stories he'd
heard. Though they were about the same age, at seventeen summers,
Ahab had already killed more men than Obadiah had ever met. The
differences between them were stark.

Obadiah was a Hebrew, a sinewy youth with bright green eyes
and curly brown hair that he combed daily. He kept his robes clean
and his face washed, although there were perpetual dark stains
on his fingers and cuticles from the inkpots he used to keep the
records. His speech was refined, each word well chosen, so that he
was often mistaken for the son of the noble, instead of the son of
a prostitute.

Ahab was not so refined. No one had ever mistaken him for a noble's son, even though he was a prince. He looked like what he was: the son of a legendary murderer, King Omri. His mother had been an Egyptian, and his father, Omri, was a mercenary soldier of unknown breeding. Omri had taken part in a coup and won the crown of Israel. Neither Ahab nor Omri were Hebrew, though, and neither looked like royalty. Ahab had met eight kings in his life, when his father was hired to fight for them, and he knew that traditional princes put attention and effort into their appearance. But Ahab had been raised in military tents, encampments near whatever battlefield his father was on that season. He wore his coarse black hair long, like military men, keeping it pulled back and out of reach. He had dark eyes that startled people with their intensity, just as his father's did. He knew his eyes gave the wrong impression, though. He was nothing like his father, not so fierce and cold. He did not like to watch men die.

He spoke very little around his father or around any older man. When he did speak, he had no distinct accent. He didn't move his hands when he spoke, an old habit from the battlefield that helped him avoid attention, which added to the intensity others thought they saw in him. He had been too young to go into battle that first year his father had forced him along and had tried to keep very still as the arrows shrieked through the air outside his tent. The habit of stillness stuck.

Ahab and Obadiah watched the puppies eat, and then the mother stuck her muzzle into each bowl, licking the sides clean. She looked up at the men, then slunk back into the night, her brood following.

Obadiah used his foot to turn over a rock on the ground. A fat glistening spider scurried out, and Obadiah took a step back. Ahab crushed it with his sandal. Obadiah walked back to the fire, and Ahab looked at the dark horizon to the north. Tomorrow he would be in Phoenicia.

In two days he would meet his bride.

Obadiah

Despite everything he had read, the road to Phoenicia was surprisingly ill kept. For all their legendary knowledge, all their wealth and prestige, Phoenicians kept terrible roads. Obadiah worried that the stories he had read about the Phoenician empire might have been exaggerated. Roads this poor couldn't lead to one of the wealthiest kingdoms on earth. The scouts had to move stones all morning to save the hooves of the animals. Tall green grasses sprouted in clumps right in the middle of the road. The land was infested too. Gnats flew into everyone's eyes, even those of the donkeys and horses, and mosquitoes had left hot red welts on everyone's arms and calves. Obadiah would not say it to any of the men he traveled with, but sleeping inside the Phoenician palace would offer him relief. Even if that palace symbolized the spiritual suicide of his own home, Israel.

Obadiah sighed as the donkey plodded steadily along. He understood the appeal of this marriage, at least when he put it into writing, in the Annals of the King. Phoenicians wanted trade with the southern kingdoms, including Israel and even Egypt. Israel wanted to sell crops and gain access to the greatest maritime fleet in the world. Phoenicians were legendary sailors and boasted the busiest ports with the best goods, but they couldn't grow their own food. Their land, Obadiah had once read, was unsuitable. He understood the words in a new way now, patting his donkey as she tripped over another rock.

Though exhausted from lack of food and poor sleep, he kept careful watch all morning, right past the noon hour, lest one of the younger servants or women suffer injury from a stumbling beast. The official wedding party consisted of twenty men, including the king, Omri; his son, Ahab; and eight of his military officials. The other ten men were elders who could conduct private meetings during the visit and arrange the first series of trades. Obadiah, of course, didn't count himself in the twenty. He offered neither advice nor assistance. As administrator, he was nothing more than an official scribe, and he hardly felt like a man in this elite company. Split between this band of men was a traveling army, half to ride ahead and half to follow behind. He prayed they would not need the security, but when the princess returned with them, it would be a wise precaution.

Four women traveled with them too, daughters of the elders; they would serve as maids for the new princess. They would help her acclimate more quickly and save Ahab from having to explain everything about her new home. One of the women was Mirra. Just thinking that name made his heart tense. He wished Ahab would keep better watch over her, so he would not have to see her face. But Ahab rode near the front with his father, and neither of them ever glanced back. Obadiah reached up occasionally and touched the scar on his cheek. Amon, Mirra's father, had given it to him years ago, when Obadiah was running messages for the court. He had brought a message to Amon, but when he saw Mirra for the first time, he lost all ability to speak. Since he had no ability back then to read or write, the message was carried by mouth. Seeing him mute, Amon backhanded him, striking him with his fat signet ring. Mirra hid behind the folds of her father's robe, her face twisted in sorrow. She had nodded to Obadiah, just once, and lifted the sleeve of her own robe. She was covered in welts. Obadiah grew to love his scar almost as much as he loved her. He had taken her father's fury and spared her one welt.

The wedding party was finally on the last portion of the long march up toward the gates of Sidon, the jewel of Phoenicia, so near the sea that they could smell the sharp tang of brine. The sky darkened, but sunset was hours away. A storm was building. The air took on a heavy, sweet smell; the trees that grew with thatched trunks began waving their fronds in the wind. Where stones had littered the path this morning, he now saw broken shells lining the road. A few of the women stopped and picked them up, clearly delighted. This was a new world to them, too. Mirra did not get down from her donkey. Her father, ruler of Samaria and the richest man in Israel, had already given her every treasure imaginable. But she looked bored. Obadiah knew that serving another woman would be hard for Mirra, pampered daughter of Amon, who was second only to King Omri and his son, Prince Ahab. Obadiah prayed that Jezebel would never hit her.

He scanned the edges of the path as the women turned the shells over and over in their hands. They were surrounded by impassable hills, which he had read should keep them safe from attack, but he had an uneasy feeling. He didn't know how to respond to it, except to look for predators lurking behind the trees. He glanced ahead. The last of the men was still visible, but Obadiah would have to hurry the women along.

He turned to call to them. Mirra was gone. Her donkey had wandered toward a clump of grass and nudged it with his nose, testing it for flavor, perhaps.

Obadiah's heart lurched into his throat.

He saw her walking toward a cave about twenty yards from the path, its black mouth yawning wide. He motioned for the women to remount and join the men. He wanted them with men who knew how to handle a sword. Then he jumped from his donkey and went after Mirra. She had disappeared inside the cave.

He hesitated at the edge of its darkness. A strange sound came from deep within. Inside, he saw Mirra strain her neck in either direction, trying to discern where the sound came from. She did not look surprised to see him entering the cave. Perhaps the wealthy were never surprised to see servants following just behind. But he did not enter the cave because he was a servant. Silent, Obadiah held his hand out to Mirra, willing himself not to tremble at her touch.

She looked at his hand, not moving, and their eyes met. He broke the gaze first, studying the little pool of water that lapped at her feet, illuminated by the light breaking in from above. The only other sound was the steady rasps of his breathing. Obadiah thought he sounded like a brute animal in the darkness. He hoped he did not frighten her.

"I'm not running away," she said. Obadiah looked at her again. She frowned at him, standing there with his hand outstretched. He felt foolish. Other men knew how to command a woman.

"I just wanted a moment to myself," she said, "a moment of

freedom, I suppose. But what could you know about freedom? You're a servant."

The wounds her words inflicted were exquisite. Obadiah's chest burned with the delight of being spoken to, of seeing her mouth form words meant for him alone. If only she had said his name! But she did not know it. She never paid him any attention when she came to court. He had stayed hidden like a good, and invisible, servant, and she had kept her eyes downcast whenever her father presented her to Omri. He doubted she even remembered that day so long ago when he had suffered for her.

She had no idea how beautiful he found her, with her long black hair, unbraided and loose tonight. Her mother was not here to force her to wear it up. She complained to the other girls when she thought no one listened, saying such long hair was heavy and the tight braids gave her headaches. He didn't mean to eavesdrop, but a small traveling party meant he heard a good bit more than he ever had before. Women were full of complaints and completely blind to their own allure—Mirra especially, with her generous pink mouth that he always fantasized was bruised from his kisses. He dreamed of resting a finger against it, of knowing if it was as soft as he imagined.

She turned to move deeper into the darkness. "I heard something."

The air whipping into the mouth of the cave turned cold. It lashed at his calves, picking up the edge of his robe. A great shadow must have passed across the sun at that moment, because the cave turned dark, darker than when they had entered. His flesh crawled for no reason he could explain.

"We have to go back, Mirra. Right now."

She turned her head back to him, a sly grin on her face. "You know my name. Do you belong to my father?"

Obadiah looked at the ground, embarrassed.

Mirra shook her head and stepped away from him again, her foot landing on something that crunched and shifted under her weight. She bent to inspect the material, and Obadiah rushed forward, grabbing her arm. It was a strange instinct. She glared at him, at the insult of a servant's touch.

Obadiah dropped her arm and bent his head.

The floor of the cave was covered in soft, chalky stones and twigs, thousands of little hollow pieces that snapped and disintegrated beneath their feet into fine dust. Obadiah tested his growing dread by taking a few more steps.

Mirra bent down to pick one up and hold it to the light. Fear made his stomach tight and cold. He reached down too, to pick up a tiny flint no bigger than the tip of his finger. It split in two between his thumb and forefinger, a tiny bit of marrow smearing across his fingertip.

"Birds?" she asked. She looked above her for signs of bats. She wrapped her arms around herself.

His eyes grew wide as he picked up another one. It broke in half and fell. He scooped up a handful and held them to the light.

"Oh, no," he groaned.

He held out one tiny speck about the size of a grain of rice. He had to be sure. Mirra squinted to see it.

"Get out!" he commanded. His tone shocked him. He didn't look at her to see what impact it had. Obadiah had read about this before, when disease had struck distant lands and the ground was too hard to dig a grave. That's all this was, surely. He had even read how shrewd merchants scooped up the bones later, grinding them and using them to make the blackest ink. The best ink, and the irony was not lost on Obadiah, whose greatest treasures were his scrolls, written by those long dead. Writing was always tinged with death. He had read so much about death, but never held it.

Obadiah pointed to the mouth of the cave. "Go! Join the others! Now!"

With a huff of outrage, Mirra left. She had not seen the skulls near her feet.

He waited until she was gone to let his knees crumple beneath him. He staggered, still holding the tiny prize. It was the bone of a newborn. Lightning exploded overhead, and in the sudden sharp illumination, Obadiah saw he was standing in a sea of infant bones, burnt and crumbling. A long brown serpent wound its way across the bones, its green eyes glittering.

He could not run for the light, not until sufficient time had passed. He had to prevent the rumor that Mirra had been alone with a male servant. Instead, he stood still, his breath like thunder in his ears, suspicion destroying the weak hope he had held onto for this marriage. The scrolls he had read, the writings that Ahab had rejected in his haste for obedience to his father, had been right. Jezebel's god ate children, hundreds at a time, newborn or youth, drained of blood or burned alive. Worshipping the goddess meant death. Entire generations died through goddess worship. The people called her Asherah, or queen of heaven. Elijah, the most revered holy man in all of Judah and Israel combined, had called her a serpent.

Jezebel

Jezebel ran the edge of the arrow along her arm. No blood sprang up, which was good. Archery was delicate work, requiring the right arrow and perfect aim. She had practiced for three summers to be able to shoot an arrow on her own. At fifteen, she was better than any man in her father's guard. She was glad she would never need those men again.

She walked along the top of the palace wall until she was at the corner, where she had a clear view of the ground below, and where no guards were posted. Her small, nimble feet moved slowly, and she eased each foot down so that she made no sound. Threading the arrow into its groove, she waited.

The bird spotted her from the sky and cried out as it flew past.

Jezebel let the arrow fly too, and the bird fell to the ground, hopping and chirping, one wing dragging through the dust.

"Did you hit it?" her maid Lilith asked, hands over her face. Though required to attend to Jezebel, she would never be compelled to watch.

Jezebel laughed and ran along the wall, down the stairs, and out to the bird, cradling it gently in her hands.

"Sshh," she whispered to it. She opened her thumbs just a bit to look at its head.

Lilith followed, though she was slower and more careful. "It's beautiful," Lilith said.

Jezebel shrugged and walked around the palace wall in the direction of the royal stables, to the first entrance far away from the other animals. This was a private room, where her father had his hunting trophies skinned and cleaned. A long, wide wooden box sat in the corner on the dusty floor. Jezebel unlocked a small square door on top and dropped the bird in.

Lilith swallowed loudly, and Jezebel turned, giving her a withering look. A loud strike jerked the box, and Lilith screamed. Jezebel smirked at her maid's weakness and lifted the lid a few inches to spy inside. She could see thick black coils and an orange head. The colored feathers splayed out from the edges of scaled lips. Death was fascinating.

A conch shell's mellow call broke the stillness in the room. The king's scout signaled that the hunting party was assembling in the courtyard.

Jezebel left the box, knowing she couldn't do anything else until the next morning anyway. The courtyard in front of the palace was a wide circular area that allowed visitors to rest after climbing the steep hill. It wasn't far from the stables, and the path she took was the best traveled in the whole palace complex. She could run here without shoes if she wanted. She had never really gotten used to wearing shoes and fine robes, but never again would she be without them. She had earned them all.

Seconds later, Jezebel bowed before her father, Eth-baal, the king of Phoenicia, assembled with the elders and their useless sons. Her father's appearance still surprised Jezebel. Maybe she still imagined him to be the father she once knew. Eth-baal's long, coarse black hair had been cut off at the shoulders when he became king. He had gotten quite fat in the last three years too, and his black beard had white streaks in it. He wore a lot of jewelry now, and not just the amulet of Pazuza, that demon that rode the winds. Eth-baal also wore a gold collar from Egypt and wide ivory bracelets from the nations below there. He had a ruby ring, a gift from the Sumerians, and it rested like a heavy flower on his right hand.

His voice hadn't changed, though. He had once had to speak for the gods, and he was always too loud, demanding silence and attention. But his eyes had an emptiness, a fixed gaze as if he was watching for something, or someone, in the far distance. His thoughts were forever elsewhere. As was his heart. The elders liked that. They had what they wanted, Jezebel knew: a king they could manipulate. Yet today, when Eth-baal looked at her, he held her gaze, which he never did. He seemed to want to tell her something, but in front of the court, perhaps he couldn't. Instead, he said that the hunt would be a good way to pass the hours. Jezebel had wanted to ask more, but the elders were so restless today.

Jezebel walked to the senior trade adviser, the elder Hetham, and he slipped her worn and fragrant leather vest over her shoulders. It had scratches from the struggles of dying animals and hung very loose, a fact that was not lost on Hetham's son, who nudged a friend and smiled. They exchanged a coarse joke, she suspected, and Hetham's son licked his lips.

Though old enough to bleed with the moon, she was no taller at fifteen than she had been two years ago when she had first bled. She suspected years of neglect had robbed her of length of bone. She stretched her neck, trying to stand tall, and though she could not look the boys in the eyes, she hoped they saw her hand go to the knife tucked in her belt.

Exhaling, she lifted her face to taste the wind and pointed the party to the southeast path into the forest. Lilith glanced at the safe palace above her and then back to them.

Jezebel sighed and moved on without Lilith. Eth-baal followed first, and then the men. An elder's son played a drum made of thick hide stretched across a hollow clay head. He played it softly in beats of three, short grunts that echoed into the woods ahead of them as daylight faded and they went into the world of beasts.

As the hours passed, Jezebel led them deeper into the darkness, her skin tingling with the delight of a moon above and the treacherous, tangled path under her feet. Other sons kept close to their fathers. Jezebel was not so foolish. Men were useless. She loved proving that on these hunts.

The wind carried a surprise, a hint of sweat and pack animals. A traveling party was nearby. Her father had not mentioned that visitors were due, but when she glanced back at the men, they did not seem to notice what she had. The travelers hidden in the forest could be scouts from an enemy in the east. If Jezebel found them, if she protected the kingdom, perhaps then her claim to the throne would be secure. She had earned it a hundred times over already, but maybe this would leave no doubt, even for the most stubborn among them.

She heard a lion's roar as she split from the party and went to investigate. If they were merely traders who brought goods, they would be in danger from the animal. They would be grateful for her protection. Many men did not even know when they were being hunted. When men slept under the moon, in her territories, they slept hard; the land was bewitching. And if she wanted, she could kill them, for any reason at all, and the earth would keep her secrets.

The earth always kept her secrets, every last one.

Ahab

The hair on Ahab's neck raised, and he held up a hand to the men following behind him, who all drew their horses to a quick stop. Birds called above them, and monkeys fled from lower branches to the higher perches. A few threw fruit at the men. Ahab heard a lion growl, but it was moving away from them. Something was hunting it.

Ahab stood very still as leaves rustled in the wind, disguising the sounds of the predator that dared to hunt a lion.

He saw a girl moving through the trees, her bow drawn tight against the gutstring, no more than thirty yards from him. She lifted her head to draw the scent from the wind before she let the arrow fly. With a glance in his direction, her eyes met his, and his heart stopped. It was more than her beauty; he had never seen a girl handle a bow and arrow like a man. He had to know if she'd won the lion. How would she drag it home? What would she do with it?

He jumped from his horse and ran after her. The forest was nothing like his arid home, and he tripped and fell as vines caught his ankles and branches slapped his face. Panting, he leaned against a tree. It was no use, and he knew he had no business trying to follow a girl anyway. He staggered back to his men, torn and bleeding.

That night he slept close to the fire, and the forest fog stole around the men as they made camp, blanketing them in the way of the wild, that bitter mother. Darkness was alive here. Eyes blinked from behind the trees. Throats opened and sang. Footsteps broke through vines and dead wood as the creatures drew closer to smell the people and horses. The horses snorted and circled.

Ahab would miss the sounds of the night. Tomorrow night he would be locked away inside a palace to sleep, unable to hear any noises except those from servants. He would be saddled with a princess. She would be a girl accustomed to fine foods, gentle games, and fawning attendants. She would see life the way a prized house pet did, measuring the quality of her life by its ticklish pleasures. If she had ever been allowed to stand alone under the light of the stars, or run, or scratch her knee upon a rock, it would be a shock to him. He watched as shadows shifted at the edge of the camp. A cloud had passed over the moon. He shook his head, wondering if his reign was already spoiled.

A thick brew was passed around, an elixir they called saddle cure because of its powerful magic, putting a trail-weary explorer to sleep in minutes and soothing sore muscles. The next morning they would feel worse for drinking it, but no man in the wild thought of tomorrow. The animals moving through the underbrush nearby reminded them there might be no need.

So Ahab drew nearest to the fire and let the other men take the outer edges of camp to sleep. He felt a few sparks land too near and brushed them away. He would rather suffer a small singe than a bigger bite. So it was with this expedition. A princess would be given as a covenant between kingdoms. Trade routes would open, a strong defense made against the brutal Assyrians, so restless along the border of his country. The children the princess brought forth would be political collateral.

Ahab spit into the fire, thinking of her, this bride of burden. He sighed and turned over, letting out an exhausted laugh at the thought that a lasting reign would depend on him procreating. After swinging a sword for so many years, this was how he would serve the nation? Israel had begun by brothers taking each other's lives. How odd that it would all lead to a marriage. And odder still was the fact that the Hebrew prophet Elijah had warned that this marriage was evil. Why would Elijah have preferred brothers spilling blood to a marriage?

Hadn't Israel seen enough bloodshed already? Obadiah had told him all the stories. Long ago, King Solomon, the wisest king of Israel, the brightest star, beloved son of David, had died, leaving his son in power. Rehoboam had been that common, terrible brew of stupidity and violence Ahab had seen many times on the battlefield. It was a fatal alchemy. The northern tribes tore away, declaring themselves to be a sovereign nation, Israel. The southern tribes became Judah and clung to the comfort that they alone controlled the temple, the seat of the one they called Yahweh, the Lord, the god of all twelve tribes. If they did not have the allegiance of brothers, or a good king, they at least had that. They had their god.

Now, to build Israel into a true, independent nation, Ahab, the son of a foreign mercenary with not a drop of Hebrew blood in his veins, had to marry a foreign princess. Together they would rule the Israelites. How strange it all was to him. Stranger still that Elijah did not care about his murderous bloodline, only about his heart. If the people's faith had not been enough to keep the tribes together, why did it matter to Elijah that Ahab had no gods?

It was deep into night, as he was dreaming of war and sorrows, when the sparks singed him along his arms. The first one was so slight that Ahab only acknowledged it in his mind and slipped back to sleep. The heat from the fire had kept the night bugs away but made him too warm to sleep in his clothes, so he bundled them up and used them as a pillow, laying his belt next to them. Inside was a bag with earrings and a bracelet for his intended bride. It had been nothing but an annoyance on the trip, reminding him that he would return with a much heavier weight to drag through his life.

He slept naked, glad to have at least that little freedom, covering only his groin and thighs with the blanket. Sparks spitted and poked into his exposed skin along the thick part of his arms and chest. Finally he sat up in disgust, resigned to move away from the fire.

The fire was only glowing embers. There were no sparks.

He heard a soft laugh catch in someone's throat, and he reached for his sword. A hand shot from the darkness and caught his. The creature, on all fours, edged closer and smiled. Ahab froze. It was the girl from the forest, her eyes reflecting the embers. Her lips were dark and sharply edged, though full through the middle. The moonlight made her pale olive skin shine like polished marble, and her hair was hanging loose around her shoulders, brushing against his arm. It had the soft touch of silk. Releasing his hand, she dropped the arrow she had used to rouse him and crawled closer so that her knees were against his hip.

Her long fingers moved across his face, and she closed her eyes when she touched his mouth. She breathed deeply, then looked at him. Taking a knife from her side she held it to his face. He did not flinch. No man in the camp made any sound beyond snoring and turning. Grinning at him, she used the knife to lift the bag of jewels from his belt lying beside him, then sliced it free. He let her take the bag because he wanted something too.

Lifting himself at the waist, he took hold of her at the shoulders and pulled that mouth to his. He kissed her and didn't let go, even when she resisted. Even as he felt her fingernails dig into his back.

Ahab heard Obadiah begin to stir, not three paces from them. The woman sensed his brief inattention and slipped from his grasp. Standing over him, she spit on him and ran into the night with the bag.

He remembered a dream he had once, when he had been a boy, of falling. In this dream, he fell from a very safe place into a deep, cold well where no one could hear him. He remembered how every revolution, every stone that passed by as he fell into the darkness marked the descent. When he awoke the next morning, he saw he had only fallen from the bed as he slept, but he cried anyway. He had wiped his tears with vigor so that his servants would have nothing to report to Omri at breakfast.

He lay back now, looking at the stars, wondering why he had ever been afraid of falling. He had just touched it, that darkness he had always feared. It was only desire, and how could any man fear that?

2

The next morning, Ahab looked up at the shimmering white palace. It sat high above him on the top of a hill, overlooking turquoise waters, guarded by green fir trees and white sea rocks. Shells of every variety lined the walking path that led up to the grand entrance. Omri waited for him at the gate that stood at the mouth of the path. He had ridden ahead with his military advisers yesterday, anxious to meet the Phoenician king and his court. Ahab wondered if Omri was not a little embarrassed by his son and wanted to be sure the Phoenicians had the right impression of Omri first. After all, Ahab knew he was not the strongest son. He was just the only one left alive.

"Leave your mounts here," Omri commanded. "You walk from here."

When Ahab and his men stepped foot on the path, their feet made that curious new sound, crunching through the shells that lined the walkway. The palace was made of ivory and white stone, with two enormous bleached bones used as door handles.

"A palace made from the dead," Obadiah murmured. Ahab suspected the altitude and humidity wore on him, just as much as the adventure itself. Ahab pointed out the serene waters of the

Mediterranean on their left, far below the path. A minstrel could be heard playing the strings near a window above. Obadiah opened his mouth as if to say something, then nodded and moved on. Whatever was bothering him would wait.

A servant at the palace door saw their approach and lifted a huge striped shell to his mouth. The call echoed around them as he ran back inside. Two Phoenician servants sprang out from the doors, causing a few of Omri's men to grasp their swords quickly, and Ahab laughed. The Phoenician servants simply grabbed the tusk handles and held the palace doors open.

King Eth-baal was easy to identify as he walked toward the doorway, wearing a striped robe and a thick gold collar. He had a simple crown, a band of gold that was tucked down around a mass of graying hair. He regarded Ahab with a detached expression. Ahab didn't know what a father felt when he had decided to trade a daughter. This man didn't look like he felt anything at all.

Omri tipped his head, already familiar with the king, but Ahab knelt to King Eth-baal, who bade him rise and extended a hand. It was a symbol of friendship, though the king's eyes were dead. Ahab shook his hand, trying not to wince at the king's sour breath. Eth-baal released him and staggered, reaching out for a palace guard. Blood filled Eth-baal's mouth and dripped from his teeth. Ahab gasped and glared at his father.

Both Eth-baal and Omri caught his expression, but only Omri laughed. The guard offered Eth-baal a cup, and he spit a thatched red paste into it. Then he reached into the pocket of his robe and held seeds out to Ahab. Ahab saw his knuckles were thick and his fingers bent, like trees struck in a storm when they were fresh and green.

"Betel seeds," he explained. "Chewing them eases the constant pain in my hands and knees." He shrugged. "Come, and let me show you the palace."

Eth-baal led the men on a tour of the most magnificent palace Ahab had ever seen. Omri shrugged when Ahab caught his eye, stunned at the wealth displayed all around—the delicate floral ivory inlays; the shimmering bronze statues of fantastic animals, lions, and bulls that lined the halls in every direction; the mosaic of blue and white waves under his feet. The trade routes Omri controlled were truly valuable to merit an alliance with this king. There was no talk of Eth-baal's daughter.

Ahab wanted to ask about Jezebel, when he would meet her, but his father's presence dissuaded him from asking any questions. Omri had little interest in the questions of a seventeen-year-old prince, one who would inherit a throne. Omri had killed for his.

"Your chambers," Eth-baal said, and Ahab realized he had become lost in bitter thoughts, ignoring his host and the tour.

"It's a beautiful palace," he said. "It's my honor to be your guest."

Eth-baal received the compliments with a nod and directed several servants who had been trailing the group to attend the prince.

"Dinner is in six hours. I trust that will give you ample time to bathe and refresh." He nodded again, without expression, and turned away.

Some kings had dozens of daughters and never knew all their names. Maybe Eth-baal didn't even remember which one he had promised. That could be true, Ahab thought, but what troubled him was the lack of life in Eth-baal's eyes. He seemed broken. But how could he be, when Eth-baal ruled so many cities and had so much wealth?

Elijah's warning stirred in Ahab's mind, as it had done several times over the past few weeks, but those words were no use to Ahab now. He had come too far to turn back.

Ahab refused all offers to assist him in preparing for the dinner. He sat for most of the afternoon on his bed, head in hands, feeling dread wash up on him again and again. He had no idea how to please a woman, much less a princess. He had bought a few women after battles and kept a few as concubines, but their duty was to please him. Omri was probably relishing the thought of his son disappointing a princess, one last test to prove again that Ahab, instead of his brother, should have died all those years ago.

Ahab hadn't chosen to survive. The sword had gotten to his brother first, that was all. Ahab knew it would come for him again one day. But this present duty, to marry into royalty and father royal children? Would Ahab ever be done proving to his father, and to the world, that he was a real man?

Later tonight, Ahab would be introduced to his royal bride. He would obey his royal father's wishes and so lose his respect. He would become a very different sort of king. He knew enough about those men to despise them. Kings had hired his father to kill for them. His father said they were not man enough to do it themselves. Kings were no better than eunuchs, he said. They didn't have what real men had. Omri had set out to make Israel into a military nation, to show kings what a real man did when he wore the crown. A real man didn't need a son to bring respect to his name. Ahab would, and Omri never had.

Ahab had chosen to be loyal to his father, even if it cost him respect. The irony was that, according to Elijah, his loyalty provoked the god of Israel, the same god who had commanded that a son must honor his father. Did no one care that this god was full of contradictions?

A servant came to escort Ahab to dinner, and Ahab was surprised to find Obadiah standing outside the door, a thin sheen of sweat visible on his forehead. Obadiah looked nervous, as if he had something important to say, so Ahab held up a hand to the servant and nodded for Obadiah to speak.

Obadiah mumbled a few syllables, twisting his lips, as if searching for the right words. That was not unlike him. He lived for words. He lived through them and with them too. Ahab shifted his weight from foot to foot.

"The Phoenicians invented the alphabet," Obadiah said finally.

Ahab stared at him. This could not be what he really wanted to say.

"I needed you to know that," Obadiah said, rushing now. "I value their contributions. I would not slander their culture." At this, he stopped, having either exhausted his thought or his courage.

Ahab moved on, pausing only to pat Obadiah on the shoulder. Whatever his trouble was, it could not compare to what Ahab faced. Obadiah slumped against the wall, defeated, but Ahab knew he would catch up in a moment. After all, this was a royal dinner in a foreign palace. Some things were meant to be experienced, not read about. As palace administrator of Israel, the servant highest in command, Obadiah had overseen all royal events but never attended a royal wedding.

Ahab was led past four bronze columns to the entrance of a temple. Inside, the torchlight reflected across white stone walls inlaid with opals and polished shells. The room glittered, alive with beauty. Three rows of polished cedar tables with ivory borders of vines and flowers were laid end to end. At the head of the rows was a massive table where Omri and Eth-baal sat, facing the guests. Ahab saw his men already seated at their tables and probably already half drunk.

Behind his father and Eth-baal, at the far end of the temple, was an elevated stage. There was an altar for sacrifices, made of gold, with tusks at each of the four corners, the sharp edges curving up over the center of the altar. Ahab did not know what Phoenicians sacrificed to their gods. Some gods liked grains; some preferred coins. Judging from this temple, these gods wanted only the best.

Next to the altar was a bowl that sat upon a stand. The stand had two rings in front in which to place torches. If these gods liked incense, he guessed that was the bowl to burn it in. Ahab was seated next to Omri, and as he took his seat, the musicians began.

Men carried drums made from tanned and stretched hides, beating the instruments with one hand as they began a low chant of two notes, high and low. They lined both walls of the temple. Dancers flowed from between the bronze pillars, weaving their way through the men, sheer veils wrapped around their bodies, trailing behind them in the air. Ahab found the dancers to be beautiful, which gave him hope. Maybe his bride would look like them, instead of the wild boar with brown tusks that he kept imagining. He pushed his bowl of beer away, his stomach knotting up, then decided he needed all the courage he could find to get through the dinner, even if that courage gave him a splitting headache in the morning.

A crescendo roll of thunder from the drummers signaled the arrival of the priest of Baal, the storm god, husband of the goddess

Asherah. Obadiah shifted noticeably in his seat, trying to communicate his panic to Ahab with his eyes. Ahab frowned at him to be still, to not offend their host. The priest was a white-haired man draped in purple linen with a sash of gold rings around his thick waist. He wore the crown of the priest on his head, a simple gold band with serpents woven around it.

The priest lit the incense in the bowl on the stage. Thick gray smoke rose, and Ahab caught the strange scent of a pungent balm, like a burning flower.

"My name is Sargon, representative of Baal, servant of Asherah. Pray and beg favor from heaven!" the priest commanded. Servants around the room fell to their knees and chanted the request. Ahab's men looked at each other and him. A few raised their eyebrows. Obadiah looked like he was about to vomit. Maybe it had been a mistake to bring the administrator on this journey.

"We beg the god and goddess to bless the union between kingdoms! We ask for overflowing abundance and great wealth! And peace from our enemies!" Sargon lifted his hands and chanted in a tongue Ahab did not know.

"Only a priest would ask for those things together," Omri whispered. "A warrior knows that the rich always get attacked. Doesn't matter who they worship."

The temple fell deathly quiet. Ahab heard crickets singing outside and dogs howling in the forests beyond the fragile walls of the temple. Looking around the edges of the room, he noticed chimes made from bones strung together that danced as a gentle wind from the beach blew through. Sargon lifted his hands above his head, and the Phoenicians in the room all bowed their heads in prayer.

Obadiah stood to leave. Ahab pointed to his chair. It was a command. Then Ahab bowed his own head lest he offend Eth-baal, who was plucking grapes from a bowl, looking bored. Ahab wondered if this was the moment Jezebel would be offered to him.

With his eyes closed for a moment of relief, he could not deny the horrid pounding of his heart, as scared to meet his bride as he had ever been on the battlefield. He would rather die, he thought suddenly, than take a wife. He wished he had drunk more beer, a lot more. He should have started drinking much earlier. His body seemed too small, his skin too thin to contain all the noise and agony inside.

Ahab felt the hairs along his arm rise as a heavy hissing noise slithered along the floor and soft fur brushed against his leg.

"Behold the mighty, fallen by Jezebel's hand," Sargon yelled. "His strength is ours tonight."

Ahab opened his eyes, unable to breathe at the mention of her name. He could not see her in the room. He clenched his teeth, suspecting there was a reason for the delay. Maybe they wanted Ahab drunk too, so they could present the ugly woman. Although he had heard that she was two years younger than himself, which would make her fifteen, so he should think of her as an ugly girl and not an ugly woman.

Servants had dragged a dead lion into the temple, past the king and onto the stage, leaving a wake of blood behind them. They lifted the animal onto the altar. Sargon raised his knife as an offering to the statue of Asherah before slitting the throat of the lion, blood raining down, red against gold. Servants used bowls to collect the blood and began circulating the cups to the men at the tables. All were expected to drink it. Ahab refused to look at Obadiah, afraid Obadiah would beg permission to leave. Obadiah would never drink blood. Another odd command from the Hebrew god, who believed in spilling blood but never drinking it, preferring that the strength of his enemies be wasted on the earth.

The drums grew louder as Sargon blew a fine powder into each torch. They exploded into blue and purple sparks across the stage, arcing over the royal table. Sargon waved smoke from the incense bowl down onto Ahab, its thick sharp scent staining the moment into Ahab's mind forever. He was shrouded in animal musk and the tang of blood in the air as he caught his first glimpse of her.

"Behold the Princess Jezebel!" Sargon called.

She rose from behind the altar. Ahab was always aware of his surroundings, yet he had not seen her come in, and this unnerved him as much as the recognition that followed. She was the girl from the forest, the one who had stolen his bag and from whom he had stolen a kiss.

He saw his jewels draped on her arms and dangling from her ears, but she was covered in many other jewels; ropes and strands wound around her body from neck to thigh. Heavy gold chains wound down her arms, with dangling ropes of rubies extending from her wrists to the ground. When she lifted her arms to bless the crowd, the rubies formed red wings that swept across the floor. She wore no clothes; against the torches she appeared as a wild, glittering red bird. The thick black curls of her hair climbed down her back. Her eyes were lined in black, each painted line extending from the corner of the eye all the way across into the hair framing her face. Her lips were painted red, brown lion's blood drying slowly in the creases where her lips met.

Then Eth-baal rose and gestured to her. "I offer my daughter, Jezebel, in marriage to the house of Omri, to his son, Prince Ahab of Israel."

Ahab rose, arms extended to accept her. She froze, her eyes on her father, who turned away and stumbled from the temple. When she looked back at Ahab, the violent flash of hate in her eyes was unmistakable. He barely heard the murmurings of the other guests, the Phoenician men especially. She surveyed the room with a cold fury, her back noticeably stiffening.

Some inner decision made, the red angel descended the stage, walking to Ahab, her mouth set in a hard cruel line. She walked to him and kissed him on the mouth, symbolizing her acceptance of the union. She took some of his lip in her mouth and bit. Ahab pulled back in shock as the room erupted in cheers. Only Ahab sensed what that kiss really was: a hard promise of pain. Jezebel didn't want this union any more than he did.

Ahab glanced to see if Omri had noticed the princess's immediate disdain. Omri sat back down, unconcerned. Omri had repeatedly said that he'd long forgotten the touch of any woman and had never chosen to remember. He acted as if he hated women, but Ahab knew the truth. Omri had loved just once, and it had destroyed all that was human and whole about him.

"Teach the gods how to love!" Sargon commanded the guests.

From the corner of his eye, Ahab saw Obadiah flee the room. Ahab kept his full attention on his bride, though he saw dancers disrobing and his men doing things with women they had only bragged about. Sargon urged them to make love and celebrate the freedom and pleasure of Baal and Asherah.

Ahab reached for Jezebel, unsure of what he was to do, if he should remove her robe of jewels in front of everyone, to lead this strange ceremony. She moved with the blinding speed of a sword, catching his hand and biting it hard. This time, blood sprang up, smearing across her face as he jerked his hand back. She stood, defiant, her eyes blazing.

Did she think he meant to hurt her? He held up a finger, as if to call for peace, and then slowly moved it toward her face. She did not flinch or pull back. He used his finger to wipe her cheek. His touch was deliberate and soft, the way he would treat a frightened, wounded child on the battlefield, one that spoke a language he did not know.

She stared at him, unmoving, but a flicker of hunger passed through her eyes. He knew hunger, but he was surprised that she did too. What did she hunger for? It was not for him; he could see that in her eyes too. He displeased her somehow. She had no choice but to accept him; she was a girl, and a royal. Could that be the reason for her hatred of him?

There was no doubt, from her expression—she had been forced to become his bride, and she did not want him. She didn't care what he could give her as prince of Israel. She needed something entirely different, but what she wanted was a mystery. She showed her hunger when he touched her kindly. Perhaps no one had ever dared touch her before. But she was a vicious girl. What man would want to touch her? A man could save a woman from any enemy, except herself.

A dark memory shook his heart. Ahab had failed to save his brother. But this was not a battlefield, and there were no real enemies here, just a frightened, angry bride and a reluctant husband.

Ahab had never fought for himself; he had always fought for others, and in another's name, but when he looked at her, he knew this fight was his. He would prove Elijah's warnings wrong and his father's disdain an error, and he would please this girl.

Jezebel

Six Years Prior
888 B.C.

Most nine-year-olds were not allowed at the temple during sacrifices. But Jezebel was not like most nine-year-olds, especially not those who had loving parents and a familiar place to sleep. Jezebel's father, the highest priest in the land, was embarrassed by Jezebel, it seemed to her. Her identical twin, Temereh, got to sleep with their father and mother in the temple's living quarters, but Jezebel had to beg for a bed among the servants. Some cared about her tale of woe; some didn't. But they determined where she slept, and sometimes she didn't get to sleep at all. She wandered through the city streets at night, peering in windows, rummaging in trash. One time she found a broken statue of the goddess, the feet snapped off, but she wrapped her in her sash and carried her about for comfort. She told herself the goddess meant comfort, and she wanted to believe that. Baal and Asherah were worshipped, god and goddess, like husband and wife, but girls were supposed to worship Asherah most of all, because Asherah symbolized the sacred feminine. Asherah symbolized all women, and all that women could aspire to be.

Asherah was the promise that someone would love her, maybe even pat her head or stroke her cheek and see something remarkable in her. All women were honored in Asherah's name, and so Jezebel knew her time would come too.

Her sister, Temereh, didn't have to wait. At her birth, a sacrifice had been burning on the altar to Baal when the priest spied the dark-haired child emerging. Temereh was born face down, her arms crossed. News spread throughout the empire, for this birth was a mighty sign from the heavens. Temereh would be able to speak to the gods and goddesses, and they would listen and respond. She would have visions of the future, of their enemies and what they planned. The Phoenicians would grow even more powerful. For nearly ten years now, Jezebel had suffered for her sister's gift. There was nothing Jezebel could do to change that.

Jezebel had been born second, and as she emerged she was assumed to be nothing but the afterbirth. Temereh loved to tell that story. Jezebel had almost been tossed into the fire. Her mother was exhausted, and Temereh was already in their father Eth-baal's arms. Jezebel had been passed off to a startled servant with her first cry. Besides, the sacrifice was for one child, not two. Jezebel was born unloved by men and gods alike.

Jezebel did not cry anymore. And tonight, the sounds of pleasure and joy from the worshippers inside the temple stabbed her heart. Jezebel pleaded to Asherah, begging the goddess not to be indifferent, not this time. How many times had Asherah ignored her? What could Jezebel do to be special, to be noticed? She wanted to be wanted more than anything in the world, but the harder she tried to earn affection, the more distasteful people found her. She was nine years old, and the thought of decades of life stretching ahead strangled her with frustration.

The sounds of dancing and wine had stopped. The rue seeds had probably been ingested and the visions begun. She heard the worshippers move on to the high place, the tallest point on the hill, outside the temple. They were bringing infants to die at the hand of the priest. Maybe it was her father who held the blade tonight; maybe not. She had not seen him in days.

Jezebel wandered through the quiet temple to the lamp of the eternal flame, a low room off to the side of the temple that was littered with clay statues of dead or broken children. The room had a closed, musty smell of clay and old incense. The floor was cold tile, and Jezebel wrapped her tunic closer in. This was the saddest room in the temple to some, but to her, it felt like the only home she had ever truly been able to claim.

When a child in Phoenicia was born with a great infirmity, or was ill beyond cure, the parents made a clay replica of the child and placed it here before the god and goddess, so that the heavens would be mindful. If Baal or Asherah should become bored or listless, they might choose to step down from their throne and heal, and a certain clay replica might catch their eye and receive the blessing. Sometimes, when no one was watching in the temple, Jezebel slipped in here and sat among the clay children. Just in case a god came down. She had so many questions, so many wounds. Couldn't there be a cure for those, too?

Statues were placed here month after month. No one ever came back to remove one, and hundreds were piled against each other, some of the heaviest ones crushing the ones beneath. Jezebel considered the clay children tonight, with their empty eyes and hollow mouths. Why was there no answer, not for them and not for her? She sat, her back against the wall, and reached for one, cradling it in her arms.

A noise startled her.

A mother was bringing her offering to this place, but Jezebel saw at once that this child was real, not clay. It squirmed and mewled from inside its blankets. The mother did not notice Jezebel.

"What are you doing, mother?" Jezebel asked, setting the clay statue aside and standing. The woman jumped, and her eyes quickly found Jezebel sitting among the ruined children, but she could not answer. She just choked back a sob and laid the child near all the clay ones. Jezebel came closer. She moved the blanket to see the little face. The child was perhaps a year old, though it was hard to tell from its emaciated face. Its eyes were sunk deep into the face, and its skin had a yellow cast, even in the dim light of this room.

"She can't eat," the mother said. "I try. But she can't hold it down. No one has been able to cure her, and I've taken her to every healer in the land. I've sold everything I have. She can't eat." The woman sounded utterly defeated.

"The father?" Jezebel asked. The mother shook her head. She had most likely conceived during a worship rite, Jezebel guessed. Most women went into those events knowing beforehand what they would do if they conceived, but this poor woman had held on to her child too long. She had grown attached. Jezebel saw how awful the pain of becoming attached could be. Women needed to be free, above all else.

Every woman gave herself, as the goddess would have her do. Any attempt to inhibit or restrain female desire was nothing more than an attack on the goddess herself. That's what her father had taught. The sacred feminine was honored when women lived such free lives, and unwanted babies could be easily sacrificed.

"Don't leave her here," Jezebel whispered. "Give this child to Asherah. But don't leave her."

The mother shook her head and began to weep. Tears ran down her face, staining her faded robes.

"Please don't let her suffer," Jezebel said, her chin trembling and a strange pain piercing her heart. She felt as if she were speaking to her father.

Jezebel led the woman by the hand as she cradled the child. The feast for Asherah continued on the high place, naked bodies spent, food passed around on fat platters, but all grew quiet when they saw the two approaching. Tears streamed down the mother's face as she approached the stone altar. Jezebel gripped her tightly, whispering words of comfort only the mother could hear. Her father was not there.

Sargon, the second highest priest, stepped forward and took the child, his eyes meeting Jezebel's. He was older than her father by a few years, but his hair had always been white, for as long as Jezebel had known him. She had always thought of him as old, and she had always wondered what secrets he kept. He was a quiet man, but she saw kindness in his eyes, and sometimes, she thought she saw sorrow, too.

With the baby in his arms, he turned, bowing before the statute of Asherah, the mother of the earth, of the gods and all creation. She stood twenty feet tall over them, made of white stone, with great naked breasts and a round protruding belly. Her arms stretched straight out, coming together at the hands, and there was an empty place where her womb would have been. Her face had hollows for eyes, too, and a hollow mouth, but no other features, nothing to hint at her disposition toward mortals.

"Great mother, look upon this child given to you. Turn your face to us at last, Asherah! Receive this child, offered in the name of the goddess."

Jezebel's heart beat faster. She had seen sacrifices, but always from a distance. She could reach out and touch the baby if she wanted to. Surely Asherah would turn her face to them now and reveal herself. Jezebel would ask why some children were born to be unloved.

Sargon made a soft swift movement of his arm. The mother wailed and collapsed to her knees, beating her fists against the earth tamped down around the altar. Jezebel fell beside her, wrapping her frail arms around the woman. "Your child was so blessed!" she whispered in her ear. "She will never suffer again. You saved her. You are so strong!"

Sargon's servants stepped behind the statue and lit a fire in Asherah's belly. It shot up through the statue so that the dead eyes came alive with yellow and moved. The priest took the lifeless dripping body and laid it into the arms of Asherah. The body rolled slowly down the arms and into the belly, a womb that consumed what another had nurtured. Jezebel stood transfixed. The heat grew with a snapping and hissing noise from the womb. The statue glowed white, the hidden wax plugs melting, milk pouring from the breasts. Jezebel opened her mouth and risked the heat to be blessed. She wanted to be first, but men in the crowd shoved her to the side, trampling her as Sargon called to them all.

"Receive what the Great Mother will bless you with!"

Jezebel crawled away, with bleeding scrapes on her knees and arms. She almost cried. The grieving mother stumbled away, wailing a prayer to the goddess, and the name of the man who had not wanted the child. Jezebel felt a blinding rush of tears sting her cheeks.

The tears had sneaked out without her permission. She beat her head against the earth until they stopped. She would split her head like an egg before she accused the goddess of wrongdoing.

Jezebel

Jezebel had led the prince to a room called The Chamber of Dreams, telling him she would return within moments. She commanded two servant girls to attend to him, not caring what they attended to first. She heard his protestations as she ran down the hall. She knew where her father would be hiding. Was this what he called power, hiding from the past in his bedchamber? From her? From those hungry ghosts, her murdered mother, and the bones of her sister, who cried out in dreams from a deep and crowded pit? Jezebel wondered all that, making the accusations in her mind dark so she wouldn't allow herself to consider the worst one of all. She had participated twice now in the fertility rites, twice now giving herself to men who wore masks and didn't care that her head pounded against a marble altar, breaking and bleeding as they panted into her neck. She gave the goddess everything. She held nothing back, nothing for herself.

And nothing had changed. Her father interrupted her when she spoke, often leaving the room in the middle of her stories, communicating to her through servants or scribes. He did not invite her to take meals with him, and he did not attend the ceremonies she presided over as the royal princess of Phoenicia. If she couldn't earn his love, she had reasoned, nor the love of Asherah, she would just try harder. She had tried very, very hard. But this last betrayal was too much.

Jezebel pushed past the guards and threw open his door. Ethbaal grunted as he saw the light from the hall cast across the bed.

"What have you done?" she shouted.

He sighed, rolling over and sitting up with some effort.

"You wanted to prove you were worthy," he replied. "The elders thought this was the best way."

"So they banished me?" she yelled. "You let them send me away to be nothing more than a wife?" The word stuck like a rock in her throat. "Don't do this! I will make a better ruler than any son in the empire, and you know it. They all know it!"

Then it hit her, a sudden drop in her stomach. "They all know it," she whispered. Of course. The elders had planned this all along. She had been nothing more than a rabbit for their hunt, to flush out the best among them. It was probably Hetham's son. It had probably been decided long ago. Though a woman could be elected to the throne, none ever had. None ever would. Not as long as men like the elders were in control. They worshipped the sacred feminine but did not want a woman in command. Jezebel's flash of insight was so cruel, it had to be wrong.

She sat on the bed next to her father, the life sucked from her body. She had fought so hard, for so long, to prove her worth. To wear the crown. And all along, it had never really been within reach.

She shook her head. "I made a promise to myself, that if a son from the elders won your approval and the crown instead of me, I would kill myself." She was surprised how ridiculous it sounded now. She wanted to live. The desire was strong. It was a strange discovery—that wanting to die didn't mean she was ready for death.

"How would you do it?" he asked, a desperate hinged note in his voice, as if he was not really entirely in the room with her.

She glared at him, at those horrid betel seed stains across his mouth and chin. He was in agony, and she knew it had nothing to do with his sour stomach or arthritic hands. She was all he had left of Temereh and her mother. Nothing could save him from the torment of letting this last little part of them go. He thought surely he could hide it from her even now. His emotions had ruined him, and her, too. If he had only kept control of himself, her life would have been different. He had always been weak, though, and she had paid that price for him. Always.

Jezebel

Jezebel lifted the snake from its cage. Her father had betrayed her. Though it would be the last betrayal, it still stung like a fresh burn, even after three days since Ahab's arrival. Her father had so frequently hurt her, the wound was never allowed to heal.

Now she had a gift to give him before she left. She did not want to do this in front of his servants, but it would be better for everyone if they watched. They needed to know. She laughed silently, realizing that even now she sought to prove herself to him.

A lump was evident in the snake's midsection, the previous meal not yet fully digested. She slowly lowered it into the open sack and picked it up using both hands because of its weight. She walked from the stables into the palace, ascending the stairs toward her father's bedroom.

He was just waking, the maids tending to him like a flock of nervous pigeons that scattered with her entrance. One of them eyed the bag with a dark scowl. Eth-baal saw it too and struggled to sit up. He grimaced, but whether it was from pain in his joints or grief at seeing her again, Jezebel didn't know. It would be over soon anyway. She was done trying to understand him.

She stood at the foot of his bed and lowered the sack to rest near his feet.

The serpent's head emerged from the sack first. The servant girls cowered in the corner, whispering in their own language. Jezebel watched as the beautiful animal slid from the mouth of the sack, gliding back and forth slowly across the linens.

King Eth-baal turned his head and would not look his daughter in the eye. She saw his chest moving rapidly up and down. His face betrayed nothing, however, no emotion. Her throat grew icy and tight from the pain of disappointing him, even now, when she was prepared to sacrifice so much for him.

"I was told that I must leave by tomorrow," Jezebel said. She hadn't seen Ahab since the feast, and it had taken a good deal of skill to avoid him.

Eth-baal did not reply. The snake moved alongside his thigh, which was hidden under the bedclothes. He refused to acknowledge it.

"You don't even know what you're losing," she said quietly, her voice barely a whisper. It roared in her ears.

"I lost everything that mattered years ago!" His chin moved as he spoke, but he would not look at her. The snake, however, watched him, growing very still near the fleshiest part of his thigh, hidden under the thin sheet. It began curling its body into a tight curved pattern. She felt the truth tightening up inside her, too, coiling, and her gut constricted violently, forcing words out in a spitting rush.

"The sacrifice of the beloved calls for a beloved child to die," Jezebel said. "If you had loved me, Father, even a little, even the slightest hint, I could have died in her place. I would have done that for you. But you didn't love me, and so I couldn't die. It was you and Mother, your love, and your hatred of me, that doomed Temereh."

"Get out!" he screamed, slapping the bed with his gnarled hand. The snake struck at once, sinking its fangs into his thigh. The king bent his head back, swallowing another scream. The snake released him and curled back onto the bed. Little pools of blood rose up on the sheet. Her father opened his mouth, gasping for air, looking at her with wild eyes. He tried to say something, but his words were caught in his fast-swelling throat. She thought he said, "Demon." His frantic gaze went to the statue of Asherah on his bedside as if trying to tell Jezebel something. Reaching out, he knocked it to the floor and slid from the bed.

King Eth-baal collapsed onto the floor, and the servants scurried to claim him and nurse the wound. They glared at Jezebel. Though they had surely heard of her strange treatments, none had ever witnessed it.

"It's an old Sumerian cure," Jezebel said, her voice sounding hoarse and old. "I traded a royal stallion for the secret. The venom will have its full effect within the hour, and his joints will be freed from the arthritis. He will feel much better for a few weeks. But see to it he never does this more than once for every cycle of the moon, or the venom will kill him. And always feed the snake first so that she will not use her full strength. I leave them both in your care."

Jezebel crossed the room and bent to kiss him on the cheek, like Temereh always used to do. Jezebel could be bold like that today, because she was leaving forever. He couldn't hurt her anymore. She inhaled the air in the room to try and capture something of him to carry with her into the strange future. She didn't smell him, though, but instead her sister and mother, something of the softness they once had. She pulled back with a frown, uncertain if it was some trick of his.

He was slipping away into unconsciousness as she walked out the door for the last time. But then, he had always been lost to her.

Ahab

Jezebel's caravan would stretch further than the length of Israel's capital city—this is what Omri had said in disgust. Ahab concurred, but said nothing. It was taking more than a hundred servants to prepare for her departure.

Omri left Phoenicia after the first army division headed for Samaria, taking five of Ahab's favorite men with him. He intended to spite Ahab, but Ahab was thankful for a reprieve from Omri. He left two days after his father.

Ahab was riding with Obadiah and eight other men, plus several pack mules and two attendants for cooking and tending the animals. It was about an hour after they left the palace, when Ahab stopped to remove a rock from his horse's hoof, that he turned and saw. The caravan of the princess numbered forty covered chariots.

Obadiah had stopped alongside him. "Most of them are for her priests."

How much could he say, Ahab wondered, without revealing his inadequacies? "I had not realized her gods meant so much to her."

Obadiah paused as if considering whether to add something painful to the conversation. Ahab waved him off. He did not need more trouble. He had assumed when he first entered Phoenicia that the princess he acquired would be willing, if not happy, to be married. He had not anticipated her wrath, although her resistance was strangely inspiring. Maybe this was what he had hated all along about this whole arrangement between the fathers; it was too easy. Ahab had grown up fighting. He needed to fight for this, too. It was an insult to just be given a wife. Ahab would win this one.

He looked forward to the battle.

He and his men had all been overwhelmed by Phoenicia, with those salacious women who were nothing like the Hebrew girls back home, and he wondered if any of the men felt relief, like he did, to be heading home. Phoenician dancers wore sheer veils and little else, and they gave themselves to men as a form of worship. So astonishing was the perversion that his men had not stopped pestering Ahab about his own experience, his first night with his princess.

"We envy you! She is so beautiful!" one of his men said. "We are surprised you have the strength for the trip home."

All but Obadiah laughed. Obadiah had been silent and pale since he first entered Phoenicia. Ahab pondered why leaving did not relieve Obadiah of his secret burdens.

Ahab was content to let all conversation die away, though. He had a secret of his own; he had received nothing on his wedding night but a vicious bite to the hand. He had been ushered into a room reserved for special visitors, where two young girls had attempted to entertain him, and their efforts had begun with disrobing. It had angered him. Did Jezebel think he was a blind man who could be content with any woman? He shoved them from the room, ignoring their sharp cries of pain from his grip on their bare arms. Alone, he waited in the room until he was sure they had given up on returning, then wandered through the palace until he found his chamber. Once inside, he had not slept well, stirred by a restless confusion of guilt and frustration and relief.

On the far horizon ahead, he spotted the first fires of the evening, which meant that Omri and his men were done traveling for the day. Omri lacked the stamina of his son, Ahab realized with a start. Omri was getting old. Ahab had never believed that could happen, but now he suspected Omri wanted to travel ahead so Ahab would not see him weary and anxious to return home. Omri had wanted to see the marriage happen, even if the trip was hard for him. He seemed determined to keep up with everything unfolding in the kingdom, but Ahab had not understood. Now he did. Aging had forced Omri to acknowledge how fast everything else moved.

"Call it," Ahab commanded to Obadiah. "We camp here tonight." He would grant himself peace from his father at least.

❧

The night air was pleasant, but a sheen of sweat covered his forehead. Ahab could feel it trickling down his chest as he walked back toward Jezebel's caravan.

Jezebel's covered chariots and litters had been brought to rest in two large half-circles. Each had a fire pit in the making; Jezebel's servants were running about in the underbrush, looking for fuel sources, chattering among themselves in a language only they knew. Ahab called to them to warn them of vipers, and a few nodded at once in thanks. Judging from their dark skin, darker than even Jezebel's, he guessed they were from the lands below Egypt. Some hurried back with dung, which made excellent fires, except for wolf dung, a lesson that Ahab had learned the hard way years ago. His father had beaten him for the mistake.

Ahab walked on, lifting leather straps and peeling back linen chariot veils, searching for his bride. Faces peered out at him from beneath folds of fabric draping over the litters, priests with painted eyes, expressionless, and servant girls with eyes rimmed red from tears. When he saw Mirra slip from a caravan, off on an errand of her own, he knew he had found Jezebel, too. A sudden rush of nerves made sweat stick, cold, to his back. He shivered and approached, his hand trembling as he reached for the veil, the same way it often shook on the eve of battle.

Jezebel was lying on cushions, alone. No servants remained after Mirra had gone out, a breach of security and protocol, but he suspected she might have commanded them to leave.

A feast had been spread at her feet, two great bowls of wine balancing on a tray of silver edged with inlaid pearls. Surrounding the tray were platters of fresh grapes and honey cakes and slivers of roasted lamb. It was not the food he usually ate when traveling. She traveled like a princess, even if she didn't act like one.

Jezebel wore a long gown of threaded gold, a thousand tiny ropes woven together, which slipped loosely across her body and glittered in the air as she raised her hand to him, denying him entrance. He entered anyway, the veil falling behind him. She watched him with the stillness of a cat, as if judging the right moment to strike.

He refused to cower. Instead, willing himself to breathe deeply and slowly, he lowered himself to her side, brushing against her. She was thunder in his veins, his skin burning where it had touched her. She had bitten him and that had hurt, but this gentle accidental touch stung just as much. Obadiah once told him an old Hebrew legend, that Yahweh had created one being and then separated it into male and female, and set each on earth to find the other. When they did, they married, and marriage reunited the whole, completed Yahweh's work again. Did others feel this too, when they found their missing one?

Ahab had not expected to rejoice over a bride, but flinching when he touched her was not what he had expected either. Omri would be thrilled to know his son was baffled by a woman. It would prove him right about Ahab. Ahab wondered if defending his own name was the real reason he wanted to win over Jezebel. Omri would know then that his son had done what Omri never could: make a woman happy.

"Israel gets port cities established by Phoenicia." She began their very first conversation. "And access to the finest fleet in the world. Phoenicia will get access to the King's Highway and all trade routes, even those that lead to Egypt."

Ahab nodded. "My wife states the agreement well."

Jezebel frowned, acknowledging the word *wife* as if it were an insult. "But I do not understand—what do you get?"

"I have concubines when I want them, a few lesser wives given as gifts. I don't need another woman in my house. Few men do."

He paused, acting uninterested, hoping she did not notice as he rubbed his palms on his thighs. He was sweating as if in a furnace.

She turned her head so that she could look him in the face. Her eyes blazed wide and then narrowed as she scrutinized him. *"What do you get?"* she repeated. It sounded like a threat.

Ahab's mouth fell open as his mind stumbled through a few possible replies. He had never met a woman who spoke as if equal to a man. Maybe worshipping a goddess had this affect. If so, he didn't know why men allowed it. Until he remembered the dancers. Men would allow a lot of back talk for those kinds of women.

"Did your father make an alliance with the elders?" she asked. "Or did you?"

"King Omri and King Eth-baal negotiated the terms themselves. I had no part in it," he replied.

Her face fell, and she closed her eyes as if he had struck her. "I might have taken the throne of Phoenicia for myself. Now my greatest achievement will be to bear a son." Sarcasm dripped from her mouth.

She lifted a wine bowl as if to hand it to him but instead tilted it and let it grow full at the rim, sorrow etched across her face, her eyes glittering with the red reflections of the wine. Ahab caught his breath, not moving. She was so beautiful. And he had no idea how to deal with her.

She tilted the bowl more with a slight bend of her wrist, and the wine trickled down and off the side, a small dark river staining the linens between them. She began to tilt it more, meaning to spill it all. Ahab reached out and caught her hand. Wine splashed between them, but he held the bowl, stopping her.

"Nothing good should ever be wasted," he said.

She did not let go of the bowl. He pulled it to his mouth and drank what was left in one gulp. When she tossed the bowl to the side, he decided to kiss her and leaned in to her mouth.

Jezebel pushed him away. "I am not your prized breeding cow. I don't even want children."

"You were born a woman!" Ahab yelled. He regretted it at once, but he yelled again. "None of this is my doing! What do you want from me?"

"Get out," Jezebel screamed. "Start with that."

Ahab shook his head and stood to leave. He wished that Omri had listened to the dire, bitter warnings of Elijah, that nothing good would come from the marriage. Ahab now worried Elijah was right. A soldier had no business marrying a princess, even if he was technically a prince. Ahab wondered if it was easier to kill a man than it was to love a woman.

He had to get back to the men and discuss their last portion of the journey. They would be close to the capital city, Samaria, soon. Making a good entrance was important for Omri. He would be watching how Ahab entered the city with his bride. If she didn't want him, she should at least have a desire for the kingdom itself, for what might be ahead.

With one hand on the veil, he turned back to face her. "When I was very young, about twelve or thirteen, I watched as my father slaughtered a thousand men. Maybe more. Maybe less. He was the greatest warrior in our army and like a god to me. I remember that the ground beneath my feet sank with the weight of so much blood. So I rose before dawn on the day after the battle and went out of our tent to collect stones. 'What are you doing?' my father asked when he found me. 'I'm making a monument to you,' I answered. It was the way of our people. My father pointed to the corpses that stretched far into the horizon in every direction. He couldn't even lift his arms that morning, so sore was he from swinging his sword for hours. But he said, 'There. They are my monument.' I saw him clearly for the first time that morning. I saw that he was strong but blind. Death never built a monument. Stones do. I will build a mighty empire, Jezebel, and my queen will never be thought of as a breeding cow. She will be the most envied of all women."

With that, he left her. He thought it was the right sentiment to leave her with, and besides, he saw her hand fumbling for something to throw at him.

4

Obadiah

Obadiah knew Ahab had gone to find Jezebel. They had been traveling now for two days, in that strange land halfway between the turquoise waters of Phoenicia and the dry brown earth of Israel. Obadiah dreaded the return as much as he had first dreaded leaving. He had gone to Phoenicia hoping that Elijah would be proved wrong and was returning to Israel knowing that Elijah had not warned them strongly enough. Elijah must have known that no one would believe him, although he had wandered far and wide and seen much. For who could believe that a prosperous people living in freedom and beauty could murder their infants, could whore their youngest women, could worship demons and drink blood? They claimed the infant deaths honored their women and allowed them to live without restraint, but Obadiah had seen no free women. He had seen numb women, their eyes glazed with animal nature. Their bodies had moved as they worshipped, but their spirits had not danced.

Phoenicia had proven herself to be a city of pleasure, but not joy.

Obadiah knew now why so many legends grew up around Phoenician waters. The sea had been a constantly changing mirage that caught the eye and sparkled. A man might imagine anything rising from its depths. Such beauty inspired the imagination. But what a terrible accusation it made against its own people. The sea of Phoenicia was no better than a mirror that reflected a painted image. What the people had brought forth from their imaginations had been horror varnished to look like worship. Thousands upon thousands of infants had died in the name of pleasure and freedom.

So lost was he in thought as he wandered through the makeshift camp to find water, that he was startled to feel a strong hand grab him by the arm and pull him behind a covered chariot.

Mirra glared at him. "You should have told me who you were! I did not appreciate an important servant knowing something I did not."

Obadiah shrugged in reply. He was speechless, and his nerves melted his tongue and his knees at the same time. It was a wonder he could even stand when so close to her.

"You are Omri's administrator."

"I am." He wetted his lips at once to keep them from sealing together. His mouth was drying out.

"Then get me out of my duties. I don't want to serve the princess."

"Your father made that arrangement himself." He did not think it was wise for a young girl to question her father. Especially when her father had a temper and a fast hand.

"My father wants me to find a husband. He thinks that if I am at court, I'll meet someone more suitable than a soldier. And soldiers are the only men in Samaria."

That wounded Obadiah. He cleared his throat.

"Soldiers can make good husbands. Though they are not royalty, or elders, I have read many stories of valor ..." he began. He sounded stupid even to his own ears. She cut him off with a look of disdain.

"Since you keep the records, write this down: I would rather die than ever have a soldier touch me. But neither do I want my father to decide my future. I want freedom, Obadiah. I don't care how I get it, but I want freedom."

She released him and stormed off. He stood still for several minutes as the blood returned to the spot where she had gripped on his arm. Lifting his sleeve as the sun set in bright orange and gold, he saw the shadows under his skin. He would have a bruise there by morning. Bruises lasted longer than kisses. He liked that thought and went back to his work.

The camp was busy with servants doing chores: waste pots being emptied far from the path, fires begun for dinner. He was glad to see the Phoenician servants already watering their animals. It meant they had found water. Their scouts were excellent at it, Obadiah knew, often scenting it in the air before ever seeing it. Obadiah relaxed a little. If all the animals were cared for, he had less to worry about, and the foreign servants needed no prompting to do what needed to be done. They might not add the burdens he feared. It was the priests who concerned him.

Obadiah knew his only moment to speak to Ahab would be as Ahab washed. After checking to be sure that Ahab's personal cooks were at work to bring up a good fire and prepare his evening meal, Obadiah was free to look for Ahab, whom he found walking among the caravan, asking where the princess was, pausing to inspect the goods being carried into the capital city. Obadiah fell in beside him, knowing he would have to write every single item in the records. For Ahab, this inspection was a show. For Obadiah, it was a month's work.

But he couldn't think of himself or the work. He had to warn Ahab that Elijah had been right but had not told them everything. Obadiah hadn't believed it, not really, not until it was real and in his hands. Ahab had to be woken up.

"She brings her gods," Obadiah began. "She has a caravan of statues of the goddess. I've heard she intends to give them as gifts to the noble women of Israel."

Ahab nodded, the comment dismissed.

Obadiah's stomach twisted. "You remember Elijah's warning. Those gods bring a curse. Perhaps she should destroy them."

Ahab caught him by the arm. "The princess is just a girl of fifteen. What kind of god would curse a girl?"

"Her gods *are* the curse. They do not worship a goddess, but a demon. They worship death and think it is life."

Ahab groaned and continued walking. "I knew you wouldn't attend their worship rites. How did you spend your time? Reading?"

"No one understands," Obadiah said as a weak defense. He was defeated. Obadiah was a quiet man. He wasn't bold, and to tell a tale of thousands of burnt infant bones required a strength of character he didn't think he had. If Ahab didn't want to see the truth, how could Obadiah force him to it?

Ahab motioned for Obadiah to keep up. Ahab moved with a soldier's purpose and command. Obadiah moved like a servant, ever expectant. It embarrassed him that Ahab was always three strides ahead, even if Ahab had no idea what he was walking into.

Obadiah saw the growing distance between them and frowned. He crushed an anthill with his sandal. An angry mob emerged from the sleeping mud to destroy him. He walked toward a cook and shook his sandal off into the fire.

Jezebel

Jezebel prepared for the final hour of their long journey to Israel. In one hour, she would be introduced to the capital city, Samaria, and to the people and nation she would rule for the rest of her days. Of course, that word *rule* was loosely applied, she knew. Position was not power, not for women. Real power had to be taken. It was never given. And even when a woman might try to take power, as Jezebel had tried time and time again in Phoenicia, men would always be there to snatch it away. The real irony now was that giving Ahab an heir was the only way to real power. The queen mother was a position unrivaled, and from that high perch she could decide whose power to take next. She had to sleep with the prince.

The problem was that she had no desire to be touched by him or anyone else. Though he clearly desired her—he nearly panted in her presence, and she remembered his desperate kiss in the woods, before she'd known that the anonymous traveler would soon become her husband—he only saw a painted exterior, her fine robes, and he smelled only her perfume. He had no idea what hid beneath. He did not see her as she was: a dismissed and nearly feral daughter, eating from the trash, sitting among broken clay children, a girl who had submitted to the gods and men and died in her heart each time. But real death, the kind that would end her suffering, did not want her, she sensed. Even death preferred her sister. Temereh had always been so blessed. Temereh would have known what to do with a confused prince. Temereh would have never been in this litter, though. Their father would have never given her away. Temereh would have inherited the throne.

The animals in the caravan were the first to register the presence of strangers. The dogs following the caravan barked furiously, and Jezebel lifted the veil of her litter. Strange men stared from the crest of a hill as Jezebel's caravan approached the city. They wore animal skins around their waists but no robes. They intrigued her, but she was not frightened, not with the army in front and in back drawing up tighter as they approached Samaria. The priests of the goddess Asherah were the next to see them, staring at them from behind the veils with fear and hatred.

Jezebel could see Ahab struggling to keep his horse moving. He yelled to the captains with him to force everyone on.

"It is just a band of prophets," he called back. There were confused comments among the priests. In Phoenicia, only priests spoke to gods. The priests were under the king's authority and lived by his grace in the royal complex. There was no role of prophet, and certainly not a prophet who wandered.

The sun had moved behind the clouds as Jezebel's caravan arrived in Samaria. Children ran alongside her litter, cheering her arrival, throwing dates and little charms tied with up string into her lap. Young men gathered in groups all along the way, eyeing her with appreciation and curiosity. She did not know how to respond.

In Phoenicia, the sons of the elders were the only young men she had contact with, and they regarded her as an unworthy rival. They remembered who she had once been. But these men were glad to see her and approved of her. Lilith seemed as surprised as Jezebel and hid behind her. Mirra sat up eagerly, probably anxious for her peers to see her riding into the city with the princess. Jezebel knew Mirra was as much a fool as Ahab. Israel might be an entire nation of fools.

Jezebel studied the women carefully whenever one approached. Dirty, in ragged robes of no distinct fashion, faces lined by hard years in the sun and with no hint of cosmetics. Everywhere she saw their hands lifted to beg her blessing, hands that were calloused and layered in dust. Her stomach flipped from the shock of seeing all of them so eager and adoring. She had done nothing to earn their love. They didn't even know her. She wished someone would make them stop. Her hands began shaking then, and a punch of adrenaline struck her abdomen. She didn't deserve this. She couldn't even make a noise that expressed the grief their adoration gave her. She sat, frozen in pain, as they cheered and called her name.

Ahab walked ahead of Jezebel into the city on foot, shaking hands and accepting congratulations, but it made her own progress slow. She cursed him. She wanted to get inside the palace, not loiter in these city streets as women held infants up for a royal blessing. Jezebel panicked. They were mocking her. She held out her hands to refuse to bless the infants, to motion the mothers back, yet the mothers just rushed closer still. Her face grew hot. She did not want to see all these newborns, their eyes wide with innocence, their tiny pink mouths making sweet sounds.

Little black bugs swirled in her vision, but no one else seemed to see them. Jezebel tried to swat at them, looking helplessly at Lilith for help. Then Jezebel realized she was about to faint.

A blast from the shofar made her jump, startling her back to consciousness. A man in fine robes approached, and the crowd parted. He bowed before Ahab and called for attention.

"A song for the new princess!"

The crowd roared. She was the first royalty ever brought into Samaria, and the first royal blood to extend the line of Omri. They had no idea of the bitterness in her blood, she thought. No idea how much blood was in her memories.

The man cued a group of musicians that had assembled in the crowd: lyre, harp, and flute players. "To the tune of Lilies," he called, and they began. He sang loud and clear, a fine deep voice that pleased Jezebel, though she hated the words.

> "The people of Israel are like a river
> Bursting its banks with joy
> We will celebrate with a poem to the prince.
> You, Ahab, are the most excellent of men.
> Your lips, anointed with grace.
> Gird your sword on your side, mighty prince,
> Clothe yourself with splendor and majesty!
> May your arrows pierce the hearts of the king's
>   enemies,
> May all nations fall beneath your feet.
> All your robes are fragrant with myrrh and aloes and
>   cassia

Brought from that fine palace adorned in ivory
And at your right hand is the royal bride in gold from
  Phoenicia.
All glorious is she, her gowns woven from gold.
Listen, my princess: forget your father and your
  father's house.
The prince is enthralled by your beauty
Honor him, for he is now your lord.
May your sons take the place of your fathers,
May the nations praise you forever and ever!"

The crowd applauded, and Jezebel knew it was finally over. She had distracted herself to keep from fainting by studying the city behind the singer. The first outrage was that the wall that should mark its boundaries and give it protection was still under construction. Workers in tattered robes and frayed head scarves had thrown down their shovels to approach Ahab, and she was able to see the dusty trench they had been working on. The wall might take another year or more to complete.

Jezebel searched the horizon for Omri's flag. His colors would fly above the palace, and by this she would know which building was her new home. She had never seen any palace except her own.

A white-haired man grinned broadly at her. He had been drinking from an old brown bowl filled with frothy milk, the white mess dripping from his beard as he grinned without teeth. Cows and goats moved between the people, wandering into tents and being shooed back out. All the revulsions of her early years flooded back up. This was a nation of feral people. There were no homes,

Jezebel realized. No one had boundaries or barriers. Yet there was no tension in the air, just laughter and children who burst into song for her attention.

Just after they passed the trench being dug for the foundation of the wall, there were rows of shields and armor on display on either side of the street. Further down there were tents everywhere, and fire pits dug at random, some with animals roasting on spits, some filled with gray ash.

As the litter crept forward, she saw what had to be homes, little squares made of stone and lumber, with two windows that faced the street, one on either side of an open doorway. These must belong to the elders. Samaria was a new city, Omri had told her that. A city still being built, a new center of power in this region. She had never realized all power was born dirty. The thought was a sudden comfort to her. Maybe that was why Asherah had never saved her. She was born for power, dirty.

At the edge of these homes, the common people stopped following her. Boundaries did exist, she realized, even if invisible.

Ahab extended his hand. She stepped down from the litter without accepting it and began moving through the remaining crowd, which consisted of older elders and their servants, those not able to make the trip north to fetch her. Searching again for Omri's colors, she saw them at last and pressed her lips together to keep from crying. The palace was plain stone, undecorated, not a bit of color, but just one square stone on top of another. She straightened her posture in resolve. It didn't matter as long as she could curl up on a bed, alone.

The foundation had been laid at the highest point on the hill that was Samaria. The dirty city stretched beneath it and behind it; Jezebel assumed the view was what Omri had called unusable land. The foundation itself was just a plain stone platform about twenty feet high, and cut into the face of the platform were two empty tombs. They looked like missing teeth against the expanse of white stones all around. One was marked for Omri and another for Ahab. That was odd. Her people only planned for their lives, not for their deaths.

The walls of the palace were as dreary as its foundation, just plain stone, with empty, dark windows, and an open rectangle for the entrance. Several sheep lounged beneath the palace, enjoying the cool shadows cast by the wall. One looked at her and bleated.

"It is not Phoenicia, is it?" Ahab slid his arm around her waist as he stood behind her, whispering. He was big; perhaps this gesture intimidated women. It only infuriated Jezebel. Her head was filled with thoughts that screamed for expression, but she shut them up and refused to speak. Every interaction with him was a fresh nightmare.

"This is not your homeland, Jezebel," Ahab said again. "Right now, that seems like a terrible fact. But if you dwell on it longer, you will begin to see it as a promise." He pulled away, giving her a small formal nod, and left to go present himself to Omri.

She was led to her quarters by a man of slight build, about the same age as Ahab. He was the only one who seemed frightened of her, suspicious.

"Who are you?" she whispered.

He bowed his head. "Obadiah. Palace administrator. Ahab asked me to see to it you had the best room for tonight."

With that, he left her. She entered a quiet chamber prepared for her with a bed, a low table, and a bowl of wine should she become thirsty.

Jezebel removed her sandals and lay down on the bed and cried until she slept.

Ahab

The wind was relentless, whistling through the dusty city below. Ahab listened to its hiss and moan as he climbed the stairs to the royal sleeping quarters for the second night since they'd arrived home in Samaria. He had given Jezebel peace last night as a courtesy. She had needed to sleep after the journey, after being introduced to Israel. She was so young, physically, two years younger than himself. Yet her eyes had shadows he could not explain. A darkness hid in her spirit. Still, Obadiah was wrong, at least about her; whatever darkness was there, it had nothing to do with death. The horror that lived in the human heart was surely not in hers. Not at her age, and not after living in Phoenicia's royal palace.

Ahab had seen new lands only when his father had been hired to kill someone in one of them. He had grown up viewing the world through the eyes of a murderer. To Omri, glory and money were always one city away. One more kill, Omri promised him each time they set out, one more death groan, and it would be over. Yet his father was never satisfied, and Ahab thought he understood why. His father wanted to die too. Every time he swung that blade it was a prayer for an enemy that was stronger. But Ahab didn't want to die, not until he had made his own name, in his own way. Omri didn't understand there could be any other way besides the sword.

He couldn't give Jezebel one more night. She shouldn't ask. She belonged to him from the moment their fathers poured melted fat on the leather scroll and embedded their seals in the shimmering warm pool. If he allowed her to resist him any longer, it would be like stealing from him. That was what he told himself as he climbed the last three stone steps and entered the hallway lit by flames. The arch of the doorway cast shadows on the faces of two guards, so that all he could plainly see by the torchlight was the shine from the swords at their sides. He saw the blades and the door and took a deep breath to shake off his nerves.

As he entered, he saw her reclining on the bed. A single oil lamp burned on her bedside table, though the moon was bright enough to light the chamber without it. She was alone, a hollow expression on her face. Her long black hair was loosely coiled and held in place by a wide ivory comb that glinted in the soft lamplight. She was staring at the blank limestone wall.

She turned to him, and he saw a look he had already come to know so well. She was in despair.

"Tomorrow we will go out riding. I will show you the city," he said, hoping to console her.

She shrugged. "I can see it from the window."

"You have not seen it through my eyes," he said.

When she said nothing, he floundered. He was at a loss, being born and bred in the military.

He cleared his throat and used his most commanding tone. "I gave you the first night here to yourself to recover from the journey. Tonight you will sleep in my chambers. In my bed." She made no visible or audible response, so he added, "As my wife."

"We can do that now if you like," she said, rising with a sigh.

He took a step backward. He had not expected that. A willing woman was a ready woman, that's what the soldiers always said, but she didn't seem to know that saying. She wasn't willing, even if she was ready.

But if he did nothing, and she told anyone, even the girl who threw herbs into her toilet every morning, he would lose respect. Or worse. A man suspected of preferring men often died of mysterious causes in his sleep, the only mystery being that no one ever confessed to slitting his throat. Ahab had seen that twice in his years of battle.

So he crossed the room and, with a deep breath, put his hand around her waist and pulled her to him. He kissed her on the mouth. She did not part her lips, nor did she close her eyes. He kissed her again, slowly this time, showing her that he was no threat, and still she remained frozen in his arms.

He stopped and pushed her back, frowning, trying to read her blank face.

"You do not want sex?" she asked. She tilted her head, as if perplexed by his odd behavior.

"I want you," he said, the honesty of his words surprising him. "There is a difference." It was a truth he had never known, and yet speaking it made it real.

A light flashed in her eyes. She was alive in there, indeed. "You don't know me," she said. "I understand what I owe you, and I will give it to you. You don't have to lie to get what you want."

It was the most personal thing she had said to him yet. He held his tongue, shocked.

"I didn't want the marriage," she added. "I was forced to accept it."

He laughed, startling her. "I didn't want the marriage either. It was my father's decision. If I had thought I could change his mind, I would have fought a hundred men to get out of it."

She looked away from him, color coming up in her cheeks. No tears ran down her face, so he did not think she was wounded by his admission.

"And then I saw you," he added. Reaching out, he pulled the ivory comb from her hair, and it fell in a black cascade around her shoulders. He saw his hand tremble as he did it. It didn't bother him now. She needed to see him weak. She wouldn't trust him until she did.

He undressed himself and sat on her bed. She watched him but did not move toward him, and once again he could not read her expression.

"I thought you wanted me to come to your chambers," she said.

"If I leave, even for a moment, you'll go back to your thinking before I see you again. You'll dwell on everything you've lost."

"And if you stay?" she asked, taking a step toward him, not out of desire, he thought, but out of curiosity.

"We can form an alliance against our fathers, in our own way."

Jezebel

The sun had been climbing in the sky for nearly five hours before Ahab left the next morning, sated and quiet. He did not seem to notice how Jezebel's hands shook as he kissed them before leaving. Her thoughts were like a thousand sharp needles scattered across her mind. Nowhere could she find comfort from what had happened.

There had been no blood. She was so used to blood when men touched her. But Ahab hadn't hurt her. He had seemed concerned with her, how she felt, how she received his tenderness. She felt like an ant caught in a jar. She had no escape from his attention. She had been too afraid to close her eyes. But he had closed his, in pleasure, and not just his own pleasure, but the pleasure of being with her. He took pleasure with her. Other men had taken pleasure from her.

Anger rose up from her heart into her mouth. She spit his taste from her tongue onto the soiled linens. She needed to act like a princess, a real one, not one that had slept near open sewers and watched infants slaughtered so their mothers could go on giving themselves away.

Last night had been horrible, an intimacy so terrible it pierced her soul. She stood now, ripping the linens from the bed, throwing them to the floor, disgusted and afraid of what they now represented.

That had been easy, those nameless offerings. Women never named the infants they planned to give to the goddess. They weren't meant to be known. *Some things are not meant to be known*, she thought. After the offerings, no one ever stayed. Mothers fled so they would not see the bodies burn. Men who worshipped through sex fled so they would not have to truly see the women they had lain with.

Ahab had not run away. He'd stayed for hours, stroking her hair. There was no shame in his eyes of what he had done to her, touching her like she was of value, instead of the rejected, despised thing she was. Marriage was worse than she imagined. Intimacy was a cruel new world. It seemed to make all her wounds and her confusion brighter, like air to a flame.

She took the oil lamp from the bedside and poured the oil over the linens. She didn't want to be known or touched or loved. Her family had judged her unworthy, unloved, less than. She had spent her life trying to prove them wrong, but last night, Ahab had proved them right. Wanting to be loved, to win approval, had led to her worst sorrows. She had been a fool to let him touch her like that, and to open herself back up to that pain, as she nearly had with Ahab. She vowed to never close her eyes, never surrender to his kindness. It was nauseating that he thought she could want such tenderness from him. She knew what it led to: only pain.

She touched the flame to the bedding and opened the door. Ignoring the shouts of the servants who rushed to extinguish the blaze, she went in search of water.

She needed a bath.

Obadiah

"I'd like to request we give Mirra another assignment, one that is not so public," Obadiah said to Ahab. It had taken several days to decide how best to approach the prince. Finally, Obadiah decided that he had to be direct and plain. Ahab was so often distracted. Though Obadiah had searched for the prince in the palace, he found him in the stables. The stables were not attached to the palace, but further down on the land below it, with other royal buildings that marked the beginning of the royal complex. There was also a storage building for grains and foodstuffs and a treasury for receiving taxes and tributes. Each was a plain rectangle-shaped building of white stone, with one main entry door. There were no windows in the food storage building, but two windows had been allowed on either side of the door to the treasury. Counting coins required light, but windows were invitations for rodents in the storage building. Obadiah had been the one to suggest the windows for the treasury. He was tired of reading scrolls by lamplight and wanted the accountants to have an easier time.

Ahab was brushing his horse, a small, wicked beast with a temperament as black as its coat. Obadiah kept his distance.

"No," Ahab replied, clearly lost in thought.

"Mirra's father wants her to find a husband from one of the visiting elders or royalty. That's why he asked Omri to allow her to serve the princess. But she has no real talent for service."

"Mirra should be pleased with the arrangement. She will find a good husband."

Obadiah lifted his hands in a weak protest. He hated to love a woman he could never have, but worse would be to fail her.

"I don't understand women, Obadiah," Ahab said, leaving the horse and walking down the center of the stable. One either side were stalls with stone walls and wooden gates at the entrance. Each had a window, and the early afternoon sunlight illuminated the dust that was in constant circulation here. The bedding was being replaced in an empty stall, and Ahab paused as the stable boy spread it out. When Obadiah caught up to him, Ahab turned his attention to him, intense and yet not focused.

"When your father died," he asked Obadiah, "why did your mother never remarry? Did no man want her as a wife? Is that why she had to sell herself?"

Obadiah straightened his back at the mention of her. "She didn't want to be a wife. It does work both ways, you know."

"Why would a woman feel that way? It's against nature."

Jezebel is anything but natural, Obadiah thought, thinking of the fire she'd set last week. Ahab told the staff she had spilled the oil lamp by accident. Obadiah suspected not, but he wasn't sure Ahab even knew the truth. She had strange responses. She did not like the servants to touch her, she did not like to eat with others watching her, she seemed afraid to take the good portions of meat, she scowled when the elders of the city complimented her. More than once he had seen her spit at them when their backs were turned.

Ahab sighed. "Women are complicated, aren't they?"

"Most of life is, I think," Obadiah said. Ahab was not listening to him anymore, not about Phoenicia and not about Mirra. Ahab had made his choice and seemed to wander in his mind now.

Obadiah wished he had a choice to make too, but all he had was responsibility. That was not the same as authority. He had to keep them all fed and clothed, the palace and court running effortlessly, and the royals free from the daily worries that could distract them. He wished God had given him choices, not just responsibilities.

He watched as a stable hand made his daily count of the bits and bridles hung on the wall.

Obadiah tasted the metal of the bit in his own mouth.

Jezebel

Ahab had left her hours ago to attend to the court's business. Mirra apparently had noticed Jezebel's boredom while he was away and offered to teach her a dice game that her people played. Lilith offered to pour a bath. But Jezebel preferred to walk. She headed out of her chambers, alone.

A month had passed since Jezebel's arrival in Israel, and she had slowly begun to feel stronger against Ahab's affections. She needed fewer little tricks to resist him emotionally. She had resolved weeks ago to survive his touch until she conceived. When she was with child, he would mercifully not touch her for months.

Until that happened, she had found a way to bear his tenderness. She closed her eyes and thought of the other men, those who had hurt her and used her but did not know her. She had been so much safer with them. When Ahab touched her, it felt as if he wanted to peel away her skin, to the part of her that could not bear even the touch of fresh air.

As she walked, Jezebel ached with longing for the solitary comfort of sitting among the clay children. She had no way to pray to Asherah, the queen of heaven, without the regular sacrifices of infants. Her daily routine was still unfamiliar, as was the religious calendar of the Hebrews. The Phoenician court had centered its days around visiting merchants and previewing merchandise and making deals. Israel was a military-based country run by an army commander who didn't give much thought to luxuries or fine foods. Or to the goddess. The Hebrews Omri ruled had fasting days and feasting days, but Obadiah had replied curtly to her that no one offered sacrifices in Israel. Only in Jerusalem, at Solomon's temple, and, he'd said, they were holy ones. She was not sure what he meant.

Which was why she had wandered to this particular wing of the palace on a late afternoon. She'd heard about Yahweh, Israel's one god—for he refused a consort—but his history was written on scrolls, and Obadiah kept them with the palace records. She had walked through the palace enough to know where he kept them, in a quiet room with only three long tables and benches for seating. There were baskets lining the walls, and crocks, all of which contained scrolls, and some of those looked very old indeed. The walls were bare stone. There were no windows in this room, and the three oil lamps that burned left dark shadows of grime on the walls.

Jezebel paused outside the doorway, a familiar wash of anticipation flooding over her. This was a room like her own, back in Phoenicia. Obadiah grew close to Yahweh through the scrolls, and these scrolls were not unlike those clay children. If only Obadiah knew how similar she was to him.

Jezebel heard men's voices coming from inside. She opened the door and leaned her head toward the opening, holding her breath.

Omri and Ahab were standing over an open scroll on the table. Obadiah was seated, watching Omri with an expectant look, a stylus poised in midair.

Omri was the one most comfortable in this room; she could see it in the way he jabbed at the scroll before him and watched impatiently as Obadiah nodded and wrote.

Omri was planning something, and Ahab paced and argued. When Ahab's eyes met hers, her stomach tightened.

"Jezebel, go back to your chambers," he commanded.

Omri glanced up. "Wait. What do you know of Ben-hadad, Jezebel?"

"She knows nothing of this," Ahab protested.

Obadiah watched her, his eyes narrowing slightly.

Jezebel had faced many men like this, men who for whatever reason were entertained by her trying to prove she was not stupid just because she was born a girl. "I know that he will soon be king of Aram," she said. "That he is not as patient as his father. That he has a taste for foreign women."

Ahab's right eyebrow arched. She had never told him of Ben-hadad. He had never asked, and she now dreaded the questions that would come later.

"When he visited our palace," she continued, "he always rose before dawn to be the first at the port as the slave ships came in. He bought at least four or five girls on every visit."

Omri's eyes were cold as he studied her. She had grown up under cold stares. She was unmoved.

"Did your father ever consider giving you to Ben-hadad? Instead of Ahab? Were promises made?"

The air in the room was like a wall of blades closing in, stretched tight across her skin, resting against it, ready to cut her. But then Jezebel exhaled quietly. Omri's intuition surprised her, but it gave her an opportunity.

The stones beneath her feet seemed more solid now. She knew this terrain, the way important men lashed out at her when afraid, and she had many good defenses.

"No promises were made. But yes, Ben-hadad pursued the union," she said, avoiding looking at Ahab. "I refused him," she added.

Omri smiled with a cold, cruel distance in his eyes. "Ahab, we may have a scorned lover to deal with."

"He was never my lover." *No man has ever been my lover*, she wanted to add, looking away when Ahab caught her eye.

Omri folded his arms.

She let the boldness come over her. She crossed the room and found Ben-hadad's territory on the map. She circled it with her finger. It lay to the east, slightly above the midpoint between Israel and Phoenicia.

"Ben-hadad has a strong army, stronger than Phoenicia's, perhaps stronger than even yours," she said. "But if allied with Phoenicia, he would have attacked Israel and tried to take it for himself. My country would have lost control of the trade routes. I advised my father to refuse Ben-hadad because of money."

Omri smirked and glanced at his son. But it was true. Jezebel had refused him, and her father and the elders had applauded her foresight. That was why she thought she could trust them. They saw something valuable in her at last. But she realized now that what they had seen was her value in marriage if sold to Israel instead.

"He wants your trade routes, not me," she added. She glared at Omri, hating him for making her confess her worthlessness.

Ahab stepped between his father and his bride. "We caught a scout last night," Ahab told her, speaking softly. "One of Ben-hadad's. The scout said Ben-hadad is interested in our progress in building Samaria."

Jezebel nodded, thankful he treated her as an equal. "Ben-hadad needs Phoenicia for its seaports," she reminded them. "But Phoenicia and Israel are aligned now. If he attacks Israel for her trade routes, he will anger my people and lose access to their ports."

"Maybe Israel is not what he is after," Omri suggested. "And *we* are your people now. Aren't we?"

"My king!" a page burst into the room, out of breath. "Elijah is here!"

Omri cursed, and his body withdrew into the hard shell of a fighter. His hands became fists, his shoulders pulled back and down, his brows came together in a fierce line. He followed the page without another word or glance. Obadiah and Ahab followed close behind, exchanging worried, quiet words.

Jezebel had heard only dark rumors of this man Elijah, but she had not met him. He had been nothing more than a ghost in the stories of the Hebrew servants, tales of miracles and children he raised from the dead. He had powerful magic, if half the stories could be believed.

Perhaps he knew of Asherah. Perhaps he could pray to the goddess for her. Her pace quickened at the thought. If he was a powerful man of the gods, he might not even need to sacrifice a child.

She started to follow, but Omri stopped and whipped back to her. "Get her out of here," he said to Ahab.

Ahab shook his head at Jezebel, stopping her from following them. Obadiah saw her take another step forward, and he moved to grab her arm, as if he was panicked.

They didn't want her to meet Elijah. They wanted to keep him and his magic far from her. But why?

When Obadiah's hand reached Jezebel's forearm, she lifted her arm and sank her teeth into his hand. He screamed, and in the space between their shock and reaction, she was already running ahead of them.

❧

The throne room was empty. Omri's plain wooden throne sat on top of a raised platform. It was the only furnishing in the room. Ahab had sent for artisans from Phoenicia to paint the walls and put ivory inlays on the throne.

Doors stood at the far end of the room, which led out to a common hall. There, elders could do business in relative quiet. Important discussions and important men, but she paid none of it any mind as the doors swung open and Elijah entered.

She was shocked to see small children circling about him, and watched as he bent down to them and whispered something that made them all go still and wide-eyed. He reached into the bag on his tunic and produced something that looked like seeds or little fruits, and they squealed with delight before taking them and running out.

She watched him, fascinated. He had a bushy white beard and a spreading, bulbous nose. His eyes were wide and clear, like a child's. Energy pulsed from him; his presence stirred the air. But he had a kind face, like a grandfather who wanted to hear a story, and she was tempted to reach out her hand to him as if he might give her something good too. He was so calming and steady. No wonder the commoners had begged for healing. He was the sort of man who made others believe such things were still possible in this age. His cheeks popped up like small red apples above that beard, and under his whiskers she could see his lips twitching. He smiled often; she could tell by the deep laugh lines all around his mouth. He was not thin, either. He had a good-sized stomach, that of a man who enjoyed his dinners. He wasn't wealthy, judging by his crudely woven robes, but he was obviously loved. Someone, maybe many people, were feeding him well.

Omri, Ahab, and Obadiah burst into the room behind her, all breathing heavily. She didn't turn around to acknowledge them, but she knew they were there. She waited, staring, for Elijah to speak to her.

When her eyes met his, his whiskers no longer twitched. His wide gaze burned her skin. Jezebel shifted her weight from foot to foot, feeling as if she should run. He took a step toward her, and she felt a fear wholly new to her. Whereas at first she was comforted by him, something about him now made her cringe. She wanted to hide in shadows; the throne room pulsed with a strange energy. It felt like a horrible guilt, but she had done nothing except serve her gods.

She gasped for air, drowning in pain. Her heart seemed laid bare before him. She thought of a worm writhing on the ground after a hard night's rain, dying in the strong morning light.

"I see you made your choice," Elijah said to Ahab in a diffident tone, as if bored by her.

"I had no choice," Ahab said. No one moved. Jezebel heard only their breath and the sound of her pounding heart.

Elijah stroked his beard and waited. Ahab said nothing else. Then Elijah spoke, in a voice drenched in sorrow. "I pronounce a curse on you. As the Lord God of Israel lives, before whom I stand, there shall be neither dew nor rain again, except by my word."

Elijah picked up the extra fold in his tunic and turned for the exit. He paused only to rest his hand on a guard's shoulder, giving the young man a look of grief. Then he was gone.

Omri glared at Jezebel, taking a step toward her, his face clouding with anger. Ahab took her by the arm, pulling her away from his father.

Her stomach churned, and she did not know if it was from her new illness, some small plague that came to her daily, especially in the morning, or from the shock of thinking Elijah could be that strong. What magic was this? From what god? She clenched her jaw as she realized she had not even had one word with him. Whoever his god was, Jezebel wanted to make a sacrifice to it at once. If she had known of this god earlier, so many things could have been different.

For this reason she was allowed to live, so that she would know His name at last.

That was a strange thought, and not in her voice.

She stopped, digging her heels back, forcing Ahab to turn to face her. She spoke with firm words, the way one would speak to a frightened child.

"I want to talk to Elijah alone."

Ahab set his mouth in a hard line and pulled at her again, to force her on. She refused, wresting free of his control.

"I have to talk with him. I want his god brought here to Samaria at once. I will make sacrifices to it. He will be pleased."

"Elijah? No. And his god is Yahweh," Ahab said. "The god of Israel. Yahweh is already here."

"That cannot be true. Why would a god curse his own nation? Elijah must serve another god."

Ahab shook his head. "He knows no one, and nothing, but Yahweh."

She had thought of Yahweh as an older god, less potent than her own, a god for a dying generation, but Elijah proclaimed a bold living curse. Withholding rain was slow death for a nation. Why would any god threaten his own people? Why would a god be so uninterested in her and yet so angered by her presence? The court around her was alive with whispers and frantic movement.

"What could have angered your god so?" she asked.

"You," Ahab replied.

The familiar taste of damnation rose like bile in her throat. Nothing had changed. She was a princess, yes, but she was still, as ever, unwanted.

Ahab

More than two weeks had passed since Elijah's visit. No rain had fallen, but it was early in the season.

Ahab could not sleep, restless from thoughts he wished to avoid. They always seemed to find him at night. He would be glad to leave for Jezreel. Jezebel slept next to him, the steady rise and fall of her breath a relief. He had not been able to look at her since Elijah's visit. He should have told her of his battle with the prophet long before the man presented himself at court with a curse for a wedding gift.

Ahab had never had a choice. Elijah had warned him not to honor his father's wishes, not to bring this princess to Israel, but Ahab was not in the habit of obeying men who did not fall in his chain of command. He took orders from his father and no one else.

And for good reason. Soldiers obeyed Omri, or they died.

Even if this land, as Elijah said, belonged to Yahweh, a man had to rule it, didn't he? Kings had ruled Yahweh's people for generations. Obadiah concurred and said it was all written in his scrolls. But those men were nothing like Omri. Or perhaps, Ahab thought, Omri was nothing like them.

Ahab crept quietly to a corner of the room, lifting a small oil lamp into the palm of his hand for light. In the corner was a table where he kept his bag. Inside were all the amulets and necklaces and stone figures of gods, twenty-three of them. He lit a piece of charcoal in the flame of the oil lamp and set it in a dish, sprinkling incense over it. The charcoal burned red and then released the white smoke that stung his eyes. Cupping his hands, he dipped his face into the smoke, waving it over each of his shoulders and then over his head.

"Which one are you praying to?" she asked. Jezebel stood behind him. He closed his eyes, annoyed with himself for getting caught.

"Go back to bed," he replied.

"I do not recognize all of the gods," she said. "They are crudely done."

"Soldiers carved them in their tents when they were waiting for a battle and could not sleep. They carved the image of their god and prayed, sometimes all night. Then they died in the morning." He sighed.

"Their gods failed them," she said. She sounded distant, angry, as if speaking to someone else.

Ahab stood and faced her. Her pupils were wide and black as she stood in the shadows. "I am not honoring the gods. I am honoring the men. They were my friends."

She shook her head, as if trying to understand, trying to push away a bad memory to see him more clearly.

He took her hand, and she did not pull away. A smile played on his lips, but he did not look at her. Wooing her was like trying to coax a frightened kitten from its hiding place. "I had an older brother. Did you know that?"

Her eyes opened wider, a flash of something like recognition. "No," she whispered.

"I did. He was older by two years, and very much like my father. That's why my father loved him more than me. When my brother died," he said, "I spent all night with his body so the animals wouldn't get it. I held his hands and rubbed them between my own, for hours, trying to keep them warm. He just kept getting colder. He didn't worship any gods, and neither did our father. That was not their way, and so there was nothing I could do for him. I think that's why gods are important. Whether they are real or not, whether they fail or not, it doesn't matter. The gods are for us."

Jezebel stepped closer, listening intently, something stirring in her eyes. "How did he die?"

"We had gone into battle, confident that we had more troops, better weapons. And we did. But he and I got separated, and when I looked up, a stronger man had him under his blade. My brother looked right at me as he died. He hated me in that moment. I was the one who would live. There was no reason for it; he was stronger and more loved. But I was the one who lived."

Jezebel reached out her arms and drew him into an embrace, and he did not resist. He felt her head rest upon his chest, bent down his own to smell her hair, perfumed and combed and glistening black in the lamplight. Her arms were strong, even as they trembled, unsure how to touch him. She was such a strange, wondrous woman. He had no idea why he had told her those things.

"Let me show you something," she murmured, pulling away. She walked back to the table where her robes had been laid out for the morning, and from a bag retrieved a stone statue no bigger than her palm. It was the figure of a woman with pronounced breasts and belly but no face. Its feet had been broken off.

"This is Asherah. I have kept her next to me since I was a child." She looked at Ahab, biting her lip, then set her Asherah among his other gods. She knelt, pursing her lips, and blew the perfumed smoke over the statue, whispering a quiet prayer.

"We can pray together," Ahab said, and she groaned in an agony he did not understand, burying her face in his legs. He stood, stroking her hair, wondering what he had said or done that had burst this heartache open. Perhaps when he had finished building the temple for her gods, she would feel better. The marriage treaty required him to do that, as all marriage treaties between nations did. The temple for Baal would be built first, and later, when the people had come to accept that even the mighty Baal needed a wife, the goddess would have her own temple. Until the Israelites understood the power of the feminine, they would not worship it, not completely.

"If your god ever asked you to kill me," she said, looking up with a face twisted by pain, "would you?"

"No." He would not. He would not even entertain the thought, or give her that strange comfort by promising he would. He could never hurt her. Something had done that enough, long in her past.

Finally, she grew still, and her breathing grew calm. He knelt beside her, stealing a glance at her face, now resigned back into its mask of indifference, before the smoke stung his eyes and he closed them for relief.

Jezebel

Jezebel hung her head over the bowl, waiting for the wave to pass. Lilith had sent for the ashipu. She needed medicine or a spell or a prayer. She did not care which. Relentless waves of morning nausea plagued her every day. Mirra encouraged her to lean back onto the pillows of the bed and offered to wipe her forehead with a damp linen.

Jezebel refused. Soon her priests would be ready to make sacrifices to the goddess. Even before Elijah appeared, Ahab had set his workers to building a temple to Baal, Asherah's husband, with a carved sacred tree and altar just outside the temple for her honor. Once the gods saw the smoke rising from Samaria, they would come. They would talk to Yahweh, or chase him away.

Jezebel drew a deep breath between waves, which helped. Her forehead was beading with sweat, and she swallowed the bitter taste in her mouth. She turned her head to look out the window; a sirocco had swept through late yesterday afternoon. The scorching wind had ripped the late summer leaves away, exposing branches that bled dark rivers. Leaves rained past her window in frantic spirals.

Jezebel wondered if she would survive the drought. A world without water, to a Phoenician, was an impossibility. Would death be slow? She was trapped here, trapped in her own body by this illness, trapped by dry land in every direction, no home to return to. Ahab still brought her to his bed at night, but he seemed reluctant to touch her. She should have been relieved, but in the weeks that had passed since the curse, the unspoken name that hovered between them was Elijah.

A joyous season was beginning for her people in Phoenicia, but the mood in the tents below here in Samaria, and in the new houses, was quiet. Word had spread about the curse. Jezebel suspected that Ben-hadad was out there too, somewhere, watching and waiting.

Obadiah entered the chamber, a red ball of flame drawing a gasp from Jezebel. He was holding the first ripe pomegranate of the season, carrying it in his hand like a gem. It was a radiant ruby that illuminated the chamber.

She refused to hold out her hand, though her body twitched from greed. He hesitated and then placed it on the bed next to her.

She sat up to grab it, feeling the weight of the juice inside, thinking of the rich seeds that would burst on the edge of her teeth. The red skin was rough beneath her fingers. It was a prize. She had not known hunger like this before. It was more powerful than any hunger in her past. She did not understand why she could feel so hungry, so fast. The drought had not yet taken hold. There was plenty of food on her table.

"We will be moving within the month to the winter palace in Jezreel," Obadiah said. "It is tradition, as the winters here are unpleasant. Ahab will go ahead of you with the army, so you have time to prepare. Will you require my assistance?"

"No." She wanted him to leave so she could eat the fruit.

Obadiah reached for the pomegranate, and she jerked it away. He held his hand out, patiently, until she saw his arm shake from holding it in midair for so long. He wasn't going to hurt her, or steal it, so she put it on the bed and rolled it to him.

He began peeling it for her, frowning softly as if a deep trouble were stirring him. He did not like her, she had known that immediately. He should have come here gloating, delight twinkling in his eyes that she had caused a conflict between Ahab and Elijah and the nation's god. Yet he had no rebuke. He was a mystery to her. Like Ahab, his kindness was unpredictable.

The dark juice stained his fingers.

He held it out to her, the top peeled back, revealing the white pith and crimson berries within. She accepted the pomegranate, careful to avoid touching him, and held it to her lips. The juice was cool and piercingly sweet. He spoke as she drank, although the relief she felt was so great it was hard to concentrate. A few seeds fell into her mouth, and she chewed them.

"Jezreel is our military headquarters," he said. "It is nothing like Samaria. The surrounding land is beautiful, but the palace is built as a military base. It is surrounded by military compounds. It will not be to your liking when you first see it."

She nodded, handing the pomegranate to a servant, who set it on the table for the princess to enjoy later. Lilith entered with the ashipu, who quietly set his bag on a table in the corner of the room, his back to the women as he prepared the medicine.

"Are you trying to keep me from going?" she asked.

"No." Obadiah shook his head with emphasis. "I am preparing you because you will go. Ahab will want you to be happy. Take whatever you think you will need, and remember we will be there for several months."

Obadiah stepped forward and lowered his voice. He spoke with urgency, but not disrespect, as if he were trying to save her. "I want to speak boldly to you."

She nodded.

"Leave your gods behind, Jezebel. You are a princess of Israel now. You belong to Yahweh."

He was afraid. She saw it in his eyes. They were her own eyes, when she was a child. No one was going to save him, though; he must have known that just as surely as she once had.

"But I don't. I gave myself to my gods long ago. I gave so much," she said, willing him to somehow understand everything she could not say.

"Israel is not Phoenicia. You can leave the past behind."

She heard the desperation in his voice, as if he were fighting for her. Why did he care? How could he find her repulsive and still want to help her? Yet it was the most intriguing conversation she had had since laying eyes on Ahab. Obadiah was speaking to her as an equal, but she was not offended. Something drove him.

"The past will not leave me," she said.

"Renounce Baal and Asherah," Obadiah insisted in a whisper, his gaze piercing. He did not blink as he stared into her eyes, searching for the soul that rested behind them.

"Surely there is room here for more than one god!" She could not stop her voice from rising, as the ashipu turned and moved toward her with a statue of Asherah in one hand, and a cup of medicine in another. Obadiah backed away, holding his palms up as if protecting himself from them both.

"I have come too far," she said, though Obadiah was no longer listening. She may as well have been speaking to herself. "I have given everything. If I was wrong, I deserve death, not a second chance with some new god. I will not make the same mistake twice."

And truly, she was not an ignorant woman. She had heard as many tales as Obadiah had read. Never had one god given his own nation such trouble. Did Yahweh not honor those who were devoted to him? If he would betray his best subjects, then Jezebel knew well what kind of god he was. He was no different than her father and Elijah—just another man anxious to see her fall. If her gods were disgraced, and his own were elevated, Elijah might ask for any sum and get it. He might even ask the elders for the crown. She had lost a crown once. It would never happen again. She had trusted a god's word once and done the unthinkable, and it had only led her here.

"Why is death the only way?" she asked the ashipu.

He raised an eyebrow, waiting for her to continue.

"In any religion there is death. Death is the only way to prove yourself to the gods." She sighed. "It's the only way to make progress."

He shook his head, not understanding. He was a healer, though, not a priest. She was the highest-ranking official of her religion in this land, being the daughter of Eth-baal. If her god was to be defended, she would have to do it.

"If you needed to kill someone, who would you hire?" she asked.

He thought for a moment, scratching his beard. "A soldier named Amun has been staying in the city. He has waited at the gates every morning for a week now, looking for work. Ahab will not hire him, though, because it is rumored he kills even young children. The Hebrews find him repugnant."

He sounded perfect. "I have a job for a man who is not afraid of angering a god. Hire him for me."

She whispered the details to the ashipu, relieved to know there was at least one man in Israel as bold as she.

Obadiah

Obadiah searched the scrolls all night to be sure of what he already knew, with only hours left before their departure for Jezreel. He couldn't bring his library with him. Never in the history of Israel had the winter rains not come. The winter rains had to come, because life could not continue without them. Rain was life. Without rain, there would be no spring wheat, or barley, or fruits or seeds or wine. Without rain, there would be no Israel.

Obadiah was half-crazed with fear, though no one paid him any mind when he spoke of ancient writings and the story they told of God. All the servants of the court, even some from the families of elders who would travel with them, had come repeatedly to him throughout the evening, and throughout the night, interrupting his reading. Many needed help finding items, or unlocking the stored supplies, or verifying what must be brought both for the journey and the stay. Obadiah stayed in his scroll room, searching frantically through the words for a solution. None could be found.

Elijah had proclaimed a curse unheard of, a blight without remedy.

"Do not make me go to Jezreel." A servant named Amitra stood in his doorway, her face tear-streaked.

He rose and went to her, taking her hand in his. She was wan, and her eyes seemed to have lost their life.

"What is it, Amitra?" The past year had been hard on her. Her parents sold her as a slave to Omri's court but had neglected to tell anyone that she was pregnant. It was why they no longer wanted her as a daughter. She would not bring a good price as a wife, but she had value as a slave.

"I don't want to serve Jezebel. I believe she lies," the girl said, almost without feeling.

He frowned. "You must never speak of the princess that way. It is disrespectful, and even if I forgive you, the king might not."

Amitra's face suddenly developed some color, and anger knit in her brow. "But she does! She told me there was a way I could be free, but I am not free! I thought I might be able to go home if ..."

Obadiah suddenly knew what the girl was about to say, and he closed his eyes, trying not to frighten her. He exhaled for strength and then opened his eyes.

She burst into tears, and he had to catch her when her knees seemed to buckle below her. "She said she knew how hard it was for me to do," the girl stammered, "that my choice would not be easy, but I could be blessed in the future, if only I sacrificed the ... child ... my child. She said it would make things better for everyone. Asherah might bring rain, even. I obeyed her." She was weeping quietly, shaking. "I couldn't stand to look at the baby because it reminded me of everything I had lost." The girl let out a quiet wail. "But now I can't stand to look at myself."

Obadiah put his arms around her, though she resisted at first, knocking against him with her shoulders, refusing all comfort, but he was patient and held her until she quieted down. He tasted the tears that ran down his own cheeks, too. It was what he had feared: Phoenician lies had appeal in Israel, too.

This girl didn't care about honoring the goddess or worshipping the sacred feminine as a bold declaration of her womanly power. She had only thought there was an easier way.

Obadiah comforted the girl as best he could, then sent her back to her quarters. He would make arrangements, he promised, to keep her in Samaria for the winter. He needed much wisdom for the plans he had to make. Ahab and Omri were worried about war. They were soldiers, and that threat seemed most real. But Obadiah was a Hebrew, and he trusted Elijah as much as he feared him. If Elijah's words were true, a drought was coming, and famine would follow. Obadiah searched his scrolls to find the words of Moses, the tale of a palace steward named Joseph who had led the Egyptians through a mighty famine. If Yahweh had mercy, it would not come to that. But if He did not relent, these words could still save many, if only Obadiah applied them faithfully.

Toward the final watch, he smelled smoke, a sweet thick smoke, like those of the cooking fires from the kitchens. But this came from somewhere else. He followed the scent until he came to a window. In the distance, a fire glowed from a makeshift altar of Asherah that Ahab's men had set up.

Obadiah retched, holding his hands against his mouth to quiet the sound. He had to keep this secret until he was sure, until he held a burnt bone here, on Hebrew soil.

Everything that defined Israel was changing. A blessed nation was under a curse. The winter rains would not come. The first infant had died to honor a foreign goddess, a demon Obadiah did not know.

Obadiah wondered if there was any mercy now to save them.

7

Jezebel

Jezebel thought about all the little birds she had caught and fed to her snake back in Sidon. Had they felt this way? Swallowed, dissolved, taken up forever into some enemy's territory. That's what it was like to lie with a man every night and grow his child in her womb. All her life, her enemies had been visible, external, people she could run from. Now her own flesh had become the detestable thing. Ahab's body had consumed hers, and this thing grew inside her, feeding off her, the lump in her belly just like the snake's.

She hated Jezreel, too, where they had relocated two weeks ago.

Its location made sense, however. Two main trade routes crossed through Jezreel. One connected the upper and lower nations, one connected the eastern and western nations. Jezreel stood at the heart of it all and had to be defended. If a nation attacked Jezreel, it would send the entire region into uproar. They'd be swarming with everyone from the beautiful Egyptians to the rowdy Arameans brandishing swords and getting drunk under the trees.

The palace was a disappointment, even more than Obadiah had prepared her for. The builders had given no thought to its appearance, or construction, or even layout. It was a military palace, built by a military man for his men. Much smaller than the one in Samaria, it was surrounded by a thick wall that had towers on each of the four corners. Like Samaria, it was built on an elevation. Anyone sitting by a window had a view of a garden and vineyard below and of the valley. That would be pleasant enough, she thought, though Omri only wanted a clear view of approaching enemies. He had not meant to give anyone happiness.

The wall around the palace had a massive gate, which she was pleased to see was finished, and in front of the wall was a deep, dry moat. A man could die from the fall into such a moat, cut from rock as it was. No army could dig through the walls around the palace without getting past the moat.

She hesitated to even call Jezreel a city. It was a palace flanked by a few buildings and residences, and outside this wall were tents for the soldiers in the valley below.

Ahab had gone out to survey the trade routes and talk to the soldiers. She was disgusted by the catch in her heart when he left her. He was familiar, and this was an unfamiliar place. That's all she felt, she told herself. She could not trust him, not if he lacked the strength to do what was right by his own gods. Her god had tested her, and she had proven herself worthy. Ahab was being tested by his god too. Any hope she had once had that he would banish her or kill her in obedience to his god was gone. This pain was hers forever.

The ashipu entered her chamber and began setting out his materials.

"Get out," she said, and both Lilith and Mirra looked up from their dice game, startled. The ashipu kept working. None of them was sure who she was talking to, so she yelled. "All of you!"

Mirra and Lilith left at once, but the ashipu did nothing.

"You cannot put this off any longer," he said.

She gave in, spitting in a clay pot, and her healer assessed the color and texture. She urinated in another pot, and he murmured over that as well. He added the blessed thistle and stirred, whispering incantations. Jezebel stared as the watery contents turned red. Next he passed a fresh liver from a recent sacrifice over Jezebel's midsection. He laid it on the table next to a clay model of a liver, drilled with holes all over. As he surveyed the sacrifice, he noted the pattern of fat and nodules and placed a corresponding peg in each hole on the model until his diagnosis was complete.

"It is a girl," the healer said. He cleared his throat.

Jezebel shook her head from side to side.

"You did it wrong," she said. "The gods are testing your skill."

The healer cleaned the table and placed the model back in his stained bag.

"I am never wrong." He smiled. "Besides, the answer is from the gods. Perhaps they test you."

Jezebel glared at him. His skirt wrapped tightly around a thin, sunken waist, and he was shaved clean, as all ashipu were, but the gray hairs grew back quickly, giving his head a dull glow when the light hit at an angle. She guessed him to be seventy, considered the most excellent age for healers, who worshipped numbers and their combinations.

She rose and went to a window and watched a stray brown dog scavenge beneath her window for bits of food the guards were tossing to it.

Jezebel turned back and faced the healer. "I'll drink the copper and abort it. I haven't told Ahab that I'm pregnant yet."

The healer shook his head. "First, the copper can only seal the womb before life begins. Once life claims the womb, it is a fierce adversary. And second, Ahab is not a stupid man. He is waiting for you to tell him, perhaps, but he already knows."

She chewed her lip, watching the ashipu. He had no solutions or perhaps refused to offer them.

"I don't want a daughter!" It was the first time she had used that word, *daughter*, and the sound of it in the room made her weak. She sank to the floor, and he rushed to help her, grabbing her under her arms, trying to lift her up, but she collapsed into him and screamed.

"Not a girl! Please! Get rid of it."

He stroked her hair and rocked her as she sucked in air between dry groans that shook her body. She didn't know how to cry without tears. And she would not let tears come.

"My princess," he said, "I will lift your name to the gods. I will order another sacrifice for you, would you like that? Perhaps the gods will have mercy."

"You are so kind," Jezebel said, hating him for it. Kindness was nothing but salt in her wounds.

She reached up and wrapped her hands around his neck, gently at first so he wouldn't realize what she was doing until her grip was perfect. Then she squeezed with all the rage flooding her veins for that baby he would not kill and the rains that would not fall. Little blood vessels burst in the whites of his eyes as he writhed in horror. When he collapsed within seconds, her grip grew stronger. He was not putting up a good fight, and she wanted someone else to hurt like she did. She wanted him to fight, but no matter how hard she squeezed, he just sank at her feet until he lay on the floor, twitching, his eyes closed. She stood and kicked him. He did not move. She stomped on his belly, hoping it would swell and hurt him. But he was dead. She bent down and laid her face against his, moaning in agony. He was so fortunate.

The guard outside her door looked when she made those noises, shocked to see the ashipu lying on the floor.

Jezebel sat up, feigning shock and grief. She had seen enough mothers at the sacrifices in Phoenicia to know how to do it. "I tried to save him!"

"I'll call for help," he said.

It's too late now, she thought.

Ahab

Disturbing news from Samaria reached Ahab a month after they'd arrived in Jezreel. Samaria was more than six weeks past the supposed start of the winter rains, but not a drop had fallen. The mood in the city had changed, his messenger said. Workers did not sing as they worked. The sounds of labor were late in starting and ended well before sunset every day. Ahab had to authorize an increase in wages to get even half the labor done. Since the rain stopped, no one wanted to work on finishing Baal's temple. He wrote to Jezebel's father, asking for additional laborers to come. Their energy and artistry would revive the work.

He was returning to their palace after a ride with Obadiah. They had been talking to the troops, checking the roads that led in and out of Jezreel. There had been no sign of Ben-hadad's scouts, but neither had there been rain.

Ahab and Obadiah rode on to the palace before dawn as Jezebel's priests began to line the roads, burning thick pots of incense between them on the ground. The air was thick with smoke. Servants held clay rattles shaped in the figures of their god and goddess, shaking them as Ahab approached. Every other priest held a torch in his hand, so that the line of torches became a flickering spitting serpent winding up the hill to the palace of Jezreel.

Jezebel stood in the path, no jewels adorning her soft, long neck. She held her hands low across her belly, and he knew she was ready to tell him.

Obadiah stopped his horse short, his face changing as he saw her swollen belly. She faced Ahab, who dismounted, kissing her hands and pressing them to his face before kneeling to kiss her womb. She did not move when he touched her. It was like caressing a statue.

The priests began a low song, a prayer for the future springing to life in her womb. The servants sang too, shaking their rattles back and forth as they chanted. The music rose as the sun did, sounding like the heartbeat of the world, and the priests danced as they received visions.

"Blessing on the house of Ahab!" they cried. "Ahab's name will be great! He does not cast off the many gods who watch, and so they will watch over him!"

Soldiers poured out from their tents. They were used to the prophets of Israel, who talked in plain terms and preferred the company of simple people and children.

Ahab let go of Jezebel and faced his people. "Everywhere in this country I find a city in ruins. Israel has faced many battles. Like you,

I was once willing to die for this nation. But the time to die for her is done. It is time to build, my friends. It is time for new life!"

The priests let out a shout of victory and filled in the path behind the king, cutting him off from the soldiers. Ahab took hold of Jezebel's hand and led her back up the plain dirt path to the palace.

"Are you pleased?" he asked her, his voice soft enough so that no one else heard.

"Are you?" she asked. "That's all that matters, isn't it?"

It was a sweet sentiment that sounded sour from her lips. She was a strange bride, he knew, but she carried his child.

Bearing children changed a woman, people always said. It gave women new purpose in life. It changed their heart, enlarged it somehow. For any other woman, Ahab thought that would be a natural progression, an easy growth. But Jezebel's heart was so guarded, so carefully constricted, he knew the growth might be slow. He had spent a full month in the beginning teaching her how to rest in his arms, how to bear his touch. He had spent months after that coaxing her to not just receive his touch but return it.

He wondered, with a sigh to himself, how much more he would have to teach her.

Obadiah

"The news from Samaria is not good," Obadiah said the following morning. "You need to act. If it rains soon we might be able to save the last half of the growing season."

Ahab drank his wine as they strolled in the vineyard below the palace and surveyed the blossoms growing heavy with fruit.

"We have nothing to worry about," Ahab said. "I have eight trackers looking for Elijah."

"What good will it do to find Elijah? It is the Lord who cursed Samaria." Obadiah could not bring himself to say that the Lord had cursed Ahab—although that was the truth—just as he had not found the courage to tell Ahab that he suspected an infant had been offered on Asherah's altar. No one could make such an outrageous charge without proof. Obadiah had gone to the altar that night when the priests were gone, and it had been swept clean. If there was no shame in what they did, why did they leave no trace? That they had hidden their actions was enough proof for Obadiah, but no one else.

"One of Jezebel's priests spoke to me," Ahab said. "He said the curse will end with Elijah's death."

Obadiah grasped Ahab by the arm. "Do you not hear a word I say? I am telling you, the Lord is doing this. He is angered by the worship of Baal and Asherah. He is angered by your marriage to Jezebel. If you kill Elijah, that will provoke Him again!"

Ahab took a long draught of wine, then deliberately shook his arm to break Obadiah's grasp.

Obadiah's voice rose as he tried to explain one more time. "Israel is not like other nations. You cannot replace her religion, because she doesn't have one. She has the Lord. Do you understand the difference? There is a living presence in Israel."

"All those hours you spent in study, I spent on the battlefield," Ahab said. "Do you think that makes you smarter?"

"No."

"Then don't tell me how to run my kingdom."

"There are things you don't know," Obadiah began.

Ahab punched him in the stomach. Obadiah fell and laid on the ground, trying to suck air back into his lungs. Ahab didn't wait for him to recover, and Obadiah closed his eyes as Ahab's steps away stirred the dust, sweeping it into Obadiah's face.

The earth was so dry, and it was going to get worse.

"What are you doing?"

Mirra was approaching with a basket of figs.

"Greetings," he said, standing up too quickly, pressing a hand to his stomach to keep from crying out. He had never been punched in the stomach, not even as a boy.

She handed him her basket, oblivious, and unwrapped her veil from around her shoulders. He could see beads of sweat on her face; the afternoon sun was strong. She shook her hair and dropped the veil into the basket. Her shoulders were beautiful. Obadiah averted his eyes to avoid shaming her.

"Can I have my basket back?" she asked.

Obadiah could think of no reply, so he held it out to her. She looked at him with a puzzled expression, then turned to leave.

Obadiah was watching her, the way her soft robes moved and swayed with every step, her loose dark hair shaking, when she turned suddenly and caught him staring. Laughing, she tossed him a fig and then went on.

Obadiah checked the sun's position. Not even noon, and he had been humiliated twice today.

8

Jezebel

Jezebel sat in her bed, propped up by pillows, reading a letter from her father. He had heard of the curse and of the rain that had not fallen. He wanted to know if he should send a man to help her. Perhaps the son of an elder? The letter had come with a gift from the elders, who hoped she prospered in Israel and gave them good trading terms. They had sent a bed made of ivory with red and purple linens tied with chains of gold across the spindles that rose high from all four corners. Fine linen hung from each spindle; she could close it when the evening bugs grew heavy or she wanted to be free from the eyes of the servants. She despised the gift even as she knew she had to accept it. It was like swallowing bad milk. And yet the palace buzzed with excitement at possessing such a beautiful item.

The servants watched all and always had. They watched as she ate. They surveyed what was left in her pot when she awoke and made water. She remembered how her own had watched her drink the copper before worshipping with a man, and watched her without moving when she was sick and retched again and again. She hated anyone who pretended to want to help her. They only wanted to watch.

She looked around the room for a way to destroy the letter, but it was vellum. Burning it would stink up the room, and she had never learned to enjoy the smell of burning flesh.

Ahab staggered into the room, reeking of beer, and she balled the letter as best she could and left it. A servant was unwinding the belt around Ahab's waist, a huge linen cloth wrapped several times around, and he rocked unsteadily on his feet as it was loosened.

In only his tunic, he stretched and reached for his lower back with a groan. She dismissed the servant. She hated a witness when he touched her, even casually.

"Are you too drunk to listen?" she asked.

"Just don't lecture me," he said, collapsing onto the bed.

"Your father is so concerned with Ben-hadad that he may be neglecting a greater threat. Have you heard of Shalmaneser's raids in the north?" she asked.

"How do you know of those?" he replied, exhaustion making his voice hollow. "You don't talk to anyone but your priests. And that ashipu."

"He died."

Ahab looked at her, perhaps expecting an emotion.

"He was old and not very good at his job. But you are not listening. I was supposed to be a queen. I know how to keep my eye on my enemies."

"You are still going to be queen," he replied, touching her stomach lightly.

"Don't. I earned the crown in Phoenicia. It's not the same here."

He sat up. "You are not going to let me sleep, are you?"

She grabbed his right hand, forcing it open with his palm down, and pointed to his thumb. "Egypt." Then to his index finger. "Phoenicia." Then she squeezed the tender flesh in between, hard, to be sure he paid attention. "You. Israel." She pointed to his second finger. "The top? This is Assyria. Shalmaneser. Below him, in between the knuckles, that is Syria. Ben-hadad. Judah and Israel are tempting conquests. Control the middle ground between the two wealthiest nations, Phoenicia and Egypt, control those trade routes, and you can control the nations themselves."

"But Ben-hadad won't attack us. You already told us that."

"Not unless Shalmaneser joins him. Shalmaneser raids the northern territories every spring, just as his father did. Every year the same cities are attacked, in the same month, often on the same day. They agree to pay tribute, and he leaves until the next year."

"Even I knew that," Ahab replied. "And I had no hopes of being queen."

She ignored his joke. "The cities of the north are forming an alliance against him. Shalmaneser will defeat them, of course, using the gold they paid him to finance his campaign. With those cities crushed, unable to pay tribute for years, the Assyrians will have to find a new country to steal from. For years your only defense has been the Assyrian preference for victims who already play dead. Shalmaneser will become dangerous once he has won a real war. I have heard tales of his atrocities that would make the hair rise along your neck. He is growing in aggression."

Ahab chewed his lip, perhaps thinking of what he had seen in battle. Surely a soldier understood depravity. She had never seen it herself, but the tales had scared her as a child.

Jezebel glanced to the window. "I met his father once, the first King Shalmaneser," she said. "He visited Phoenicia to discuss trade. He was a sharp-toothed man, with a muddy beard and yellow eyes. He had bruises all over, the way some men have tattoos. I did not like him. His son was there, though he hid behind his father's robes and leered at me. He stole sweets from the table when he thought no one saw, while the men talked and spit seeds on our floor. It is this boy who is in power, and takes his father's name."

"The Assyrians will never conquer Israel," Ahab said. "I have seen the conclusion of more wars than he will ever begin. That is why I want to build the cities to make Israel great. Every wall I build? Two rows of stone. Every tower? Archers, boiling oil, heaving stones. Every gate? Even the gods have to knock. No Assyrian will come near my cities or my bride."

Jezebel leaned back on her pillow. She was sleepy, though it was an early hour for her. Her body had changed so much, it was a stranger to her. "What news of Samaria? Has it rained?"

Ahab's muscles tensed, and he turned on his side. He fell asleep, leaving her alone with her sorrows in the still, quiet room, voices of the soldiers outside carrying through the walls.

The child within her made her stomach feel tight and unsettled. Thankful no servant was in the room, she knew it was time for what she had planned to do. There was something poetic about Ahab in this bed with her tonight.

She reached under the bed for a little dish she had hidden. She had brought it from Phoenicia, almost as an afterthought, realizing it might be of use if she needed to hurt someone. She just hadn't known that someone would be herself. She hadn't understood, then, that losing one crown would not be as painful and horrible as wearing one here.

Jezebel sighed as her hands cupped the small round bowl with a carved head of a crouching lioness on top. Inside were a small ivory spoon and the powder she had left over from a sorcerer's trade. She had given him her fattest emerald for this.

Jezebel lifted the lid off the bowl and shoveled the powder under her tongue. She was breathing hard, frustrated by having to teach a man, frustrated at her own body that made her a prisoner, frustrated at being eaten alive from the inside, every day this thing growing and squirming and kicking her. She spooned a second batch of the powder made from the waxy green flower and waited. If the child died, it was no loss. Not to her. Not even to the kingdom. If Jezebel died, it wouldn't mean much more. She wanted to feel death in the room with her, to believe escape was possible. She hesitated to reach for the spoon a third time, however. She wasn't sure she trusted death any more than she trusted any other deliverer.

She'd finally decided to reach for the spoon a third time when the drug blew through her veins, knocking her back onto her pillows as her back stiffened and she bit her lip. Blood ran down her chin, and she tried to wipe it, but could only swat loosely at her face with her limp hand.

But she didn't sleep. She lay there all night, with blood smeared across her face and the life within kicking her. Toward dawn, as Ahab stirred, she managed to turn away from him and face the wall.

Ahab was gone when she awoke. The sun lit the room, making the colors too bright for her sore eyes. She called for servants to attend her and vomited up the breakfast they brought. Lilith laid wet cloths across her forehead and asked Mirra to send for a crock of warmed water.

Mirra waited at the door for the water, and when it was delivered, she stood at the window, looking out, as Lilith began the slow, warm pour down Jezebel's spine.

"May I ask you a question?" Mirra asked.

Jezebel looked up to see her staring at her with intensity. Although Jezebel did not reply, Mirra continued. "You left your home, you rule a people you barely know. We are so different from Phoenicians, aren't we?"

"You are Israelites," Jezebel said. It was a clever reply, true and easily mistaken for polite discussion. It revealed nothing of what she thought, her disappointment that she had not bled on the sheets, that the child still kicked, that her own heart still beat. Jezebel wondered why, after all she had done, the goddess did nothing to help her. Asherah had yet to perform one wonder in this land, to offer one reassurance to Jezebel that all would be well.

"But we are not Phoenicians." Mirra sounded wistful. "In your country, there is wealth and exotic visitors, and entertainments, and every freedom."

Jezebel snorted in disdain but raised her fist to her mouth as if coughing. Lilith narrowed her eyes, but Mirra did not seem to notice.

"There is freedom, yes. Women are free to do whatever they like. They are free to dress as they want, free to share their bodies, free to refuse a pregnancy. But do not confuse freedom with having what you want," Jezebel said. "People are weak." Jezebel shook her head, and her eyes burned. She was as weak as any of them. "They get swept into lives they never wanted."

There were no altars in Jezreel, no way Jezebel could alert the goddess that she was in distress. No hope of making an offering. Jezebel hated the sight and sound of infants. Ahab blamed her nerves as a first-time mother. Jezebel only resented that she could not offer a child up and end her misery.

"I wouldn't know," Mirra said. "I don't have any freedom at all."

Her question stirred Jezebel back to the moment, remembering what it was like to be a girl and have to trust a man. It was not any easier than being a woman and trusting a goddess. "Are you promised to anyone?"

"No." Mirra shrugged. "Omri has surrounded himself with soldiers. The elders are bringing in more visitors from other nations, but my father has not met anyone worthy."

Jezebel signaled for Lilith to be done. "Do not trust your father. He'll do what is best for himself, not for you."

"If I was more like you, strong and wise, he would listen to me. I wouldn't be so afraid of being given to some man I despise."

Mirra was like a vague shadow of the girl she might have been.

"How frightened are you?" Jezebel asked.

Mirra's chin quivered. She had plenty of tears.

Jezebel smiled. "Fear can be strength. Fear will make you do great things."

"Call Obadiah to us," Jezebel instructed Lilith. "Mirra wants to send a message to her father."

Lilith raised an eyebrow, but Jezebel scowled, sending her off. Mirra was still protesting, horrified, as Obadiah entered. Lilith had draped a tunic over Jezebel, and was circling the princess with a sash worn low to accommodate her bulging stomach. He should have been red-faced to enter as his princess was being robed, but he did not seem to notice Jezebel at all.

His face was very still, unreadable, yet his eyes betrayed him. They followed every breath that escaped Mirra's lips.

"Mirra, do you have a message for your father?" Jezebel asked.

Mirra froze, refusing to say anything.

Jezebel did not try to hide her disappointment. "Obadiah, I apologize. I thought Mirra was going to send a message, but I was mistaken."

Obadiah backed out, with a furtive last glance at Mirra, whose tears ran down her cheeks. Jezebel had the feeling that Obadiah blamed her for Mirra's distress, but he could not know. Mirra needed to suffer. She needed to feel enough pain to make her rise above any feeling at all.

That was the only way she could save herself.

Obadiah

A great black shadow crept up Obadiah's back. Above him, a flock of birds migrated for the spring, just as the court now did. The winter had drawn to a close, and the court rode back toward Samaria after nearly six long months in Jezreel. He stretched up, sitting tall in his saddle as the birds flew overhead, and for one second, his shadow was lost in theirs.

The journey back to Samaria was a long, wearisome one. The court could not move fast, though many of Jezebel's priests and servants rode camels. Camels covered a lot of ground with each step. Obadiah wished that there were more riders and fewer singers and dancers who announced the princess's progress with every step taken. Ahab had hired them, thinking it would cheer Jezebel, who seemed distressed and despondent as her due date came closer.

Ahab was anxious to return, to hear news from the scouts who were watching for Ben-hadad. Ben-hadad had waited for the winter rains to pass, as all kings did. If he knew of the curse, he had not believed it and had stayed home.

Obadiah hoped for news of the first drops of rain. He looked back, straining to catch a glimpse of Ahab. Ahab rode with his father, and his defiant glare warned that he wanted no interruption.

Obadiah knew the reason for his banishment on the journey. He had, just last night, warned Ahab to send Jezebel's priests back to Phoenicia. There were hundreds, Obadiah had pointed out, and if a famine came, the court could not support so many without burdening the people. It was an excellent argument. The people supplied the food to the court and would be frantic to feed their children. Being forced to feed hundreds of foreign priests, while Elijah was whipping up passions against them, would push the country into civil war. This was Obadiah's prediction and the reason for his punishment today. Ahab confused a legitimate concern for the people with antagonism for Jezebel's gods. Maybe Obadiah did too, he thought. Those were closer than Ahab admitted.

Toward dawn on the third day of the journey, they passed a
white-haired Bedouin man milking a camel as a calf nursed on the
other side, forcing the milk to flow. Beside him, a woman in a black
veil sat on the ground, shaking a goatskin bag to make butter or
curds. On this day, no less than six families traveling the road asked
for, and received, permission to fall in behind the royal caravan.
A royal caravan of this size was security for the lonely roads ahead.
One mother had introduced her daughters to Obadiah, all six of
them, with a hopeful gleam in her eye. He felt nothing but pity as he
looked on their crooked faces. None were as beautiful as Mirra, but
that thought seemed shameful to him, so he was especially kind to
them all. Her first four daughters had inoffensive common names,
after trees and flowers, but the fifth was Zaoule, "the nuisance," and
the sixth Tamam, "please, no more."

He wished them well and kept the caravan moving with a shout.

The sky was dark gray, tempered with white edges. The hills
beyond were shrouded in darkness; the trees that stood in the distance looked black. At noon they stopped to rest near a well and
watched as a woman attempted to draw water. She pulled on the
rope that twisted around an old, thick tree branch braced above
the well. The water bucket came up fast and swinging. She peered
inside, then lifted it to her mouth and shook, a scowl on her face.
Her children stood at a distance, huddled together in dirty tunics,
their faces confused and afraid. Ahab shouted the command to move
on without waiting for Obadiah to do it.

They had left Jezreel's green world and entered the world of rocks
and snags and dust. There were tricks waiting here; rocks the donkeys did not always see and stumbled on, thorns instead of blossoms.

They entered the region of Samaria by noon. The afternoon shadows were long and dark. The hills were lower, and there were olive trees in groves but no green gardens to play in. The drought was revealing itself in a slow brown spread.

The wall had been built up, though Obadiah felt cold disappointment to see the meager progress that had been made. Not as much as Ahab would have been able to accomplish had he remained here, without a wife, without trouble. Obadiah paused at the gates, which had not yet been set on their hinges but rested against the wall, which was only halfway to its proper height. He sat up straight, keeping watch over the caravan as it entered the city, conscious to keep his eyes on the horizon as Mirra passed.

The gates seemed to him like judgment. The court was not entering Samaria; they were all passing into darkness.

Jezebel

Jezebel instructed Lilith to give extra attention to her hair and cosmetics on the third morning of the return journey to Samaria. No one in that city had set eyes on her for six months. Perhaps they would see her and know what she had done for them, her bulging womb a blessing to them, and proof of the injustice she suffered. She was meant for more, but this was all she was reduced to. She hoped they saw her condition and wept. She hoped her father heard of her pregnancy and realized all he had wasted.

Lilith plaited her hair and pulled it back, using red cosmetics on Jezebel's lips and cheeks and nails. Jezebel instructed her to use Egyptian green for her eyes, sweeping it far back into the hairline.

She would ride in the litter with the curtains pulled back so the people could see her.

Obadiah walked past Lilith at her work with the cosmetics, and Jezebel called to him.

"Find Mirra and bring her," she said. "She should ride with me."

Lilith chose this moment to apply the malachite to her eyes, so Jezebel did not see his reaction. He probably blanched or swallowed hard. It must be a terrible humiliation to love someone.

"I have not seen her," he replied.

Jezebel stayed Lilith's hand and opened her eyes. "I did not ask if you had seen her."

His face was red, but he turned quickly away, into the sun. He returned with Mirra.

"Help her into the litter," Jezebel said. "Lilith, ride behind us. Borrow a donkey." She motioned for Lilith to be gone. Obadiah did not reach to help Mirra up. He seemed frozen. She grabbed his hand and did not see him flinch as if bitten. How long had he loved her? Jezebel wondered. Did he have a plan to end his suffering, or was he going to be its victim forever?

Lilith grunted in disgust as she set off to find a donkey.

As they approached, Jezebel sensed that a spell had been cast over the city. Instead of cheering for her, the people acted offended by her. As she was carried through the city's main road, no one ventured past the door of their tent. They looked at her with dark, wounded eyes. But all had fat on their cheeks; no one looked gaunt or hungry. It had not rained since Jezebel's arrival, but no harm had come. Everyone was still eating from last year's storage. They had no emergency. They accused her with their eyes but refused to see what she had done for them, what she was giving them. Even if it was a girl, it had some value. It had Ahab's blood.

Jezebel had seen no barley growing in the fields as they approached, nor wheat. She stirred, uncomfortable to think that this spring would bring nothing but horrors. Hunger and a girl as the firstborn to the throne.

As they made their miserable progress through the half-finished wall, Jezebel was careful to smile, especially with the daughter of richest man in town beside her, past the display of shields to the right, which would grow bigger now that they returned with soldiers. Mirra was a guarantee that the elders would not turn against her without forewarning. Mirra loved to talk of what she felt and what she thought and what she worried over. Jezebel would help her, yes, but Mirra would help her, too. Mirra would remind the people that their elders had supported this marriage.

Ahab rode in front of her litter, sword at his side, his back straight and defiant. His throne was secure. He had held Jezreel for another winter. Now he returned to see that Samaria had almost finished her transformation. He had reason to be proud and certain. Yet he slowed when he turned past the display of shields and headed toward the palace, unwilling to speak with the people.

Jezebel felt Mirra shift and saw her start to eye the ground, thinking perhaps she should now walk alongside the princess, instead of being elevated above the people she knew. Now that Mirra had seen into Jezebel's eyes, she seemed to want to pull away. Temereh had wanted to pull away too, Jezebel remembered. She realized that she didn't push Temereh into the fire pit; she had only let Temereh go.

Jezebel grabbed Mirra's hand and gripped it tightly, preventing her from pulling away.

The procession from the gate to Omri's palace took no less than two hours to complete. Jezebel was pleased to see the amazed expression of the people as they saw all her priests and artisans traveling behind her, no fewer than five hundred souls. King Omri did not wait to speak to the people, did not even wait for Jezebel to get out of the litter before he entered the palace, but she knew he enjoyed the impressive entrance. A true king commanded vast resources.

To the left of Omri's palace, a small, modest residence had been built. It needed much work, Jezebel knew, but she was so grateful to have a private residence like a real queen. She sat up, thinking of all that must be done, including receiving whatever news from her prophet-killer. She needed to sit up to relieve her throbbing head. Lilith had perfumed the litter for the entrance, and it stank. Jezebel had lifted her head to catch a clean, pure breeze when she saw them. Men were appearing, one by one, on the low hills surrounding the city. Without a full wall blocking their view, they could see everything. They looked like black moving trees from this distance, but by instinct, she knew who they were. Prophets. Dozens of men like Elijah.

She did not see Elijah, the plague prophet, among them. But she could not believe he could resist the chance to look on their glorious return; she narrowed her eyes and searched the hills again. He had to be among them.

The child kicked within her, and she grimaced, anxious to be out of this litter. Panic began to rise, forcing bile into her throat. The people shifted and swayed in her vision; the litter was tossing side to side. Mirra grabbed her, calling for help.

Jezebel couldn't help the scream that escaped, shattering the silence of Samaria.

The pain was like a vengeful knife thrown to rip Jezebel open, to force her into the pit with her sister. In her panic, she thought she saw a god, its flashing white teeth at her stomach and throat, tearing her apart, as the child began its bloody fight to emerge. Pitching to the side, clutching her belly, she was in danger of falling off the litter. The men carrying her stumbled at her scream, and she began to slide off. Her priests, traveling behind, were already racing toward her, taking hold of her shoulders and supporting her. Several grabbed the poles of the litter, elbowing the servants out of the way. The servants screamed at them and grabbed again at the poles, and mayhem broke out. Priests swarmed the litter, cursing the servants as others supported Jezebel and maids chanted in frightened, high-pitched tones. The screams came so fast and hard her head was forced back. She hadn't thought the baby would come yet. The ashipu died without telling her the date. He had betrayed her.

Jezebel was going to die in the dusty streets of Samaria.

Ahab was off his horse, shoving men out of the way to get to her. She heard him scream her name, watched him moving as if the world had slowed to a crawl, as if the distance was too great. Confusion took command; none of her priests or Ahab's soldiers or the commoners moved out of his way or obeyed. Everyone was shouting orders to the others or reaching for her. Hands grabbed at her from all sides, and her gown tore at the shoulder as someone grabbed the sleeve and pulled.

Then she saw deliverance. Ahab's sword, the sword of Moses, flashed in the afternoon sun like a silver strike of lightning as Ahab unsheathed it, the muscles of his broad arm pumping as the sword began to cut through the men. He smashed it against shoulders and heads and used it as a club to reach the litter. The men fell away like broken dolls, dropping silently as Ahab leaped up, his eyes telling Jezebel that he was stronger than she knew. Maybe he said something, but she heard nothing except the pounding of her heart and the explosion of staggered breaths. She reached for him, keeping one hand on her belly to stop the pain.

His sword sheathed, he wrapped his arms around her as men lowered the litter to the ground. With no other choice, she sank into Ahab's arms. He lifted her without effort, carrying her up the steps into his palace. Looking up into his face, with its grim determination to safeguard her, to rescue her from the people and the pain, she felt a new pain. When his eyes met hers, she knew the truth.

He did love her, a real love. Nothing good had ever happened in her life, but she closed her eyes and told herself not to try to hold onto this.

She was going to disappoint him.

9

Inside her chambers, Jezebel was on her side, her face buried in pillows. Sound carried in this so-called palace; it still had so few furnishings and carpets. She screamed into the pillows, refusing to let servants hear her and doubt that she was strong enough to deliver a child. She would come out with a child even if it took her life. Her name would not suffer.

Sargon entered the room, and Jezebel's heart leaped when she heard his voice.

"You're here," she whispered, having little strength to speak.

"I wanted to see you wearing a crown," he said. He was wearing his necklaces, and the fat gold ring that signified his position of chief priest of Phoenicia. How good it was to see those ornaments again.

She tried to smile, but the pain was too much.

He leaned over her, smoothing her hair back. Seeing his eyes, which were like none other, comforted Jezebel. Blue they were, and they flashed like lightning in his face, which was handsome and weathered, his age being hers plus forty. His hair was pure white, kept neatly groomed, and his beard disguised a wry red mouth that reminded her of home.

"Your husband is outside," Sargon said. "He demands that a Hebrew midwife be sent in. What is your wish?"

Jezebel clenched her teeth to keep from making a sound as a wave of pain hit. "What is yours?"

Sargon tilted his head to one side, thinking. "Birth is sacred and magical. Midwives serve their gods, and the Hebrew god does not like you." He looked at her. "I am not scolding you. Your father should have warned you about this Yahweh. He knew. He sent you because he thought you were the only one strong enough to face Yahweh and defeat him."

Jezebel caught her breath for a brief, bright moment, the air sweet and cool. Her father had seen something worthy in her.

Sargon continued. "The Hebrew midwife must not enter. Do I have your consent to lead?"

She nodded.

Sargon's voice rose above the others, a deep comfort to her. "It is the seventh day of the month; a day of powerful magic for the Hebrews!"

The other priests quieted to listen.

"You do not understand the forces at work against us on this day," Sargon said to the other priests. "Seven is a holy number to them, the number of creation. But this god Yahweh has no companion or rival. What he chooses to create, he can choose to destroy. To deliver her child on the seventh day puts Jezebel under Yahweh's power."

"What do we do? No one can stop a birth," another priest asked. He was one of four who huddled around, worthless. They had been the ones her father had sent, and her father never had given her the best of anything. Until Sargon's arrival.

"We will try to delay the birth until the moon sets tonight," Sargon replied. "Can you prepare anything?" She thought he must be speaking to an ashipu.

The pain was intense. She begged for relief. There was a drug of forgetting that the ashipu prepared for wealthy women; she could sink away from the pain.

Sargon's hand rested on her head. "Let us wait. You are strong. Fight to hold the child in."

She moaned in agony.

Ahab could not, by his nation's Hebrew law, enter the birthing chamber, but she could hear him pleading with Sargon, begging that a Hebrew midwife be permitted inside. She glanced up to see Ahab standing in the doorframe, looking like a child caught stealing. He cleared his throat and pushed a woman forward.

"Her name is Deborah. She is an excellent midwife." Ahab nodded and left, not bearing to look at Jezebel. Deborah came to the princess at once, feeling her forehead, urging her to sit up and drink some water. Jezebel turned over a little, trying to shield her belly from this woman.

"Everyone out! I have work to do," the midwife said, shaking her finger at the men, with the confident tone of a woman who had delivered every child born within the city. Sargon turned to an ashipu and nodded. The ashipu moved fast, crossing the room quickly, and brought something to Jezebel's lips. As Jezebel drank, she saw a priest grab the midwife, his hand over her mouth as he pushed her from the room. As the door opened and closed, and Jezebel's eyes grew heavy, she felt the air stirring around the bed.

Death was in the chamber with them. She knew that as she slipped away. She knew his smell, the way he reeked of old nests and smoke and stinking fruit. He was there, and he was hungry. Jezebel wished now she had not desired him months ago. She knew why she was in this rat-infested city with a prince she had not chosen.

She was here to destroy a god. She would live for that.

～✣～

Blood ran from the soft folds of Jezebel's robe onto the floor. She woke in a dark chamber lit only by oil lamps scattered on tables throughout the room. Glancing at the window, she judged the hour to be before dawn. Instinctively, she reached for her stomach. The child had not yet been born. The day of awful magic for the Hebrews had passed; the potion had worked, allowing her to deliver hours later, when the moon had changed and it was a new day.

She lurched forward, screaming. The air was heavy with the odor of sweat and vomit. Pale-faced attendants laid wet linen strips against her forehead as she cursed them. A large roll of dirty linens was carried away by two male servants who strained as they lifted it.

She screamed again, a sound of fury meeting pain, and gripped the arms of her servants so tightly that they would not be able to carry her goblets for days. Her eyes rolled back in her head as she gave one last desperate push and expelled the child onto the blankets. The baby let out a tinny cry.

Jezebel's eyelids fluttered, and she fell into a strange vision. Far from the room, a serpent moved in the shadowlands, its mouth opened wide, venom spraying softly from its fangs in the moonlight.

Sargon tended to the baby, severing the cord and using salt water to bathe it. The smell of the sea overpowered the room, transporting Jezebel home. Ahab had given her this child, that man whose body had once been the sea, his strong waves breaking over her, and she was returned to the churning depths, this treasure revealed, this wailing red siren that captivated Sargon. His face shone with pleasure when he saw Jezebel watching. He used an ivory dish shaped like an ibex to pour olive oil over the child's shivering body, then set to work with his right hand, rubbing it in. The child turned its head, and Jezebel looked into its eyes for the first time.

Jezebel felt nothing, which was sweet relief. It opened its mouth, a soundless little gesture, as if forming a word for her.

"It is a girl," Sargon said.

Jezebel brought a hand to her face to hide her shame.

He presented the infant first to the statue of Asherah, lit from within by a yellow candle, and then presented her to the princess. Jezebel looked at the child, who squirmed and cried. She caught sight of herself in the mirror hung low by her bed and saw her hair disheveled, the tiny blood vessels in her eyes burst from the exhaustion of birth, the dark rings underneath. Temereh had looked prettier than this when she died. Temereh had not been strong, though. She had not been chosen. She had only been born to speak for the gods, not kill one.

Jezebel reached down to touch the baby, and servants huddled around, smiling nervously. Jezebel pinched the infant, who screamed.

"Welcome to Samaria," she said. She waved the baby away. "Take her to a nursemaid, and send for an attendant to wash me at once. And bring me a bowl of red copper to drink lest another child see the womb empty and desire entrance from the other world."

She slept then and woke sometime later, groggy and sore. Her groin burned and throbbed in agony. Her head pounded as if someone had smashed her brains in with an iron. Opening her eyes, she saw she was alone with Sargon. She had not been alone with him since she left Phoenicia.

"How much do you know of my trouble here?" she asked.

He looked up from the papyrus he was reading. With a gentle smile, he set it on the table beside his stool and crossed to her, bringing his stool with him. He sat next to her.

"There are fanatics in every empire," he said. "Elijah is yours. He is your best chance. If you can get rid of him, you'll get rid of the god. No one wants to worship a god without someone to lead them. That is human nature."

"Why wasn't I warned?" she asked. "He's cursed the people with a drought, and they think it is my fault. And there is Shalmaneser, and Ben-hadad … my father did not prepare me for this."

He reached out and touched her cheek. "I think he prepared you very well."

Outside the chamber, a bird sang, a pure and sweet song. A peace descended in the stillness of the room. They were alone, yet Jezebel sensed something more, but it had a lightness to it. She saw her reflection in Sargon's eyes, this man who had taught her to sacrifice, who had led her into the world of gods and goddesses and visions. In his eyes, she saw she was still a young woman. A thought came to her, clear and soft: her past did not have to be her future. Maybe she had looked at life through the wrong eyes. Maybe there was something more. Something else.

She wanted to ask Sargon if he had ever heard strange, peaceful whispers, but something told her he hadn't.

Sargon laid his hand on her shoulder, and as he blinked, her reflection was lost. Smiling up at him, she remembered who she was, what she was born to do. Jezebel was born to reign.

The bird beyond her chamber fell silent.

Ahab

Ahab sat on his throne as two advisers argued and five elders presented their requests. So many voices made it hard for him to think,
and he rubbed his forehead for relief from a growing headache. Omri
had retired an hour ago, worn out by the bickering that could not
be resolved with a sword. Ahab was thankful. He was embarrassed
by the truth, which was that it had not rained for nearly a year. The
pregnancy and the move to Jezreel for the winter had disguised the
passage of time, but this was the truth. Jezebel's body had given up
its secrets, and the passage of time had given up Ahab's.

The drought was real.

A curse was upon Israel. Ahab had chosen to obey his father
instead of Yahweh, and because of his choice, people would suffer.
Ahab had seen lands wiped out by drought and famine. He had never
forgotten the children with bloated bellies and flies in the corners of
their eyes, sitting next to dead mothers. Women went looking for
food or water and died in the streets.

Jezebel entered, her body still clearly weak from giving birth only
two days before. All the men dipped their heads once in respect, stepping back from the throne. Ahab had allowed a smaller throne to be

built for her use in court, and she sat in it warily, keeping an eye on the men. Ahab cleared his throat, hoping to remind her of her manners. She still couldn't be trusted to be civil with men she did not know. In fact, she still couldn't be trusted to be civil to men she did know.

"Welcome to my future queen!" Ahab said. The men murmured in forced concurrence.

Ahab stood to make his announcement. "Next week, as some of you may know, is the Feast of First Fruits, an important day for the Yahwehists. I plan on holding a feast here at the palace, for everyone in the city of Samaria. We will celebrate the birth of my daughter, who is to be named Athaliah, or God is praised."

There were whispers from those who frequented the temple of Baal, but Ahab was ready.

"I am not a Yahwehist. I am a ruler. I want peace. Let her name signal that we want peace with the Lord. I have seen drought, my friends. It is a terrible way to die."

He judged by their faces that they were considering his words. He continued.

"This feast will appease Elijah. It will give our people cause to stay in Samaria for the event and not travel to the temple in Jerusalem as they have in the past. Their money will remain within our borders, which is good. We need every resource right now, including Elijah's goodwill."

Mirra's father stepped forward. "We must conserve our food. I am loyal to you, Ahab, you know that, but I believe Elijah. If he says the drought will last, it will."

"Do not be troubled, Amon," Jezebel said, placing her hand on Ahab's arm. "My priests have made an offering to my gods, who control the rain. They say Baal is well pleased at the construction of a temple in his name here. His wife, Asherah, has accepted our gift. It will rain."

Ahab leaned in to her and whispered, "You cannot promise rain. If you don't deliver, they will be at your throat."

Jezebel turned to face him before speaking. He wished she would keep her voice lower. "This is your kingdom. Not Elijah's. It doesn't belong to a wandering band of prophets, either. You should never have let any of them live. And you have to make bold promises if you want to keep the throne."

Ahab took her hand. "I can't speak for gods I don't believe in."

"The time will come, Ahab, when you will have to believe in one. Life forces everyone to that moment."

Ahab crushed her hand in his and pulled her to him. He pinned her other hand, and he wrenched her closer yet to whisper in her ear. He saw out of the corner of his eye that the elders noticed this display of displeasure with his wife. Her eyes went dead as he touched her like this. She did not seem to stay in her body when handled roughly. He had spent more than a year now trying to unlock her secrets, to discover what she hid and what she loved, but if he ever pushed her too far, her soul evaporated before his eyes.

He paid no attention to anyone else, not caring what they saw.

"Listen to me," he said. "All my life I was forced to worship a man ten times as big as me, ten times as bitter as a scorpion. When he handed me the crown, there was a sneer on his lips. He knew it would be too much for me, that I could do little but bear its weight and suffer. And yet I have built new cities. I have filled the treasuries and brought to my land a princess of Phoenicia. I have done all this, and I have done it without god or man. Do not tell me I will be forced to do anything. I will never be forced again."

He let go and saw that she was breathing hard, her eyes alight again, lips parted. She looked as if she felt desire for him, but how could that be? He had admitted a weakness to her, and she was not a woman who respected weakness. What did she see in him in these moments of confession?

She faced the court with a face like stone, betraying nothing of what she felt.

He turned and addressed the court once more. "I will amend my plans. Let us invite all people, from all provinces, to celebrate the birth and the feast at the temple of Baal and the shrine to Asherah, which are almost complete. After all, Athaliah does not belong to Yahweh. She does not even belong to me. She belongs to the nation."

Jezebel reached for his hand, and a flush of warmth came over him.

Obadiah

Obadiah grieved to see the priests of Baal and Asherah moving through the new temple, preparing for the Feast of the First Fruits. The temple was an abomination. Built for Baal, it had two columns in front, leading to an open area. Along one side was an archway opening into a room of tile mosaics, with couches lining the walls.

Straight through the main room was a smaller three-walled chamber where a stone altar rested. Tonight it had two bowls for incense. Beautiful, ornate bowls with ivory designs of flowers and vines, Obadiah noted, meant to distract the new worshippers among the Israelites. Behind the altar was a fire pit that went down deep into the earth. It was above this that Baal's arms extended as if to hear the prayers of his people. Obadiah noted how close the hands were to each other, slightly cupped. Here, he knew, they would place an infant. He had read too many accounts to have any more doubts that such evil could be embraced as good and necessary.

Asherah's tribute was outside, a slender statue of a tree of life. Artists had worked hard at the beautiful deception. Gone was the makeshift altar.

The statue of Baal rested on a throne, with his ugly head of a horned beast and his body of a man, but no man Obadiah would ever see. Baal had the body of one of God's great messengers, like the angel of the Lord. Obadiah shuddered at the thought. Whatever sat upon the throne, it was not from the Lord.

Outside the city gates, he heard the prophets of Yahweh wailing, tearing their sackcloth and smearing ashes on their faces, warning the people to flee. The people kept their faces down as they hurried toward the temple.

Obadiah wondered who would sacrifice their infant tonight. He understood the appeal now; to be free of a burden or a mistake, to pray that the future would be brighter. And when the priests promised it was a freedom they had long deserved, the women believed it. Sentiment was growing, Obadiah knew, that Jezebel had brought the future to Israel, and the future was the delusion of freedom for women.

Obadiah alone knew what this freedom would cost them, the cost of this night of feasting and the drought ahead. He not only read the past records, he kept the records of present and saw the prices driving up every week, quantity and quality growing less. He sweated at night as he reviewed the scrolls, trying to feed the court plus the four hundred priests of Jezebel, plus one hundred artisans. Ahab was in grave financial danger. Ahab was in every kind of danger, though, and Obadiah knew that Ahab didn't care. Didn't care, or refused to speak of it. Obadiah was abandoned with his scrolls and his knowledge and all his fears.

The priests lit the incense in the heavy gold bowls, and its sharp, thick smoke rose, snaking through the air. Obadiah closed his eyes in prayer that the fire pit would stay cold and dark tonight.

He watched as Jezebel smiled and held Ahab's hand while people arrived and bowed before them, laying gifts of gold and fruits at their feet. The tax law required these offerings, yet many were slow to release their goods from their hands. Obadiah understood. The people were bringing the best of what they had left, and what was left was not much. They offered it to please Ahab and Jezebel, to please the gods, to urge whatever powers ruled Israel to send rain.

Obadiah's heart burned. There were children in those homes, children who would not eat because their parents gave their food away. Those were the lucky children, though. They had a chance to live. They would never know the terror of resting in the hands of Jezebel's gods.

The people wandered through the open room of the temple and ran their hands along the smooth walls of the Chamber of Dreams. They admired the Asherah pole that stood outside the temple, the carved tree of braided limbs and wooden fruits. It looked pleasant to the eye. Obadiah watched as Sargon surveyed the temple and blessed it, then retreated into the shadow far away, as Jezebel received the attention.

She and Ahab presented the infant Athaliah and spoke of the future. Obadiah had not yet seen the infant close up; she was always carried about by a milk nurse or servant. Never with Jezebel, though, he noted. The darkness that had always hovered around her now seemed thicker, malevolent, as if birthing a child had brought something else with it for her too. Something disturbed and hungry.

A young girl he had seen many times in the market, a sweet girl who helped her father sell herbs, came and bowed alone before Jezebel and Ahab. She looked up at them with admiring eyes, seeing those jewels she had heard tell of, he was sure, probably smelling a perfume too rich for her means. He saw that she was dazzled, and it grieved him further. She was lovely in every way, too lovely for this nonsense.

"I have no offering, save my devotion," she said.

Jezebel extended her hand and smiled at her priests. "The throne is pleased to receive you," she said.

The girl's father soon came beside her, presenting a modest gift of wine at the feet of Ahab. Ahab nodded his acceptance, and the man stood to walk away.

"Nothing for your princess, not even a kind word?" Jezebel asked.

The man hesitated and turned back to face her. "I am afraid," he replied.

"Of what?" she asked. "I do not wish harm to you or your god. I only ask that mine be allowed too."

"It sounds good to my ears, princess, and I mean no disrespect, but it is wrong. I hear what the women whisper. They say your gods allow every pleasure, but I worry that that brings suffering. I cannot honor them."

Obadiah's heart jumped a little. He was not alone! Someone else saw as he saw and dared speak.

Jezebel spoke. "This land will not be ruled by ignorance."

He bowed to Ahab. "I am not an ignorant man, as Ahab knows. Let me tell you a story of Israel."

The man turned and faced the people, clearing his throat. His daughter shifted from one foot to another and caught the eye of a certain priest.

"Long ago, in a cruel land, we were ruled by one who said there was none to worship but himself. He was Pharaoh, and we were his slaves. We made his bricks and built his shrines, and he took our strength and our children. We cried in the silence of our hearts for our God. Did He not see the one who claimed to displace Him? Was He not angered that one claimed His throne? But the years passed and our fathers died under the sun, until one day when Pharaoh provoked God for the last time. God answered then, blanketing the land in darkness, frogs, pestilence, blood, locusts, flies. That is why I fear this temple, for His love rages as fiercely as His anger, and He will not suffer long one who leads His children into danger. I would rather face a man's wrath over my own wrongdoing than a father's wrath for having wronged his children. He moves among us and will not long be silent."

The people were motionless, only exchanging glances.

Jezebel stepped down toward him and moved to hold her hand out to him, to silence him perhaps. He backed away.

"You are unclean," he said. Obadiah cringed. That was true, but who would dare say that to a princess?

"We call our gods by different names, but do we not all want the same thing?" Jezebel said. She spoke like there was an unreasonable child before her.

The man backed out of the temple, shaking his head. "No. No, we do not. Forgive me, Ahab. I honor you as prince, but I cannot honor her gods."

Jezebel clapped to signal for the feast to begin, cutting Ahab off from further dialogue with the man.

The musicians began, and plates were passed among the people, plates of sweets and cakes, wines and soft stewed lamb. The priests passed between them a great goblet of offering wine, taking long red drinks before pouring the rest of it out at the feet of the Asherah tree.

Obadiah retreated to an empty, dark spot just outside the temple, trying to catch his breath. The man had spoken truth plainly. Why did Obadiah struggle to do the same?

The priests began dancing and fell into a trance, cutting themselves and begging for a vision of the new year. Would Asherah send rain and harvest? Would there be life in the wombs of all those who loved her, the women and the cattle, the sheep and the goats who grazed on her goodness abounding in the fields?

Obadiah moved to keep an eye on the young girl who had blessed Jezebel. She followed the priest she had watched, seeing him cutting himself across the chest, receiving supposed divine words he could not utter. The priest saw her through his trance and reached for her. Obadiah felt his face flush.

When the priest reached for her robe, she hesitated.

The priest leaned near and whispered in her ear.

She turned her head and kissed him, removing the robe.

Obadiah put his hand over his mouth and turned away.

Ahab

Later that evening, Ahab found Jezebel wandering along the temple's gate, having climbed to the guard's post and plank, watching the lovers below as they enjoyed the night air. He was glad to see her spirits so light. He could barely remember the last time she had smiled.

"It is pleasant here, is it not?" he asked. An odd little moth flew near, called from the desert by the flames beneath them. It flew near and alighted on Jezebel's cheek. She cursed, swatting it away.

"It stung me!" she said. A welt rose beneath the spot from which it had fled. Ahab cursed the air around him and tried to comfort her. He stroked her other cheek and softly kissed the one bitten. She turned away. He wrapped his arms around her and waited for her anger to soften. After a moment she eased into his grasp and looked up at him.

"You have done well to lead the people tonight," she said.

"Some will resent me," he replied. "They want me to choose."

"If a healer listened to the pleas of his patient, no one would ever be cured."

Ahab kissed her. She pushed him away, her hands running over the royal insignia of his robes. She was no longer as hostile to his advances, but she did not desire him in this moment. She had grown to trust him a little, that was all. She had begun to see something in him that made her soften when he reached for her, and for now, that was enough.

"Jezebel," he said, "you know how different our kingdoms are. Our daughter is beautiful. We can marry her into any kingdom we choose, but she will never rule Israel. I need an heir. A son."

She removed herself from his reach, as if repelled by the thought of what must happen again.

"Are you not inspired by the worship beneath us?" he asked, leaning against the stone wall with an easy smile on his lips. He reached for the sash of her robe, and she brushed his hands away. "I thought you believed in Asherah," he teased her. "I thought you believed in her gifts."

Her easy expression turned almost instantly to sorrow, and she slapped him. Through the sting of his cheek he saw an unbelievable sight. She had tears, real tears that were welling up in her eyes.

"I did believe! I did everything I was supposed to. Even when I came here, I did everything I was supposed to. And what has it gotten me? A mewling stinking daughter and a husband I did not want!"

Her words hurt. He had thought wrong. She wasn't opening up to him; she was still his vicious bride who refused all tenderness.

He walked away from her, down the stone steps, past the temple and back toward his chamber in the palace. She threw her royal ring after him, and it thudded into the dirt near him as he walked.

"Take this to a concubine and bid her give you a child in my name. It would be an honor for her."

"What is wrong with you?" he turned, shouting. "You are strong, but that does not mean you must be cruel. Everyone suffers, Jezebel. Everyone is disappointed by their god. But you and I can do something about our disappointment. We reign."

He watched as his words sank in, and sank in they did, her face changing again as she listened, that strange softness returning. She needed to hear what he said, but he wasn't sure why. Maybe he never would be; maybe all wives were mysteries.

He kicked the ring away with his foot and continued inside. As he walked, something troubled his spirit. It was a vague suspicion, like a growing darkness on the horizon, that Jezebel's mysteries would not remain hidden forever. Whatever plagued her would one day burst open over them all.

Jezebel

Jezebel rose early the next morning, unable to sleep during any of the night's watches. She dressed herself and went to the courtyard, where servants spied her and rushed out to bring her warmed barley and fruit. She brushed them back like irritating little birds and listened to the night.

Below the palace the villagers slept. She could hear donkeys dragging carts across the dirt paths sometimes—vendors moving to the open stalls before sunrise. She listened to the chants of insects in the distance, high and keening, and often she heard something stir the trees that was more than the wind. This was a land of unbreakable will.

She had been wrong; it would never be enough to only be permitted to worship as she pleased. Permission was not acceptance. She wanted acceptance, and, even more, she wanted her religion embraced. It was an odd irony, she realized, that men like Elijah were content to wander alone, convinced of their truth, while she needed people to believe as she did. She could not tolerate the dissenters.

She had to see that everyone embraced her gods. She had never been more convinced of that than she had been last night. The few who worshipped were not enough, and neither were the few sacrifices. She needed the people to believe with all their strength, to pursue Asherah and Baal with all their hearts. If they didn't, if she was alone, she might never know if her gods failed everyone, or if they had failed only her. She had always been second, from the moment of her birth. Asherah and Baal were second to Yahweh in this land. She was second to Ahab.

The only way she would ever have peace was to do what no one else was willing to do. It had always been that way. Distasteful work had been her birthright. She wanted a crown that no man had given her, and so she would push these people to accept gods they had never known. She would encourage sacrifices that made their stomachs turn. She would win a lasting reputation, and that was a crown no man could give—or take away.

She motioned for a servant.

"At first light, call to me all the priests and priestesses of Baal and Asherah. Summon every sorcerer and magician in my employ. Find also one hundred men from the army who love gold more than honor. And tell no one."

To kill a god, she would kill his prophets. In the silence that would fall, she would hear the voice of Asherah at last.

Obadiah

Obadiah refused sleep. He stood all night, weeping for the sins of his people. The Feast of First Fruits had been polluted, the sacred festival trampled. What good was the truth when no one listened? He tried to tell Ahab so many times, but when a heart is hardened, words cannot break it open. The greatest test of Obadiah's faith was to be this: to bear witness in evil days, and yet believe that the Lord was good.

"But Ahab fought battles," Obadiah whispered in prayer. "He has the ease of a man who has fought and won. He struck his enemies, and they fled. Give me something too, Lord. Do not ask me to suffer if I cannot fight."

The night air was quiet, the golden light of dawn illuminating the horizon. Camels on the hills were lonely black silhouettes, the morning mist swirling around them in a peaceful haze. The day came, and there was no sign that the Lord had heard his prayer.

Jezebel

Jezebel slept much of that day, until night returned and insects once again blotted out the sounds of servants who ran to fetch little comforts for her. She joined her priests at Baal's temple. Inside the temple, the last of the mercenaries entered as oil lamps were lit and set high on perches all around. The tables were swept clean of food, holding nothing but amulets, powders, and the mysterious hoards of the magicians. The mercenaries stared at the strange piles of feathers, bones and sticks until a sorcerer threatened to hex them all and covered the tables with the magician's cloaks.

Priests swept the room to the edges and placed bowls at every corner, every crack in the walls, to catch spirits that might enter unbidden.

Priests held their thumbs, the most magical finger, and keened quiet prayers as Jezebel took the throne she had placed here. It had winged lions for feet, polished gold, and her purple robes made the lions flash dark, as if shadows invested them with her thoughts.

The priests whispered spells over water and doused the mercenaries, moving through them, making sure each was anointed on his body, his sword, and his armor. Jezebel stood, and a priest sprinkled the water over her hands in a blessing.

In a corner, minstrels played the lyre, a sad song, Jezebel thought, of a lover lost at sea. She silenced the singer, and the musician played the lyre more carefully. She moved away from the throne, waiting at the altar for the priest to finish his blessing of night and of darkness.

A priest stepped forward to wash his hands over a clay bowl, careful to catch the water for his spell. Jezebel's womb ached, and she rested her wet palm against the altar for a moment of support. When she lifted it, she saw that it had left a dark imprint on the stone. She smiled to see herself embedded with Baal. Then it evaporated in the dry, waterless air, beginning at the edges until the air had consumed her entirely. Her mouth grew hard.

Standing at the altar, Jezebel surveyed the power of her name. She had summoned mercenaries to do her will, and sorcerers who would conjure the unseen world. She could command men with gold and bribe the gods with plunder. Ahab had wanted to drink tonight with his commanders. It was just as well. She alone wanted responsibility for the murders. Some deaths were necessary. The people would see that she alone had saved them.

"Behold!" she commanded, standing and spreading her arms like wings so that the purple sleeves of her robe draped below her. "A curse has been called down on the people of Israel. One man, with one god, has caused us all to suffer. He has called men to his cause. The women of Israel will burn with thirst, their children will die at the breast, and there will be no food because the fields will be dead. Is this what a good ruler should desire?"

The mercenaries looked at her and each other, not accustomed to speaking before an altar, even if a woman, and not a god, stood before it.

Jezebel continued, moving down to walk through them, exhilarated by the way they looked at her. They respected her, she could tell. Their eyes watched her as a beast recognizes a lion before its death. She moistened her lips with her tongue and ran her fingers along their shoulders, snaking between them, turning them different directions, keeping them from uniting in will just yet. She despised them for moving so easily beneath her fingertips. She was used to men who fought her.

"Ahab knows the power of this man Elijah and his so-called prophets. Yahweh is the god of Israel, and Ahab is its prince. Now, Ahab can't go to war with Yahweh. But neither can he seek Yahweh's favor as long as these prophets call down curses in Yahweh's name. So we must be wise. To catch a rat we must think like a rat. Why does Elijah warn Ahab to worship no god but Yahweh? Isn't it because Elijah would lose power? He resents that I have four hundred priests of Baal and Asherah who are fed and housed, who win the hearts of the people by performing acts of kindness and protection. Elijah's days are numbered, and he seeks vengeance on us."

One mercenary—the oldest, she thought, though attractive, his hair gray at the temples, his forearm still thick as a cedar—stepped forward. "What would you have us do?"

She stroked the muscle that ran down his arm, stopping when she got to the wrist resting on the hilt of his sword. She didn't mind touching a man when he was prevented from touching her back.

"Find the company of prophets. Kill them all. The curse will be broken when Elijah and all who think like him are dead. Then we will gather the people to Samaria and let them choose the god they will worship."

"What of Elijah?" a man called. "He does not camp with the prophets. He stays hidden."

"As I would want him to do," she replied. "I have sent a mercenary to kill him. Elijah will never be seen again in these lands."

She nodded to two priests who stood near the altar, and they brought forth a chest. Lifting the lid, the soldiers saw that it was layered elbow-deep in silver and gold coins. She watched as greed leered on their faces and they passed the coins around, filling pockets and satchels. The priests wrote the names of each man on a strip of cypress, along with the name of Elijah and his men, and set the strips on fire.

As they did this, Sargon entered with a bundle in his hands. Jezebel watched, transfixed, as he peeled away the linens to reveal a pink newborn, squirming and blinking in the sudden light. He lifted it high in the air before offering it to Asherah and Baal, and then disappeared into a chamber in the back of the temple.

A few of the men ran outside, and Jezebel heard them retching. She remembered feeling that way, long ago. The feeling had passed. What had seemed so unnatural and evil the first time she had witnessed it had become good and right to her over time. All it took was education, a constant flow of reassurances from wise men who understood the gods. In time, Jezebel had accepted it. By the time she had learned her letters, she was also learning to embrace it. These men had not seen enough, had not been taught enough to embrace it. That would change.

The remaining men touched swords and bowed before Jezebel as they left. One door resisted them when they pushed on it, and Jezebel watched as they forced it open, nearly smashing it to the other side. She followed them out and ran her hands along its frame until she found it. A small scrap of fabric, a plain linen weave, had torn away against the iron pin of the door. She smelled it and looked into the courtyard before tucking it inside her sash.

"May the strongest god win," she whispered into the night air. Silently, she worried that none of the gods really cared.

Obadiah

Obadiah was slow to move away from Jezebel's temple. He had listened from outside the door, but his ears were not sharp and he had strained closer and closer to hear what Jezebel said. He realized almost too late when the last of her words had been spoken. The door began to open, and he shoved it back; a stupid instinct, he knew, but it confused the men just long enough for him to flee. He ran for the palace stables without stopping. The mercenaries would not be as fast, for they would stop and linger to taste the water from the spring in the center, or search for a forgotten grape on the vines that ran from the timbers. The mercenaries, their pockets filled with coins, would linger to experience this place and imagine that they owned it. After all, if the most natural law, the love of life, could be broken here, any law could fall. And these were men who knew what to do when laws fell.

Once these men, mercenaries like Ahab, had been his heroes. He had dreamed of being like them and living their lives. Now he would battle them though they would never know it. The Lord had granted Obadiah not strength but a quick mind, and he prayed it would be enough.

Obadiah found the horse he needed and rode hard for the lands beyond the valley. He had to move the prophets to safer ground by morning, then return to find the evidence he needed. Ahab would believe him, if he, too, held a bone.

❧

The next morning, Obadiah walked through the remains at the temple with a clenched jaw. Ahab, hungover, had wanted to practice his sword fighting this morning, so Obadiah had to oblige him. Thankfully, Ahab's reflexes were terrible after a night of hard drinking. Obadiah beat him. After that loss, Ahab wanted to be left alone to sulk, and also to practice, as Obadiah knew he would. When the wound was to his pride, Ahab nursed the wound for ages.

Walking through the temple, he was relieved that no one else was there. His eyes went to the chamber inside the gated doors in the back of the temple, inscribed with the image of the great bull El, the form Baal was said to take when he prowled the earth among men. The handles of the doors were bronze horns, and Obadiah tested one to see how easily they swung on the hinges. The Phoenician workers had excelled at this, too, and it moved as loosely as a bead on a wire. The floor was a mosaic of ivory cut into shapes and laid into black stones. Every step showed a new wonder: sparkling images of coins falling into an open lap, pregnant women, pregnant animals, men rising from sickbeds, children laughing. There were the Egyptian gods, too, even Osiris's eye, and the Greek gods, and the gods of all the Levant as well. Jezebel had taken pains to honor all gods except Yahweh.

He smelled blood, his skin crawling as if alive with prickly bugs. Obadiah moved carefully, looking for the evidence, praying suddenly he would find nothing. He prayed he was wrong, that the presence of so many strangers had made the sacrifice of a child unthinkable.

He moved back into the open air center, where the four-horned altar sat surrounded by bowls to offer burning incense. It was here, in the center, that he saw the remains of their sacrifice. A single bone had fallen, missed by whoever had cleared the rest of the body. He bent to pick it up, barely aware he was holding his breath. But it was too big, not at all like the bone of a child. Not a man's bone, either; perhaps, Obadiah thought, the bone of a jackal or big cat. He exhaled in relief and straightened his back.

A lyre was discarded in one corner, and the incense still smoked, though it was but a small black, oily mound in the bowl. One bowl caught his eye: a shallow bowl rimmed all the way around with bull's heads that tipped and moved. A tiny bit remained of the offering left in the bowl. Trembling, Obadiah dipped a finger in and swiped the sides, first smelling his fingertips then tasting them.

"Olive oil," Mirra said, entering the temple.

Obadiah spun and reached one hand to his heart in shock. Mirra laughed and walked to him, taking the bowl from his hands.

"You don't need to clean," she said. "The priests do that."

Obadiah's face flushed. He was not here to clean, but what could he tell her?

She scooped two handfuls of olives from a barrel nearby, placed them into a press, and moved the bull's head bowl to catch the extracted oil. A basket of flatbread was near, and she dipped some into the oil, tasting it and smiling. She offered the bread to him next.

"Jezebel paid a fortune to have these olives brought in," Obadiah said. He shook his head and began to step back, when she lifted a finger to bid him wait. She pressed more olives, and pressed more again until the oil reached the rim of the bowl. The bull's heads began to bob as the olive oil ran through the hollow rim, making the bulls appear to drink.

Obadiah laughed at the trick, and Mirra smiled.

"Jezebel held a service here last night," she said. A shadow flitted across her face. She looked uncomfortable. He hoped it was not too late to turn her back to the truth, to what was right.

"You worship her gods?" he asked.

She nodded. "My father would sell me as a servant if he knew," she said. "I only watched from that room."

He moved to the altar and ran his hands along the horns, testing their strength and build. He wished he could tear this temple down with his bare hands, but somehow, he sensed it would make no difference. These temples would always stand, somewhere, whenever people preferred pleasure to truth.

She moved until she was next to him, looking up into his face. He did not move, his chest rising and falling rapidly.

"It's all right, Obadiah. I was silly to imagine there was any hope. What was decided for my future was decided for me long ago." She smiled, a sad twist on her lips. "It was decided the day I was born and they realized I was but a girl. So I will serve Jezebel until a match is made for me, then I will be sent away. I want to be strong and accept it. Pray for me."

He hesitated. He didn't know how to pray for her. What she feared was not the greatest threat. She had no idea that her mind was being filled with lies, and he had no idea how to convince her of it.

"Besides," she continued, her voice wistful and soft, "Jezebel says that no matter where you run, your worst pain still comes with you. Do you think that is true?"

A bird flew in to steal a bit of discarded bread. The sudden flapping of wings distracted Obadiah, and Mirra turned to walk away.

He had not answered her. He wasn't sure he could.

Jezebel

Jezebel felt her heart continue to wither and dry as another month passed and the cracks still appeared in the dry earth below her window, and trees in her garden began to brown. She wept when the last leaf fell from the fig tree nearest the palace, then caught a tear in her palm and held it to the light, amazed by it. It was warm and spread on her skin, settling in the lines of her palm.

Was this a good sign, she wondered, or a bad one? Did it mean she was learning to feel more like the real people did, the ones with a thousand different emotions? Was she becoming like them?

She licked another tear from her lip, startled that two had fallen on the same day and then, on impulse, bit her upper lip, a sharp fast pain that split the skin. That would stop them. Pain was needed in life, not tears. Pain was progress. Which was why few could ever be great. So few could bear the pain that she could. She had been well trained.

There was work to be done, so the distraction of tears did not matter anyway. All the ivory had arrived from Tyre, and artisans had been focusing on the queen's residence. She loved the smell of cedar being cut for furniture; the smoky, metallic smell from the strike of

a hammer; the tang of pungent oils as they were mixed and applied
to the walls. She understood Ahab's love of creating. He built cities,
but she didn't need a city—just one residence filled with comfort and
color and distractions. A palace built for forgetting.

Ahab had a meeting this afternoon about sending more men
to continue work on Jericho. Word of the drought in Israel was
spreading, and enemies were circling. A drought meant famine,
and famine meant easy pickings for predators. She hoped he would
add to today's agenda the need to continue working with the elders
to finish the city wall and gates, as well as design better homes for
them near the palace. She urged him to consider the commoners,
too, that when all was finished, he could promise them modest but
clean and comfortable homes. Keeping the people happy, including the elders, did not guarantee loyalty, but it was a modest effort
to gain it.

Of course, before any of it even began to take shape, the court
would be forced to return to Jezreel. She longed for cooler weather,
for Naboth's gardens and all the green shaded retreats, the peace she
thought she remembered there. There could be no drought there,
not in that rich green world. She would not even have to wait for a
servant to feed her! She could pluck a fruit straight from a tree and let
the juices run down her chin. She would loosen a sandal and run her
foot through the cool, soft grasses. Jezreel was a promise, a promise
that she would be free of petty torments.

The land here was a curse. No barley came in. From her perch
on the roof, waiting for Lilith to bring water for a bath (and she was
slower every week returning), Jezebel acknowledged that the goddess
was still ignoring her. What more did Asherah want from her?

Elijah had not been found, either. He was as elusive as his god. Although she had been promised that the mercenary she hired was a skilled and wicked hunter, completely unprincipled, making him perfect for this job, he had not returned anything but letters. Every time a scout entered the gates with only a slim bag, she knew Elijah yet eluded death. Her mercenary sent only letters to her, never a head.

The Israelites knew nothing, of course. They still thought she wanted all the gods worshipped. She didn't, not anymore. At this point, she had realized, she just wanted Elijah dead. A dead Elijah would mean freedom for Israel. A silenced Yahweh would give her a lasting reputation, that most permanent of crowns, and that was all she wanted. She wanted relief, to know all her suffering had won that for her.

The Israelites probably agreed with her, she thought. Daily they brought meager offerings to the temple of Baal, the Asherah shrine, and even the golden calf of Yahweh, which Ahab had erected long ago to keep them from traveling to Jerusalem. The young people were the only ones who seemed to appreciate the freedom for their bodies and freedom from their wombs. Jezebel was beloved among them.

So, she knew, the drought was not the real problem. Yahweh was, the way his name incited men to madness of incredible depths. It was unthinkable, what Elijah had done. Jezebel and her gods had only promoted happiness and pleasure, and Yahweh's prophets had started a war.

But she was comforted that today Ahab would focus on Jericho. He had never asked what she knew, but of course she knew that Baal was also Yarech, the moon god, but in another incarnation. Ahab had built a city for Yarech, the name of Jericho being a loose dialect's name for this god. Yarech would answer Ahab's prayers, laid out at his feet in stone and lumber, even if hers were ignored.

As for Yahweh, if he had any weaknesses, Obadiah's scrolls would reveal them. She would search the scrolls that Obadiah loved so. Every god has its secrets; how well she knew that! She would find whatever answers were there. She would seek Yahweh and find a way to destroy him at last.

Obadiah

A table was set in the throne room, which was stuffy from the summer heat. Obadiah waited for Omri to be seated, then Ahab. Obadiah stood behind the table to instruct servants as they set out the meal. He hoped he would not be criticized for the lack of variety. He had bought the best the market had to offer, and that was not much. Jezebel was brought in last, and she took her place at the table next to Ahab without a word. She had seemed anxious, brooding more than usual on something hidden. Mirra was attending her, looking restless and thinner, too. She had spoken to him of accepting her fate, but her strength was faltering.

Obadiah watched as Omri bit into a roasted leg chop spiced with vinegar sauce and spring onions; he had to try twice to tear away the meat. He tossed the bone behind him on the floor, and at Obadiah's nod, a servant stepped forward to collect it. Obadiah hoped he would throw it out to the dogs circling the palace, whose ribs were showing. Those dogs looked like they would eat anything.

"The meat is tough," Omri said.

Ahab agreed.

"It was the best at the market," Obadiah replied.

"I doubt that," Omri replied. Obadiah's movements slowed, and he watched both prince and king carefully.

"I trust him," Ahab replied.

"I think," Omri suggested, "that you should accompany Obadiah to the next market. See that he really does buy the best. See that he gets a good price, too. The merchants probably see a man like him and know they can take advantage of him."

Obadiah's hand shook as he refilled the wine. Omri had never attacked him before. He cleared his throat and lifted the skin of wine away, back to his side, replacing it in its stand.

His pride wasn't the most worrisome injury. He had a modest talent for treason, but no talent at all for hiding it. Everyone in the market knew Obadiah was buying extras and sending the goods to the prophets, who were hidden somewhere in the caves outside the city.

Jezebel could have had his head for that, for using the crown's resources to supply the prophets of terror. But if she did, he would reveal her secret. She was paying to have them hunted and exterminated one by one. The jackals in the hills were the only animals in Israel growing fat.

Ahab sat in silence, then stood, facing his father. "Obadiah is a good servant. You have no cause to insult him. If you're angry about the drought, Father, deal with me."

No one moved. Ahab had never confronted his father in the presence of others. Omri set down the bowl of wine he was drinking and stood as well, facing Ahab, his expression unreadable.

"You blame me, don't you?" Ahab said. "It was your decision. But you've always punished me for your faults."

Jezebel's eye lit with that strange fire. Obadiah did not know if it was fueled by compassion or rage; they both looked the same on her face.

Obadiah saw that Omri's legs trembled. He was growing old, too old for fighting, even with words and not swords. Omri left without response.

Ahab watched him leave, his shoulders sinking as if he'd been holding his breath. Jezebel stood and hissed at him. She swept part of the table clean. Ahab glanced down the hall where Omri had exited, and Jezebel grabbed him again, her hands like claws sinking into the flesh on his arms as her mouth found his.

Obadiah took hold of Mirra and escorted her away. Once outside the dining hall, she fell into giggles. He frowned at her reaction.

"You act like you've never seen such a thing," she mocked him.

"And you shouldn't," he scolded her in return.

"Don't speak to me as if we are equals," Mirra said, removing her arm from his hold.

Obadiah grabbed it again, harder. He couldn't believe he was doing this. He couldn't believe most of what he had been forced to do.

"We are not equals. I am older, and wiser, and I know right from wrong. You have a lot of catching up to do," he said.

She pulled her arm back to slap him, but he caught her hand. Her chest rose and fell as she stared at him, blinking rapidly in shock. Tears came to her eyes, and she moved to him, pressing her body into his, so that he felt her soft curves and the fast beating of her heart. She lifted her mouth to his, her body shaking, and the soft sweet lips moved across his own, stealing his breath. He had never kissed a girl, and the sweetness was disorienting. He lost his place for that quick moment, lost who he was and what he was. But his mind had always been stronger than his heart, and it jolted him back to what had to be done.

He pushed her away. "You belong to another man."

"I belong to no one!"

"But you will someday, Mirra. A better man than me, someone who will give you a good life." The words tore through his heart. The truth was bitter and vile, especially when said out loud. He was ashamed of himself for loving her touch so much when she could never be his.

She ran from him. He let out his breath and felt his body collapse in, like a wounded man in a fight.

If he had done the right thing and spoken what was true, why did it hurt him so much? Why was the truth never anyone's friend but its own?

Jezebel

The next morning, Jezebel rose before Ahab and made her way to the administration rooms. She had not slept, not even in the third or fourth watches of the night. The drought made everyone restless, without enough to eat or drink, and the servants had been noisy all night.

She was pleased to find Obadiah's records room empty and took a torch off a wall bracket from the hallway. As she lifted it, the flickering yellow light filled the room with gold. That was appropriate, for here were records of all the gold in Omri's empire, plus the scrolls she

sought. She would learn about her enemy, the Lord. Who had made
him? What enemies in the heavens pursued him?

On the long table against the wall, dozens of clay jars rested,
each containing a scroll. Pulling a scroll from a clay jar, at random, she spread it out and read.

> Fifty jars of olive oil
> Three hundred loaves of bread
> Ten sheep
> Ten geese
> Twenty fowls
> Ten curds
> Fifty eggs
> Ten pots honey
> One hundred fish
> Fifteen crocks goat's milk

All were purchased with the agreement they were to be delivered to the palace.

It was dated from the last month. Obadiah kept detailed
records of his purchases at market, the money he spent from the
royal treasury to keep the palace occupants fed. Dismayed, she
pulled another scroll free and read it. It was much the same, just
another list of foodstuffs bought at market. This one, however,
was dated from three years ago, before she had come. Obadiah
bought so much less, spent so much less, before her. Jezebel knew
she had imported four hundred priests and dozens upon dozens
of artisans and servants; but never had she seen the costs recorded

in such clear detail. She placed a great burden on the people. She was only a little surprised to notice that she didn't really care. These were necessary expenses.

She freed another scroll and read, and repeated this over and over. She spent two hours reviewing records that were honest and accurate. But where Obadiah kept the history scrolls, the ones that told of all the Lord's weaknesses, was a mystery. Groaning that she had lost sleep and gained nothing, she rolled a papyrus up and grabbed a jar, preparing to stuff it inside.

But there was already a scroll in the jar. A small scroll, rolled neatly and left at the bottom. Her breath caught as she reached for it. Of course Obadiah would hide such information about his Lord from her. She began to read it, but it was nothing more than a record of food bought and delivered—but not to the palace. Her mind began to work as footsteps in the hall approached, and she heard the guard exchanging words with someone.

She stuffed the scroll into her sash and left the room. Why would Obadiah be buying food that was not sent to the palace? Who else was he feeding?

The prophets. The realization incensed her. He was using her money, Ahab's treasury, to keep her enemies alive. Obadiah was not as loyal as she once thought. And then she laughed; he was a man, after all.

Jezebel

The horse did not slow as he approached, his mane carried by the September wind, whipping his rider, who bore the flag marked with the sign of the house of Eth-baal. The women at the well stopped and watched him, and children abandoned their games to see the rider flying toward them like a polished stone loosed from a sling.

Jezebel watched from her window as he rode to the gate of the palace. She was removing her robe, letting the breeze cool her shoulders. With a sigh of aggravation, she pulled it back on and instructed Lilith to call Ahab.

"He is walking in the stables with Athaliah," Lilith replied.

"Who?" Jezebel asked, then nodded. Of course. But it was foolish of Ahab to invest time into a girl. She would only be sent away. The thought occurred that Ahab might grow to love the child, and then he would suffer when she left. Or worse, he would not make a wise match because of his attachment. Jezebel groaned, thinking what trouble Ahab's emotions had given her.

Outside, she did not wait for Ahab but motioned for the rider to approach.

Kneeling, the rider kissed her feet.

She extended a hand, and he rose. He trembled whenever his eyes met hers by accident.

"Shalmaneser has defeated the kings of the north and begins his invasion. He demands more than tribute; all kingdoms will cede their rule to him or be destroyed."

"My priests predicted that months ago," she replied. "You must bring worthier news than this. The guards say you rode with astonishing speed."

The rider nodded and kept his face low.

"Ben-hadad hosts a war council in his palace. He says his intention is to guard against the advances of Shalmaneser."

Jezebel exhaled, the name stirring her blood. "But?" she asked.

"But it is your name on his lips when he thinks he is among friends. I fear he has no good intentions for Israel."

"Or me," Jezebel said. Being carted off as war spoils would destroy all her work.

"He often says that for you, though for no other queen, including his own, he will ride out against Shalmaneser. But he needs allies. Ben-hadad will come and ask for safe passage, that Ahab will recognize him as a friend as he crosses over your borders."

"Safe passage will be given," she said, pacing. She dismissed the rider, giving instruction to her servants to see to his needs and those of his animal. She turned for the palace. She had given the command, but Ahab must give his seal. It was an unfortunate technicality.

Ahab

Ahab sat in bed, turning the sword of Moses back and forth in the light. It had not rained in almost two years. Every day he woke thinking that the drought could not be real and could not really be the hand of the Hebrew god. Every night he slept, listening for rain, and woke discouraged. What would Solomon have thought of him? How had Solomon governed all the tribes and kept hundreds of foreign wives and never had this trouble with a prophet or a god? What made Ahab and his bride so different, so repulsive to the Lord?

He could hear the sounds of the workers outside his window, carving ivories for Jezebel's residence, and the guards cursing as another stumbled during his efforts to practice swinging a sword of heavier iron. Yes, the marriage had brought greater access to material goods. It had brought new gods and more ways to worship. Yet all anyone wanted now was rain.

"How else may I please the king?" the girl asked. She was the same age as Jezebel but had lighter eyes and a soft set to her mouth. She was a simple, sweet thing, won in some battle he could not even remember. He had been glad for her back then, before he had even heard the name Jezebel. He thought she would help him remember those days. He gestured toward the foot of the bed.

"Dance for me," he commanded.

She did. A smile was on her face that did not move or change character, a smile he had seen on blind men at the city gates who never were sure when a kind soul might drop a coin for them. He turned away, and she moved, her arms and legs light as the dust in the morning sun.

"You do not watch," she said.

Ahab frowned and tossed her robe to her. "Your dance does nothing for me."

A guard stepped forward to escort her from the chamber as her chin trembled, the first true expression he had seen.

Ahab rubbed his eyes and stood. "Give her an extra portion of food this week, and a token of the king's affection."

Another guard stepped aside, and a messenger entered.

"Jezebel seeks an audience."

"Does the princess now command me?" Ahab snapped.

"No, no, my lord," the messenger said. "A rider from the House of Eth-baal brought news that she says she must share with you."

"Tell her to make ready to leave for Jezreel." Ahab needed no news from his wife. He was the prince. He wore the crown, not her.

"But the message—" the messenger began.

Ahab threw the sword, and it hissed through the air, sticking in the cedar beam that ran just over the messenger's head.

The messenger bowed and left.

12

Heavier than usual rains stalled both Shalmaneser and Ben-hadad. All the rain due to Israel had fallen upon their enemies instead. Jezebel watched the trade roads daily in Jezreel in vain. Little traffic ever appeared to give her hope. Israel suffered from depleted supplies, with foreign merchants prevented from getting there. Foreigners had been so blessed by rain, with plentiful crops and pockets of gold. She hated them, imagining them staying home and getting fat.

Jezebel, like everyone else at court, was hungry. She ate no grapes, no melons. No figs or fruit of any kind. The court had exhausted the remaining supply of dried grain and meat. A few herbs survived, but these were cruel reminders of the food she once had. Seasonings only, no meat or bread or vegetables. The administration chambers were crammed with advisers. Ahab called every wise man he could find, but they all said he had to make peace with Yahweh, which meant destroying the other gods. Jezebel reminded him of the covenant's terms. To take her as a wife was to take her gods. And, she reminded him, to refuse the people a choice was to take away their freedom. Ahab had chosen this road. He had to follow it to its completion.

As did she. But as yet, if Yahweh had a weakness, she had not found it.

They passed two more winters this way, every month bringing bad news. At night, restless, she walked. Ahab wanted little to do with her. She suspected that he blamed her. Everyone did, their thirst and hunger and creeping poverty nudging each to madness. She had always known that drought meant dry land; she had not known that drought meant depression and despair without relief.

When they returned to Jezreel in the third year of the drought, Jezebel rode in a litter with the curtains drawn. No gifts were thrown to her, no shouts of praise and welcome. She rode alone, a prisoner behind walls of waving purple silk. She prayed that Asherah and Baal would open their ears to Sargon as he made sacrifices.

Leaving the outer edge of the territory of Samaria, she saw that a brush fire had destroyed fields for miles in every direction. The landscape was black, like the world of nightmares. Clumps smoldered in the sun. As they rode silently past, she recognized the forms. They were people. Sometimes animals, too, although by now most people had eaten their animals. It was better than watching them die from starvation.

She hoped Sargon would keep up the sacrifices. Jezebel urged him in letters to stay strong, to comfort mothers in their sorrow, to help them see that what was necessary was not always easy. They had chosen not to end a life but to prevent suffering. What god would refuse to honor such a choice?

Above all, she had written, he must alleviate their growing suspicions of Baal and Asherah and their princess. She vowed to see every tribe survive. Those who survived could start over. Babies could always be made again.

Ahab

Ahab tossed his goblet into the corner, listening to it ring as it rolled in short revolutions to a resting place. There was not even enough wine to leave a trail on the floor. Obadiah had spent the early morning hours, he'd said, tending to the animals in the stable before sunrise. Another had died as it slept. One animal, a donkey, had gotten out and not returned. It had probably wandered off, looking for water, and been torn to death in a moment by the dogs who watched the stables at night. No one could stop the wild dogs from taking lives. The elderly were warned not to walk alone. The young had to stay inside. The nights became a recital of pained, hungry wails from animals and children alike.

Obadiah returned now with a wet rag. It was a high offering, though not as welcome as a cool bath. Ahab rubbed the back of his neck and face. This was not Ahab's fault. He could not control the heavens and make rain in a drought. He doubted that any god could, either. The people had prayed to each god, hoping to cause one to rise to action, as if such things could happen. Ahab felt with conviction that they did not. If prayers were really answered, he would not have seen so many young men die in agony, the name of their god on their lips. He forsook making offerings for the dead boys at night, willing a ghost to stir and eat him or whisk him, too, to the underworld. Any death was preferable to this, the slow death of his name. Every eye in Jezreel met his with a cold stare. The people might pray to gods, but they looked to him for the answer. Faith that led back to him was foolishness or madness, he knew, and so all faith seemed horrible.

"We'll go through the country," he sighed, turning to Obadiah. "We'll find every spring and every stream. Let's see if we can find enough grass to keep our horses and mules from dying."

Obadiah did not hesitate, which surprised Ahab. He had expected resistance from Obadiah, who had no experience finding water in the hills. He didn't even know if Obadiah had ever been to the hills, with those dark, forbidding caves. But the drought made even a man like Obadiah desperate.

It took but a moment to divide the country between them and begin the search. Ahab was glad to be free of the palace his father had begun in better times and of the people he had inherited.

Leading out from the stables, he nudged his horse and thought with satisfaction that if he never returned, the people would at last be confronted with the truth. It was religion that destroyed Israel, not Ahab.

Obadiah

Obadiah and Ahab parted, each hoping to find water. They would blow a shofar if they did and wait for a return signal. Then they could lead the other to the water, blowing the shofar at regular intervals to act as a guide. Obadiah suspected Ahab wanted to sulk in private. Ahab had been powerless too many times in his life to know how to deal with it. His father had ruined him for power.

Obadiah saw a man walking toward him, his clothes fresh and clean, his face recently washed, as if such a thing were even possible. The man was whistling, his step light and easy, as if he was well fed and rested.

Obadiah got off his horse and fell to his knees. "Is it really you— my master Elijah?"

"Yes," said Elijah. "Go and tell Ahab, 'I've seen Elijah.'"

Standing on the hot, blistered earth, dead vines tangling at his feet, Obadiah saw that Elijah looked well. He did not look like he had suffered in the drought or known a moment of want. And yet Obadiah had gone hungry and thirsty and had stolen from the palace treasuries to sustain those who belonged to the Lord. He had done bad things, for good reason, but the scrolls, the laws of Moses, did not address this. Obadiah assumed that the stain of guilt was thick upon him. He did not want to look at Elijah and did not want to bring word of his return to Ahab.

"Hasn't anyone told you what I have done, how Jezebel was out to kill the prophets of God, how I risked my life by hiding a hundred of them, fifty to a cave, and made sure they got food and water?" Obadiah said. "And you're telling me to draw attention to myself by announcing to my master, 'Elijah's been found.' Why, he'll kill me for sure. I don't want to risk my life again. Too many people depend on me." Obadiah thought of Mirra, and then blushed, hoping Elijah could not read his thoughts. "The minute I leave you, won't the Spirit of God whisk you away to who knows where? Then when I report to Ahab, you'll have disappeared, and Ahab will kill me. And I've served God devoutly since I was a boy!" Obadiah stood, and his face felt red. He was yelling at Elijah.

Elijah stood still, his smile twitching under his white beard. He reached out then and took Obadiah's hand, patting it as he would a frightened child's. Obadiah backed up. He did not want to do this. To put Elijah and Ahab together now was like setting fire to what little remained. "As surely as God-of-the-Angel-Armies lives," Elijah said, "and before whom I take my stand, I'll meet with your master face-to-face this very day."

Obadiah's chest heaved as he felt the smooth, warm hand around his own. It was Elijah and not a mirage. Elijah had always had a strange gift of giving strength to the weak. Obadiah fell to his knees once more and kissed his feet. It was Elijah, who understood it all, even weakness.

Obadiah blew the shofar.

Ahab

"So it's you, old troublemaker," Ahab said to Elijah and spit on the dusty road. Rocks framed the horizon, and Elijah seemed as one of them, native and unyielding. Ahab's words felt like sand in his throat, scraping as they came out. Life had been a river flowing through his hands until Elijah had appeared long ago, and the kingdom slipped through his fingers. Now this disgrace stood in front of him.

"It's not I who have caused this trouble in Israel," replied Elijah, still standing in the road. "It is you and your government—for the comfort of a woman's bed, you've abandoned Yahweh and embraced Baal."

"I am guilty, yes. Guilty of being a king. I worry about the people I can see, not gods. People who fill my treasuries. People who live in my cities. People whose lives are in my hands."

Elijah shook his head. "Ahab, the Lord knows how to care for these people. And He knows how to care for you. He has seen how you suffered as a boy, how you suffered seeing so many of your friends die. You could not save anyone. You were not born to be a savior. But you were born to be a great king. Obey the Lord, and He will guide you."

"No," Ahab replied. "I will never serve a god who inflicts suffering, whether it is on a boy who is crushed without mercy or on a nation without water."

Elijah's face was swept with sorrow, and Ahab felt a red shame, the shame that had haunted him since he was a boy, his father home from war and staggering, drunk with blood, through the tents, screaming for his coward son to come out. Ahab had been no taller than his father's sword then. He remembered how his elder brother had laughed when he had wet himself in fear, how Omri had spanked him with his sword just for the amusement of the men.

"Here's what I want you to do," Elijah replied. "Assemble everyone in Israel at Mount Carmel. And make sure that the special pets of your Jezebel, her hundreds of prophets of Baal and the whore goddess Asherah, are there."

Elijah was picking a fight. Ahab searched the face of the old prophet, a strange feeling that he should be grateful coming over him. Elijah was trying to rescue Ahab, the warrior prince. But from what? His vicious bride? Or an angry god? Ahab's heart stirred, as if to tell him the answer, but he swallowed it up. He had made promises. He had to love her, because he knew what it was to be unloved. He couldn't leave her to face that alone, and worse, he couldn't leave her to face the Lord alone.

Ahab knew the Lord might kill her.

Jezebel

The dust from the roads clung to Ahab, thick and flaking in patches along his knees and elbows, settling into lines along his neck. He had been gone a week looking for water. Jezebel had wondered if he had died or run away. A land without rain was no land at all. Why would he bother to return?

He dismounted with a sour expression. Jezebel bit down on her cheeks, drawing them between her teeth. She would not flinch in embarrassment for him, that Ahab would reveal weakness with all the people watching and the soldiers milling around at the gates to Jezreel. He was displeased, and it could only mean she had displeased him.

She had spied his return from her window and walked out to him, though she was big again with her second child. She thought the sight of her swollen body would please him. He had liked her pregnant, seemed to be even more gentle with her then, as if he was waiting for a softer woman to emerge instead of a baby.

But despite his expression, he opened his arms to her and buried his face in her hair. She knew she smelled of sandalwood and musk, a perfume she did not usually wear, but even the women who sold perfumes had suffered in the drought, and their wares changed daily, dwindling, less expensive oils used in the mix. Obadiah had done well to procure even this.

"Jezebel," he whispered. "Jezebel, I have met our enemy today, the man who has caused this great drought. He proposes a match between the gods, between Baal and the Lord, at Mount Carmel." He looked into her eyes now, desperate. "Tell me your prophets will agree."

His hand went to the back of her neck, forcing her face into his chest. He knew her well now, trying to silence her. She bit him, and he jerked her head back. Tears of pain came to his eyes, but he did not release her.

Ahab continued. "Listen to me, for once! It is a good offer! All the priests of Baal are to assemble on Mount Carmel. Elijah will come alone. The priests will call upon Baal to send rain, using any method they wish. If Baal sends rain, Elijah will leave and never return, and the people of Israel will worship Baal and Asherah only. But if Baal does not send rain, Elijah will call upon the Lord for rain. Elijah says whichever god sends rain is the one god that Israel will worship. But only that god, and no others. It is not even a fair battle, four hundred prophets against one. But it is a good offer, and we must take it."

"Carmel divides the land," Jezebel said, "between Phoenicia and Israel. Does he think he can humiliate me? Don't even reply. Such an offer is an insult to the crown."

Ahab released her. His decision was in his eyes, a calm rejection.

"I accepted his offer. Tell Sargon to get your priests ready. We will set out in three morning's time."

Jezebel grabbed Ahab's arm, making sure her fingernails cut him. "Do you think Baal or Asherah will come when called, like a pet? You will provoke their anger. Worse things will happen!"

Ahab shrugged as if he did not believe in Baal. As if he only believed in Elijah's power to end the drought. He had never loved her, probably, even though he said he did. He might have taken bribes from the elders, with promises to humiliate Jezebel. Elijah might have done the same. She looked around for any familiar Phoenician faces. She was being poisoned here, just as she had been at home. She had never been loved. Used, but never loved.

"You were not born to royalty," Jezebel shouted. Ahab wrapped his arm around her waist and forced her to walk, nodding with a calm assurance to the soldiers who kept guard.

"We can argue in private," he said to her. "I was not born as a royal, but I do know how to control my wife."

She huffed, her chest constricting with pain. He was an enemy, just like every man she had ever known.

"You want to embarrass me," she said. "But you are the one who will be embarrassed. Elijah's first aim is to strip away all choice from the people, to force them to recognize one god alone. The Lord will not answer you. You'll know what I feel like."

"I would love to know what you feel," Ahab said. "I have only guessed at it, and I have never been right. I hoped you would welcome the chance to end the drought, to show the power of your gods."

She wavered, wondering if she should trust familiar hatred or her husband. He said many things, but he had not made her happy. He had not removed the shadows that plagued her even on bright and clean days.

"And what will you do, husband," she said, "if this magician wins and calls down rain? What will he want then? Any man who brings rain will be more powerful than the king."

"I doubt he wants to be king," Ahab said.

"I doubt you do." She made her words sharp, hoping to wound him. Wounded men were dangerous. They fought harder and with less discrimination. She wanted a warrior like that, not this thoughtful prince at her side.

"You wanted to end the curse," Ahab said. "Prepare your priests, instruct them to represent Baal well."

"You built that temple," she said. "You built the pole to Asherah, too. Will you allow yourself to be tested? Your judgments questioned?"

"People are dying, Jezebel! What do I matter?"

"When Elijah kills you for the throne, he will kill me, too. Athaliah will die." She rested one hand on her womb. "You will never see the face of your next child. You will never know if it was a son. You will never know how close you were to a real reign."

"Without rain, what good is a child? What good is the throne?" Ahab asked, his head dipping down in defeat.

She spoke gently. "Without an heir, what good is a king? Do not give in, Ahab. A child will be born to us. Perhaps we will have a son, and your throne will be secure at last, and forever. You are so close to having everything you want."

He looked at her, his eyes searching hers. "I think what I want is a god named Yahweh."

She gasped, trying to step back from the searing betrayal, but his hold on her was firm.

"If you do this, you will go to the contest alone," she said, picking up the edge of her robe and shaking it once, letting the dust mark the boundary between them. "And you will remain alone." She placed such emphasis on her last words that he could not miss her meaning.

His expression shifted. He felt something new for her, she saw it in the way his brows raised and his lips parted slightly. It looked like pity. She had hated it as a child and hated it now.

"I have always defended you," Ahab said. "I may be the only man who has ever truly loved you. Do not throw me away for a god who hasn't even answered your prayers."

"Betrayal is not love!"

Ahab's voice was soft. "This time, it is."

Jezebel

Jezebel waited for Ahab to sleep that night, unwilling to talk to him further. He did sleep, after six bowls of wine. He had complained that the wine tasted like vinegar. Everything was spoiled here. He was restless; his legs kicked at the linen coverlet. He groaned as his dreams began, and she wondered what his mind showed him. What was it like to live with so many deaths to his name? What did he feel? Temereh's face floated to the surface in the dark waters that were her dreams. Her sister was bloated and her skin raw and red, as if drowned in a lake that burned.

As she listened to Ahab's labored breathing, the strange voice whispered to her. A desire to listen shamed her. The silence in this black chamber was a grave to her. She rose, letting her feet touch the ground without a noise. Opening the chamber door brought only a faint gold light into the room. The nearest guard was at the far end of the hallway, under a torch in a bracket on the wall. He stood and bowed when he saw her. She lifted one finger to her lips and closed the door behind her. She said nothing as she went past, only lifting her hand to indicate she did not wish to be followed.

She pulled her robe up to keep it from dragging along the stone as she took the main steps down and out of the palace. The guards were not pleased with her insistence that she go into the night alone. They would have thought her mad if she tried to explain, but she was certain the voice wanted her to wander tonight. The sound of thunder, a low grumble in the distance that meant rain was coming. In the open night, insects chirped as the wind blew a fetid, warm breath.

She followed the main path, past the nobles' houses, past the military quarters. As she neared the gate, a journey of about thirty minutes, for she was weary and slow, she knew why she had really come.

A golden calf stood on a wooden platform with wheels. The calf was about the size of a donkey, plainly designed, one of the two golden calves Ahab had allowed for the worshippers of Yahweh. He hoped to keep them and their offerings in Israel, and she had hoped that was all their god required.

She stood still, listening for the sound of rain. The cry of an infant somewhere in the distance was an accusation, and she put her hand over her womb by instinct. The city was black, darker than she had ever seen it. Omri had forbidden fires even though they drove away the biting plagues of night insects.

Stopping her breath, she listened again. She did not hear thunder, or even feel the promise of rain in the air. She looked to the heavens, those bright stars sheltering the city, then looked back to the calf, a bright yellow god bathed in starlight. So this was the god of the Israelites. She walked toward him, her heart rising in her chest. They were alone, this calf-god and the princess. She stood before him, staring into his blind gold eyes. She reached out her hand, touching him, and found him cold.

She stepped back, confused. This could not be Yahweh. This calf was no god. Her mind flashed to Baal and Asherah, and what the revelation meant of them, too.

Lightning flew across the sky, the explosion of sound on its heels. She fell to her knees in terror. Her enemy was alive and near. She had not seen his face in this calf, she knew that, but he had seen hers, and he was out there, waiting.

And he was angry.

Jezebel

Jezebel paced in her chamber the following day until Sargon arrived.

"To send even one priest will legitimize Elijah," Sargon said.

"I agree," Jezebel replied, "but Elijah is not our real problem anymore. The people are. They will follow anyone who delivers rain."

"We need magicians," Sargon said.

"We need gods," she countered. "The gods you always promised me were listening."

Sargon did not answer. Jezebel had to calm her mind without him, without words or comfort or promises. Why had his confidence faded? If someone asked her to prove the sun existed, she would have pointed to it, unafraid. Why was Sargon afraid to prove his gods? Where was his certainty? Where was hers?

Together they assembled the priests outside of the queen's palace that night. All lined the steps, and Jezebel spoke to them words of encouragement, while messengers ran up and down the steps and elders and commoners milled around, a nervous, excited energy palpable. She looked back at her own holy men. They had no excitement, no visible hope of miraculous events to come. They just took long, steadying breaths and spoke very little. Some chewed their lips, and some talked to themselves under their breath as they cut sharp, disdaining glances at the people gathering at the palace.

"The people did not call for this contest," Jezebel reminded them. "Do not be angry with them. But do not disappoint them. Or me."

She called for Athaliah from the nursery. She had to be guarded should events turn sour. It was strange to look at her, to see how she had grown, with dark hair and dark eyes, able to say many words clearly. Many words except *mother*. Jezebel would teach her what *mother* meant for her, but later.

Later in the evening, Jezebel wanted to see Ahab and called for him but heard words exchanged outside her chamber door as the servant left to deliver her request. She knew then that orders had been given, probably by Omri, to isolate her from Ahab. Her fate would be decided without her because she was nothing but a female, born to be ruled by men.

She cursed the burden of being born with a womb.

She tried to sleep, but there were nettles stinging in her stomach and cold fears that seized her. She had planned on ending the reign of Yahweh here in Israel, and now she was caught in his trap.

Ahab

The day of the battle arrived to clear and silent spring skies. There were no clouds and no winds. Nothing moved above them, not even a bird.

All wildlife had fled; even the birds migrated elsewhere. There was no life to sustain their journey here. Dead brown plains surrounded Mount Carmel in every direction. The skeletons of dead shrubs stood twisted toward the approaching people with gnarled branches that clawed the air as if crying out for water that never came.

Many from Samaria and the surrounding land had come to witness the contest because there was no way to plant a crop in the brittle, dry earth. No berries grew, no lettuce sprouted. There was no work, there was no food, and there was no relief. The contest had at least brought hope, and the people had been stirred by that. Ahab fought the resentment that built in his chest, swallowing the dry air to hold his curses inside. What had they come to see, really? he asked. A prince lose the kingdom, or a prophet make a fool of himself?

They walked to reach Mount Carmel along roads that led toward the cool Mediterranean. Such a journey should not have even been possible; it was the rainy season. The roads should have been impassible, but they were dry and hard and cracked. Some whispered that this was a sign. If the Lord had once destroyed the earth by flood, he now displayed his wrath through drought. Mount Carmel stood before them, a wide flat mountain that looked more like a giant table for the gods. *Fitting*, Ahab thought. Mount Carmel would offer everyone a good view of the destruction about to occur. Whether it was an inheritance or a reputation that was destroyed, all would have a good seat. The only modest rise was near the center, just above a spring. As the people climbed, the sound of trickling water caused a riot of screams and activity, fathers pushing their children to the front, mothers cradling infants and stepping over the elderly to get to it. The spring emerged from a trio of flat rocks nestled at the base of a broom tree. The water bubbled as it came up and flowed in a steady stream down the mountain, being absorbed into the earth again before it reached the plains.

The people knelt along the edges of the spring, scooping up the water with their hands, gulping and gasping for air. Ahab saw tears running down their faces, especially the mothers with young. He bowed his head in shame to see what the drought had done to them. Athaliah had not lacked water.

Ahab rode through the slow-moving crowd, noting how their bones stood out at sharp jagged angles. When they turned their faces up to look upon him, he saw their moist eyes, dull and yellow, the hunger eating through their bodies, picking them off one by one, starting with the weak and old. He saw few infants among them, but he did not think infants could thrive if mothers had no milk. The rumors he had heard that infants were sacrificed to Asherah were exaggerated. Maybe one or two had been; he could not help what people did when driven mad by hunger, and the hunger was Elijah's fault, not his. But he did not believe that it was becoming accepted, not among the Israelites.

He spurred the half-dead horses that pulled his chariot, flanked by weary guards, and arrived above the spring where Jezebel's priests had assembled in a seething mass. He remembered seeing maggots churning in a festering wound on a soldier. That was what these priests resembled, with their white robes and blank dark eyes.

His own royal robes hung loose around his wasting body, and he stepped down as servants moved to carry a throne to place it at the foot of the modest peak. He watched the faces of his people as they assembled beneath him. They were drawn and hungry, and he felt his throne could not be placed on steady enough ground. If these gods did not make rain, the people would look again to him, and his time as king would be over. It would be a small matter to kill him when all were promised water and water was denied. The sound of the spring drove the point home.

The drought was worse for the thought of it ending, and the soft shade and sweet sharp smell of trees that were still green here made them believe mercy might come near. They trudged on with tired, thin bodies and wondered how they had left this path so willingly. The Lord would refresh the land at home, the mothers promised the children. The smaller ones cried, terrible visions of gods at war filling their minds and rooting their feet to the path so that the fathers had to carry them the rest of the way up. Battles the children had all seen; Ahab knew no child of Israel grew up without watching his father fight. These children knew what it was for men to brandish swords, for chariots to plow through lines of soldiers, knew what it was to see blood smeared across the land. But this thing, a war of gods, this was a thing that had never entered into their minds. It was a new age, some mothers whispered, when gods would fight and men would rest.

Some were speaking of Mount Carmel in the old tongues. It had once been called the Holy Head, the highest of the mountains here, and in the world before that the Egyptians had named it the Nose of the Gazelle, a brilliant shining mount that rose from the hills leaping behind it. It was a rich place, ministered to by the breezes of the sea, offering grain, olives, and grapes to those who loved it. Mount Carmel was a generous place, too, that should have stood aloof above men but never ceased to give them comfort and food. To the poorest, it was a reflection of Yahweh, and they had worshipped here with awe, trembling that they were allowed so close and blessed so well.

But when the people came to Mount Carmel they saw the stones that had once been the altar to Yahweh scattered along the mountain. The priests of Baal had thrown them down and greeted the people with firm nods and hard smiles. A priest kicked at one of the twelve stones to send it rolling away, as if the altar was rubbish that would be dealt with at last.

Elijah parted the people and ascended, his eyes on the stone's revolution before it came to rest near his feet. He lifted it, lifting it above his head, so that all below could see it, then carried it up the mountain, to the base of the altar's intended home, the place destroyed by the priests of others. Elijah set the stone on the ground and lifted his hands in prayer as the people watched. The cornerstone was in place. Men moved from the crowd to collect the remaining eleven stones and heaved them, rolling them up to Elijah, who reordered them and placed them together, the altar taking shape before them all. At last it was done. The morning sun was high, and the limestone glared against the red soil at their feet. The altar, blazing white, rested in the red pool of earth, and the people felt the stir of fear.

Elijah did not wait for Ahab to settle his thoughts. He stood at the altar, his weathered face unreadable. Only his eyes were alive, surveying the crowd with an emotion Ahab did not recognize. It seemed like compassion, but Ahab had never felt that when he had gone into a battle. Elijah was a strange man.

Elijah stood before the altar and called out. His arms were relaxed at his sides. Ahab saw that whatever Elijah believed would happen today, it had already been decided in his mind. How could a man, even a prophet, have peace on the first moment of battle? Ahab ran his hand through his hair. He was not in control, and he had no idea if control was even possible now.

Elijah began. "My people, how long are you going to sit on the fence? If God is the real God, follow Him; if it's Baal, follow him. Today you must make up your minds!"

No one said a word. Ahab felt he should say something, but Yahweh was not his god. Neither was Baal or Asherah or any other of the carved things men carried about. He was, however, the prince.

"I will not be angry," Ahab called. "You are loyal to me, to Israel, no matter which god you serve."

Elijah folded his arms, scowling at Ahab. The sun was bright on his face, and the people had to shield their eyes to look at him. He was illuminated in white light, a trick of the afternoon sun, Ahab knew, but it was a clever ploy to position himself there.

"Isn't it Baal who makes the rain, and Asherah who brings new life? Let us test them," Elijah said.

The priests of Baal spit in his direction and called down curses under their breath. They chuckled among themselves. Ahab knew the sound of that particular laughter, the sound of men anxious to see another man die.

"Let the Baal prophets bring up two oxen," Elijah yelled. "Let them pick one, butcher it, and lay it out on an altar of firewood—but don't ignite it. I'll take the other ox, cut it up, and lay it on the wood. But neither will I light the fire. Then you pray to your gods, and I'll pray to God. The god who answers with fire will prove to be, in fact, God."

Ahab saw his people exhaling and clasping hands. They seem relieved, nodding and talking quietly. An elder from the city yelled back to Elijah.

"A good plan—do it!"

Ahab saw there was more power in Elijah's scowl than in his scepter, but he didn't feel offense, though he searched his spirit for it. What he found instead made him blush. Elijah seemed more a father than a cursed prophet. Ahab felt the red shame rising, that he should have secretly grown to admire a man who could take his kingdom from him.

Elijah, as if hearing his thoughts, turned to look him in the eyes. A softness came over the old prophet's hard face, a compassion that made Ahab's shame worse. Elijah was doing what Ahab should have done as prince of Israel, and yet Elijah did not try to humiliate him for his weakness. Elijah just saw it and did what Ahab would not.

Priests led two oxen through the crowd, placid creatures unaware that the fate of the nation would be written in their blood. Gods or men made no difference to them; they knew only how to be led and had no mind to see who held the leash. They picked their way up the mountain, their flanks sweating in the sun, another day without water for them, like every day before it.

The Baal priests took their ox and slit its throat in a fast motion. The sun on the blade cast a sharp reflection that stung the people's eyes, and they grimaced, covering their eyes as the blood boiled onto the ground. The smell, sweet and salty, mixed with the scent of the sea. Ahab felt his stomach turn as the beast was quartered and landed with a wet thump on the stone altar of Baal. He alone did not cover his eyes. He saw Elijah watching him, seeing him in his shame. Elijah's face remained still, hearing but not adding to the devouring voices in his head.

The priests prayed to Baal and Asherah, beginning with loud invocations, until their prayers became shouts.

REIGN

"O Baal, O husband of Asherah, answer us!"

The priests held their thumbs and whispered the sacred incantations. "Virgin, dog, serpent! Eternal key, garlands of green, sorcerer's
wand! Grant us favor!"

The morning remained resolved in its stillness, and the sun grew
strong. The priests of Baal became desperate, stomping on the altar.
The blood shot in all directions as the ox meat was pulped and beaten
beneath their sandals. The blood flung up their legs, covering their
robes, and they invoked the people to dance for rain. A few bold women
played their tambourines and danced as the priests sang the songs of
Baal's lover, enticing him to appear and show his strength. The voices
of the priests calling to this god filled the mountain as women began
dancing, swinging their bodies, tempting the great god of pleasure to
reveal himself. Their robes slipped off their shoulders sometimes, and
they did not pull them up, nor did they blush as they lifted their robes
and exposed their legs to the men. The priests moved through them,
engaging some in deep kisses, pulling some to the ground.

Elijah turned his face away.

The morning burned on, and the priests seemed to have
exhausted what songs they knew and whatever passion they possessed. Some of the older ones had to sit, too weak to lift hands in
prayer. Some closed their eyes, and Ahab suspected they slept more
than prayed. Still he stood, watching Elijah, watching the kingdom's
foundations shaking and splitting.

At noon, Elijah began taunting them: "Call a little louder—Baal
is a god, after all. Maybe he's off meditating somewhere or other, or
maybe he's gotten involved in a project, or maybe he's on vacation.
You don't suppose he's overslept, do you, and needs to be woken up?"

The people laughed, relieved, as the children imagined gods fumbling for their morning milk and waking too late, as they often did. A child suggested a swift rod to the backside would get Baal's attention, and the children were lost to everyone, giggling uncontrollably. Mothers tried to shoo them out of the crowd to the edges, where they could be silenced with a stern look and threat of this same rod, but Elijah stayed them with one hand upraised.

The priests of Baal, their faces red and pocked with sweat, prayed louder and louder, screaming their request, cutting themselves with swords and knives until they were covered in their own blood. The children stopped giggling and watched in horror. Now Elijah did not stop the mothers from shooing the children from the crowd.

The bloody show continued for over an hour, until the blood of the oxen had turned dark and the blood of the men painted it bright red again. Every prayer, every incantation they knew was flung to the heavens, or called down as curses on the place. The morning had left them, but she was followed by the afternoon, and he proved as quiet. The priests staggered and clung to each other for support. No women danced now or played tambourines. Three years of drought leading to this, a day of draining blood and bleeding prayers, emptied them of all hope. Baal would not accept their sacrifices.

The people murmured, and Ahab felt their disappointment like an accusation pointed at him. There could be no war between gods if none arrived. If Yahweh was reluctant to accept their sacrifice, they would have traveled for days only to die. And Ahab had allowed it, just like he had allowed the drought.

Elijah did not yell. The people were eager to listen, eager for him to act.

"Enough of that—it's my turn," Elijah called. "Gather around."

He laid firewood across the stone altar. Carmel was generous with dead, dry wood, and Ahab watched with sorrow as Elijah stacked the dead reminders of days when the spring had run fuller. Elijah dug next, a trench around the altar. The people watched in silence as Elijah's back flinched and flexed, his burned shoulders shoving down as the shovel dug into the crumbling red dirt.

The ox was silent as Elijah slit its throat, resting his hands again on the animal's head, praying with quiet words. The beast fell to its knees, then its stomach, looking at the people in ignorance and awe as it heaved to one side and died. Elijah plunged his dagger deep into the thigh and began cutting, cutting each leg free, clearing away the entrails, laying each dripping piece on the firewood. Ahab was transfixed, and Elijah's words did not register at once.

"Fill four buckets with water, and drench both the ox and the firewood."

Elijah waited for a moment before a man to Ahab's right understood and obeyed. No one else moved. Some of the priests of Baal sat, their stone faces cold and hard, while others laid in the shade of a few last trees that still fought the drought. No priest had the strength to move or curse.

Then he said, "Do it again."

The man, still holding his side from his labors, exhaled and ran back to his buckets. Elijah counted each load off as it was poured in: one, two, three, four. Elijah was a man who picked his way through rocky paths because he took no pleasure in the softer ways. His faith was more like a taste, a preference bred for another place and time, and he had no patience for the confections men like Ahab lived on. Elijah wanted the hard and narrow path. He always had.

Then Elijah said, "Do it a third time."

Ahab heard a woman gasp and the priests cluck their teeth, that he would waste a day and make his inevitable humiliation greater. Children licked their cracked lips, seeing so much water flow.

Water brimmed to the very edge of the trench, and Ahab knew the horror showed on his face as water dripped, mixed with blood from the ox. He followed each drop with grim fascination, as if waiting for the one that would cause the trench to spill, and the spill to pick up speed, until they were all covered in blood and salted water.

Elijah prayed loudly, "O God, God of Abraham, Isaac, and Israel, make it known right now that You are God in Israel, that I am Your servant, and that I am under Your orders. Answer me, God: O answer me and reveal to this people that You are God, the true God, and that You are giving these people another chance at repentance."

A star of fire, burning and popping, exploded onto the altar, showering sparks among the screaming crowd. Ahab gripped the sides of his throne and willed his legs to move but could not feel them.

The fire, white at the center but burning blue at its tips, ate it all: the offering, the wood, the stones, the dirt, and even the water in the trench. Hissing steam roiled out and down, enveloping the crowd. Mothers were screaming for their children, who had dropped their hands, and men cried out for wives bent in the mist, searching for missing children. The steam was gone at once, but the fire remained, and they felt it burning something away, something living among them, in them, not a dead thing sacrificed, but something resistant and spitting, pulled away like a gorged tick; and this thing the fire burned before them cauterized the wound before they could cry out in pain.

All fell on their faces, Ahab first among them. He was not humiliated. He was convinced.

"God is the true God! God is the true God!" The words were on all hearts, and their mouths freed the song with relish. Every fiber of their bodies sang, and their ears heard harmony in a world they knew not.

14

Ahab fell as a man and was raised as a king. He felt it in his blood. Elijah's steady, unyielding face brought him pleasure now, and he knew it was true. The Lord reigned in Israel.

Elijah yelled to the people: "Grab the Baal prophets! Don't let one get away!"

The priests of Baal had already begun to run, split into panicked flights. Some ran southeast toward Muragen, the name mothers spit, another place where these priests had coaxed children away and given them as burnt sacrifices. Some ran northeast to el-Qassis, an esteemed mound where priests gave offerings of grain and oil. These two places had been their sacred sites here on Carmel and they fled for them instinctively, but the people knew how to track frightened prey and found the unholy ones, dragging them back to the brook under Elijah's command. The priests begged for mercy, but the crowd swung stones down on their heads without remorse and thrust daggers through robes dried with ox blood.

Ahab walked up the mountain, picking his way through the people's bloody business. The altar smoked though the flames were gone. The trench was empty and dry, and Ahab set one foot in it carefully as he reached to touch what remained of the sacrifice:

tiny embers that shone brightly before their death. He touched the side of the altar, its twelve white stones. How had he come to this place, he wondered, a godless son of a foreign mercenary? How was it that God had called to him at last, in this season of his life, when his path was already decided? What would this God want from him?

A priest screamed, the sound thick and stuttering as he choked on his own blood. Death was never as fast as the dying wished. Ahab shuddered with the memory, for he had been dying for years until today. The name of the Lord and the fire from heaven had sent new life through his veins. Israel was worth dying for, yes, but she was worth living for too. Ahab had never realized how afraid he had been of living.

He was not a stone, he was not of the twelve, but he would sacrifice himself, just like the oxen, to serve them. Whatever it took, he would be the king they needed. He fell to his knees and tried to make praise to Yahweh, but he knew nothing to say and so offered his silence as what worship he had.

A hand on his shoulder did not startle him. It was Elijah.

"Up on your feet!" he said to Ahab. "Eat and drink—celebrate! Rain is on the way; I hear it coming."

Ahab smiled, his eyes closed, wishing he had always known what it was to have comfort like Elijah's hand on his shoulder. *Yes*, he thought, *rain is coming*, and wiped at the tears in his eyes so Elijah wouldn't see.

He stood and faced Elijah, who motioned for him to take up his seat. Ahab's legs felt unsteady as he picked his way back down and saw the throne as if for the first time.

Elijah commanded Ahab's servants, who watched him with careful fear and scurried at once to obey.

Ahab ate and drank, roasted grains and thick wine stewed with heavy spices, the last of his supply. It burned going down. He watched as Elijah climbed up the mountain, nimble and quick, his feet finding steady ground between the rocks, his face tilted up toward the top, not caring to see where his feet landed.

At the top, Elijah bowed in prayer as Ahab watched. A boy approached Elijah—Ahab had seen him arrive with Elijah today. Elijah prayed for several minutes before the boy reached him. Elijah said something to the boy, and the boy went away to look to the west. He returned, shaking his head. Elijah sent him once more, and the scene was repeated again and again. Ahab sat up in his chair, wondering what was happening; what was this boy denying Elijah? The boy ran to the western edge again, than ran back shouting. Elijah stood, pointing down to Ahab.

Ahab shoved his bowl back to the servants. He started up the mountain as the boy flew down, stumbling too many times for Ahab's exhausted mind to bear.

"My master Elijah says, 'Saddle up and get down from the mountain before the rain stops you.'"

Ahab bowed his head, trying to remember what water felt like when it fell from the skies.

The sun dimmed quickly as a bird screamed, flying across the sky. Clouds veiled his vision, weaving and shuttling across the heavens until the sky was thatched in darkness, the clouds heavy and sagging.

Ahab ran for his chariot, landing in it as the horses jerked forward violently, causing him to clutch the sides as he tried to hang on and find a certain grip. The chariot rocked back and forth over the road, the horses racing under the stinging whip of the driver. The sky darkened, and the air grew cold.

Ahab stood and saw the figure of a man racing ahead of the horses, the lightning illuminating him as Elijah, thunder chasing him but not fast enough. Together the men cut through the gusts of rain, and the horses followed Elijah as he ran along the Kishon River, running straight for Jezreel.

Jezebel

Jezebel's fingers bled as she waited to hear the news from Mount Carmel. She chewed her nails to the quick, tearing them with the edges of her teeth.

The day wore on. The sun melted across the dry brown landscape beyond Jezebel's window. Shimmers of heat over brown-and-white buildings made her servants squint to see the horizon. The only visible clouds were clouds of dust stirred by those animals that remained, the ones that had not died or been eaten, roaming the empty streets like crying ghosts, bleating skeletons of the past. The city was quiet. All had gone to watch the gods compete.

The palace was quiet too. Jezebel had never known silence like this before, like the expectant hush before the answer to a question. The servants spoke in whispers, even those from Phoenicia like Lilith. The brown fields beyond her window swayed in the hot breeze as dead stalks rubbed against each other, a raspy accompaniment for the insects who would keen their one note over and over, all night.

She had hated those insects when she first arrived here, hearing only them and not the sound of ocean as she slept, but their true advantage had become plain enough within the first month. They sang this way as long as nothing moved through the grass around them. When predators came near, they silenced. She admired that nature had found a way to stop its enemies. Surely those beasts that ate the smaller ones had not sprung from the same womb as the others. Asherah had birthed men, perhaps, and even other gods, but these smaller hungry things had come from another mother, intent on death. But this Jezebel wondered in secret, for no word had ever been spoken of another goddess. There were only other names for Asherah, not other incarnations. There was much that could not be explained by Baal and Asherah, and Jezebel had learned not to try.

The afternoon sun was still too high to consider going to bed, but there were no servants to amuse her. She sat on the edge of the bed and waited. She stopped chewing her fingernails when the blood ran down her palms and into her sleeves. She felt it drying in the cracks of her mouth and licked at the crusts. It was salty and tasted like the metal of a knife.

Lilith motioned to the servants to change Jezebel's robes. They seemed alarmed at the blood, and Jezebel laughed at them, smearing her bloody fingertips across a girl's face, slowly dragging a finger across the girl's mouth until it dripped red.

"You look beautiful," Jezebel whispered. The girl trembled, and Lilith pushed her away, scowling at Jezebel.

The other servants worked without words, trying to avoid touching her, slipping a fresh robe on their princess, rubbing away the mineral pigments on her eyes and mouth with a bit of linen dipped in olive oil. They complimented her loudly and too often. They rubbed the green oil then into her face, gentle circles that lifted away the dirt and blood of the day, bringing roses to her complexion and a glow to her cheeks. They moved next to her hands and feet, then smeared a thick perfume paste onto the top of her head. A comb of ivory spindles wove through her black mane, carrying the scent down to the ends, until her hair smelled of frankincense and sage, a rich scent that made her think of hunting in dark forests. She sighed as they left her, bowing as they exited, leaving her in her chamber with its bed canopied in linens, and her tables for the vanities of cosmetics and gods. She had a clay statue of Asherah that she kept in one corner, the face painted as her own, an oil lamp always burning before the little goddess with hollow eyes. Athaliah did not like it and said the stone holes followed her around the room. No, Jezebel had told her, they follow you farther than that. They follow you deep into your soul, and you must appease her or she will see what is in your heart. Goddesses were hungry, angry things. They ate what you loved.

The sky seemed to read Jezebel's thoughts, turning dark even at this hour, and she felt the air in her chamber change. It was heavy and cool. Then she understood. It was going to rain. She turned to Asherah, still standing on the table, still impassive, and she blessed her loudly. Throwing open her chamber doors, she yelled for her servants to attend her at once.

"The blessing of rain has come!" she shrieked to them, clasping her hands and swirling as she prayed, chanting the name of Baal, the name of the god who had finally given Asherah the word to call out for rain. "Now will Asherah refill our bowls with grain and the jugs with wine! Now the people will serve me with one mind!"

The servants rushed to the window to witness the sky. Lilith was beaming with pleasure for her mistress.

The servants raced outside, dancing, the rain soaking their robes and splashing into their open mouths. Jezebel pulled herself to the window and made sure of what she saw.

The older women stood on the balcony of the courtyard, holding jugs out to be filled, gathering empty pots and stashing them, filled, as fast as they could, shouting to the others to stop their dancing and help them. The younger servants, for once, had the bad ears and did not hear them. They danced and laughed, their wet robes slapping as they weaved and skipped.

Jezebel watched as darkness crept toward the palace. The dark clouds stormed past the city gates, coming for Jezebel, the storm growing in fury. Her hair blew straight back in the wind, baring her throat. She raised her hands to cover her throat, unsure of this strange answer to her sacrifices. Lilith's hands turned white as she gripped the windowsill, seeing the storm that approached.

"I want the people to see me when it rains," Jezebel said. "I want them to know who ended the drought."

Jezebel and Lilith made their way through corridors that echoed with rain as if a thousand angels stamped their feet on the roof. Outside, a raindrop hit her right in the face. But rain could not insult her, she thought. Wind drove the rain, not gods. The noise of fat, heavy drops hitting hardened, dry soil sounded like small explosions, loud and close. Jezebel moved back up several steps, trying to get under the roof, to save the royal robes and the cosmetics so carefully applied. The rain changed direction. It drove in sideways, pelting Jezebel in the face, ruining her makeup until black rivers of kohl ran down her cheeks and she lifted her arms over her face for protection, the posture of an adulteress caught in her shame.

"Asherah, save us!" Lilith cried.

In the distance a dark shape ran, an animal fleeing the lightning and rain. It moved with strange grace. Jezebel watched it, mesmerized. Thoughts fluttered in her head like a wounded bird in the path of horses, but she could not hear their words. The animal drove closer, in a straight line, a tall animal with long hair. The animal ran closer still, right for her, and she felt his eyes were upon her, and that his eyes were lightning. It was Elijah. Behind him, in a chariot, was Ahab. Her heart leaped up. Ahab was running Elijah down, driving him to his death before her! Yes, that was why she trembled! The rain had come for her enemy!

Lightning split the sky, illuminating everything. Jezebel turned to command Lilith to help her escape, but she was gone. The servants were fleeing. A single guard remained with the princess, his face pale as death. Jezebel motioned for him to step aside so that she could enter the palace and find shelter. The guard stood immovable, his eyes fixated on Elijah, whose hair flew behind him in the dark storm as he flew along the main road with unnatural speed.

Ahab shouted something to her, but his words were carried away by the wind. Elijah was no less than a few hundred paces from Jezebel when she shoved the guard back and fled inside. She shut the main doors to the outer entrance and drew the wooden bolt to lock them. She grabbed a torch off the wall and held it to the doors. Made of wood that had dried in the drought Elijah had called down, they burst into flames.

The storm howled outside, and the doors shook in the wind as the flames grew wilder. At once, the wind blew the doors open. Burning embers flew at her, singeing her hair as she screamed and ducked behind her arms. Rain pummeled the entrance, driving at Jezebel as the wood hissed all around her, her fire killed by the drenching rain.

Trails of smoke snaked around Jezebel's ankles, their soft licking dying as the rain soaked her robes. She ran for the safety of her chamber, and the rain came on and on.

Obadiah

When Obadiah entered the princess's chambers that night, he saw Lilith sitting in the corner, her face against the wall, still weeping over the thrashing Jezebel had given her. The servants had all heard it, even over the constant sound of rain. Ahab had retreated to another chamber and did not call for Jezebel. Obadiah would be forced to tell her himself.

Jezebel looked out over the city. Her calm was the stillness of a corpse. The darkness that had always been around her now resided within her. She had breathed it in for so long, walked under it for so many years, that at last she and the darkness were one.

Obadiah approached, saying nothing. No one in the streets moved below. In the distance, he saw people returning to the city in small groups that moved slowly, from exhaustion or grief. Death was a terrible thing to witness, made worse by the knowledge that they had once encouraged those priests. The people made their way inside their homes, and yellow lights illuminated each, one by one, until the darkening city looked like a blanket of stars resting on the ground.

He envied them, envied their light. Their houses looked warm and solid and small, made without room to whisper those words of betrayal or make deals, one against each other. Obadiah wished he had a small home, a small life. He thought of Mirra. The Lord had given Obadiah so much, but He had not given him Mirra. He was grateful she had not seen the gruesome end of those priests.

"It was not Baal or Asherah, was it?" Jezebel broke the silence. "They did not send this rain."

"No," Obadiah replied. He should have hated her. Other men did. But the time spent studying the scrolls, the laws and history of this great unseen God, made Obadiah love his enemy, for she lived without knowledge of Him. It was a poverty so unimaginable, so heartrending, that Obadiah could not hate.

"The Lord sent the rain. The drought is over," Obadiah said. "The people have chosen to worship Yahweh."

Her temper flared as she turned to face him. "I never told them not to! I only asked them to accept that there were other paths and other truths. Ask Sargon. Ask Sargon how much the people loved his temple rituals and prayers."

"Sargon is dead," Obadiah said.

She gasped, her hand coming to her mouth to cover her scream.

Obadiah continued. "They are all dead. Every one of your priests either died or fled. I doubt they will ever return. Elijah challenged your prophets, and they failed. Baal never showed up. Elijah gave them the entire day to call on him. But when Elijah spoke, just once, fire fell from heaven. Yahweh was there, Jezebel."

"It was a trick!" she screamed, lunging for her little statue of Asherah, flinging it at his head.

He ducked.

"I am not here to gloat, princess. I am here to help," Obadiah said.

She laughed until her voice trailed away into a sigh. She sounded broken deep inside, in a place she would never reveal. But brokenness meant that something in her was torn open, that light might penetrate her heart at last.

"It is not too late," he said. "I can teach you about the Lord."

A fierce resolve stirred in the darkness of her eyes as she stood and addressed him clearly.

"Tell Elijah that by my gods, by this time tomorrow, he will be dead. I will see his body dragged through the streets and hung up to burn before this is over."

Obadiah excused himself and left, his heart stricken. He would deliver the message, not in obedience to Jezebel, but because he feared for Elijah's life. Something frightening lived in Jezebel, a madness that surfaced and made his blood run cold, rather like reaching into a dark sack of grain and finding a serpent.

Jezebel

Like all men, Omri underestimated her. He had assigned a guard to keep Jezebel in her chambers and away from Ahab. But the guard was young and afraid to hurt her. When he tried to keep her from leaving, he merely placed a hand on her arm. She grabbed it and bit until he screamed and released her, and she turned to spit his own blood at him before moving on. Lilith chased her, with Mirra clinging to the chamber's doorway in horror.

Jezebel paused only long enough to command Lilith to fix her princess's lipstick. The guard had squirmed terribly. It was probably a mess.

Once assured of her appearance, she completed a calm walk to Ahab's chamber. The guard outside was startled by her arrival, unsure what to do. He reached for the door handle to hold it tight, exposing his left side. Right-handed like most men, he kept his sword there, so Jezebel found it easy to lift it free and run it through his thigh. He made an odd sound as he grasped his leg, the blood flowing like wine.

Ahab's concubine screamed to see Jezebel enter with a sword. Jezebel looked down and noticed that her robes were spattered in blood. She dropped the sword, grabbing the woman by the hair, dragging her, naked, from his chamber. She threw the woman outside and closed the door behind her.

Ahab sat up in bed, naked as well. She could not tell if he was pleased to see her. He looked surprised, though.

"Did you mean anything you told me?" Jezebel asked. "When you promised me a future here, and your love?"

Ahab lifted his chin, watching her. "The Lord won on Mount Carmel. I've decided to follow Him as my God. Not just the God of the people, Jezebel—as my God."

Jezebel removed her shawl, letting it fall to the floor before she crawled into bed beside Ahab. He moved to one side to make room for her, but he did not touch her.

She turned to face him, placing her hand on the curve of his lower back, pulling against him, drawing them together.

"I've lost everything because of you," she whispered, her raw fingers caressing the skin on his back. It hurt to touch him.

Ahab hesitated, as if confused. Jezebel waited for his body to take control of his mind. She would never allow him to humiliate her again. No one, not even a god, would take from her what she had earned. Nothing Ahab had ever said was true, and she would not trust him again. She didn't need to.

Yahweh might give rain, but Jezebel might yet give Ahab an heir. She placed his hand on her stomach, a reminder that some things could not be undone.

Jezebel

Late in the night Jezebel heard the alarm sounding from the walls of Samaria and froze in bed, stiff with dread. A ram's horn had pierced the dark silence of the late spring night in three long blasts, the signal of danger. Ahab was already throwing on his robe and running from the room.

She lurched up, fully awake. There were more sounds in the distance, real sounds, the noise of hoofbeats. An army had surrounded the city.

Quickly she rose and threw on a robe over her linen shift. A guard already had a torch down from its bracket, and Jezebel saw the terror in his eyes as he led her to the throne room in the palace. Lilith and Mirra stumbled out of the servants' room, looking about wildly, disoriented. Mirra seemed ready to collapse. She cried that she did not want to be given to a soldier as nothing but war spoils.

Messengers and guards sprinted past as Jezebel entered the corridor leading to the throne room. No one spoke as they passed. She heard the fast slapping of sandals against the mosaic floors. Whatever was happening at the outskirts of the city, she guessed, was urgent, but no one had died yet. Everyone rushed toward the throne room to be advised or to deliver news. She passed a young boy of about thirteen posted outside the door leading from this interior corridor into the throne room. He had wet himself, but he had not abandoned his post. Tight, nervous energy pulsed in the air. Voices were soft and urgent, and everyone moved with speed. On the throne was Omri, looking disheveled and tired. She had not seen him in four months, at least. He looked much older.

Ahab was consulting with three or four soldiers. Each had dirt clinging to his robe, and none had hair or beards that had been groomed in preparation for admittance to this room. Whatever was out there was coming fast. Obadiah stood to Ahab's left, nodding as he listened to the soldiers' reports, whispering sideways to Ahab, perhaps filling in details.

When she stepped closer in, the voices stopped. The nervous energy turned on her like a needle-sharp arrow pulled tight across the string in its aim. Ahab looked past his men, his eyes meeting hers for the first time since they had returned from Jezreel.

"Jezebel," King Omri said, loud enough that all stopped and watched, "Ben-hadad entered our gates tonight."

"I tried to warn the court," she replied.

"Ben-hadad was going to come for Israel someday," Ahab said. "We both knew that, Father."

"Are you questioning my loyalty? Or admitting your incompetence?" she mocked.

Omri stood, his old face red with fury. Unable to speak, he pointed at her, and guards moved to escort her away. She held up a hand as the other cradled her womb.

"Be careful how you handle me. I carry Ahab's child."

Whatever happened, Jezebel knew Ahab would either realize she had been right all along, that Elijah had weakened the kingdom and therefore should be exterminated on sight, or Ahab would be carried off into exile, and she would belong to a new king. The child within wouldn't survive, but she would, and those who survived could start over. None of it mattered. Everyone would have to honor her no matter who won.

Omri commanded the guards to assemble along each side of the room, to defend the king if needed. No one trusted Ben-hadad, even if he offered good terms to stand against Shalmaneser. Jezebel stood behind guards posted along the left side of the room, close to the door she had entered through.

Ben-hadad was announced as if he were a royal visitor, not a king ready for war. He entered wearing a solid blue tunic down to his ankles with embroidery at the edges and a fringed shawl draped over that. He wore a collar of metal circles chained together, stretched tight over his neck.

He bowed before Omri, and formal courtesies were given.

"Why have you come?" Omri said, lifting one hand to gesture toward the city.

"I did not come alone," Ben-hadad replied. "With me, I have brought thirty-two kings from all the empires. Each wants defeat for Israel. Each one could join Shalmaneser. But they listen to me."

Jezebel fought the urge to laugh. She doubted there were thirty-two empires in all the known world. Ben-hadad had a gift for skewering the truth. He always had; when Ben-hadad took the throne from his father, Eth-baal had ordered every one of his trade payments to Tyre inspected twice. It was not unusual to hear of a layer of gold coins covering what was only, really, a sack of flaxseed.

Omri's face lost a shade of color as he listened. He tilted his head, waiting, revealing nothing.

"Your silver and gold are mine," Ben-hadad said. "As are the best of your wives and children."

Ahab moved one hand slowly toward his sword. She doubted he was even aware of it. Ben-hadad noticed it, however, and only smiled.

"I am sorry; were you in the room a moment ago? I brought kings from thirty-two kingdoms. Every one of them would seek your destruction. But I can negotiate on your behalf."

"It's not negotiation," Omri interrupted. "You want blood money."

Ben-hadad just shrugged, uninterested in the distinction, his eyes wandering around the room, noting the decorations and display of wealth.

"Call on Egypt, if you must. Hire an army, if you like. I will give you time to weigh your choices, and then when you realize my terms are generous, and convenient, please prepare the goods. I'd like a list of the women and children, their names and ages. It does displease a woman to be called by the wrong name."

Ben-hadad looked at Jezebel then. She saw the smirk he made so little effort to constrain. He thought he knew women, and he believed they found him charming. She looked away, before he told himself she desired him too.

With that, he left the court, the clanking of his guards' armor the only sound anyone else could have heard.

But all Jezebel heard was the scratching sound in her throat as she silenced a laugh. The Lord had tried to drive Ahab away from her, but Ben-hadad would drive Ahab right back. He didn't like being bullied any more than she did.

~☙~

"You won't obey me, will you?" Ahab asked Jezebel the next day. He had summoned Jezebel to the administration quarters after she had refused to leave the city for refuge.

"No," she answered him. Her stomach was sour. She did not know exactly how far along she was, having no priest to divine it for her, nor to tell her the child's sex. The asu and ashipu had fled as well, fearing the god of the Hebrews. Lilith had no idea how to judge such matters, and Jezebel had grown so tired of Mirra's whimpering that she had sent her back to her father's house.

"I won't let Ben-hadad take you, nor any of my wives. But neither will I march out against him," Ahab said, gesturing to the scrolls laid open on the table. She went to the table and looked at the writings. He had maps of the surrounding lands, plus working sums of soldiers and weaponry.

"It seems you are always running," she said, her fingers tracing the border of the kingdom. "Running behind some other great man. Never leading. I would like to bed a real leader for once."

"You are still grieving the death of your priests, so I forgive you," he replied in the calm manner of someone unwilling to fight. "I know my soldiers, Jezebel. I have served with them. I know their wives; I've held their children. It is easy for you to send me to war, because you risk nothing."

"My reputation is threatened, here and back in my real home. Where did you go, Ahab? You were a fighter once. I thought you might even fight for me."

Ahab stared at her as if summoning the courage to hate her. But he was bound to her, his own life sheltered in hers, his great name growing in the darkness of her womb. She placed a hand on it, a smile catching and lifting one corner of her mouth. If Ben-hadad won her, they would kill the child at once. If Ahab held on to her and his money, she could give him another child. She could not lose either way.

A nervous-looking young messenger took one step into the room.

"Ben-hadad has sent another message. He says, 'I sent to demand your wives and children, your gold and silver. You have not complied. By tomorrow I will send my officials to search your palace and the houses of your elders. They have orders to seize everything you value and carry it away.'"

The boy stood there on trembling legs, waiting for the reply.

Ahab sat on a stool near a table. "Go back to your residence," he said to the boy. "I must consult with my father."

The boy cleared his throat. "Do not be angry with me, my king!"

Ahab frowned, looking up at him. "Go on."

The boy glanced at Jezebel and then spoke again to Ahab. "There is one more thing. A prophet of the Lord is here. It is not Elijah, my king. He says he has received a word from the Lord for you."

⊶✱↦

Jezebel had followed Ahab to the throne room. The prophet was a short man, with a big bald head and one good squinty eye, and failed at simple courtesies. He lacked the power of Elijah, but she had chased Elijah off. He had not been seen or heard from in months. This man was a sorry replacement.

He delivered his message as Omri sat upon the throne. Ahab stood on the step below, wearing his royal robe. An official from Ben-hadad's court stood below the throne, alongside the most prominent of Israel's court.

When the prophet spoke, his voice was too loud, like a man who thinks he will only be heard if he shouts. Clearly he had no confidence in the message, she thought.

"Hear the word of the Lord! The God of Israel says, 'Look upon the vast army. I will give it into your hand, and then you will know that I am the Lord.'"

Jezebel pressed her lips together. Yahweh was going to fight for Ahab? Ahab would not even have to suffer or fight for the victory himself? What kind of god wants a half man? She groaned. She hated Yahweh.

Ahab turned to consult with Omri, quiet words no one else could hear. The guards in the room, and the other elders who had gotten here in time, all shifted from foot to foot, waiting to hear what would be said next.

Ben-hadad's official looked amused.

The prophet raised an eyebrow at the man's confident sneer. "Ben-hadad will return, of course," the prophet added. "He will need to be defeated more than once before he understands the power of the Lord."

Ahab looked up as he listened, then returned to his position and addressed those present. "We refuse Ben-hadad and his demands."

Ben-hadad's official, an elegant man who looked no more than forty, with dark features and piercing green eyes, stepped forward in alarm. "Your army is small, weakened by drought! This city cannot be defended. Ben-hadad seeks money and a woman, not your death."

Ahab stepped down from the throne pedestal and shoved this man in the shoulder with one hand. Murmurs shot through the room. Jezebel felt a twinge of pride. It would be good if Ahab killed him, and the prophet, too. Ahab needed to get back in the business of killing people. He would remember what power was for, and he would be a better ruler. She would love a man who killed his enemies.

"Tell Ben-hadad we are not afraid of him. We are the people of the Lord." Ahab glanced at the prophet, looking as if he expected a nod of approval. He got one.

"But there is no time," the official pleaded. "You cannot even call for reinforcements."

"We need none. We will march out tomorrow. Tell Ben-hadad he will regret ever setting foot near Israel."

Guards began stamping their feet, the sound ricocheting in the room, thunder growing in power. The official shook his head, marveling, and left.

Something stirred in her blood. Ahab's eyes searched the crowd until he found her. Prince and princess looked at each other. His expression was unreadable. But something stirred in her heart and his. She could not deny that.

Obadiah

Two of Ben-hadad's scouts circled Samaria to the north and east three days after their arrival. Obadiah knew what they were doing; they were to make sure Israel had no forces hiding in the hills. And none were, so the men turned their horses to return to Ben-hadad.

Obadiah saw it at the same moment they must have—tracks leading into a cave. They rode to investigate. Obadiah dismounted his donkey, leaving her behind a tall cluster of rocks. He crept on behind the men, slower but quiet. He had been sent out this morning to negotiate the month's rations and secure whatever foodstuffs the army would need. But a sense of dread had led him here, and he did not know why. He had no business with Ben-hadad's men.

The horses pawed at the earth outside the cave, made nervous by something Obadiah couldn't see. One of the men dismounted and silently urged his companions to follow him into the cave.

Obadiah crept nearer still, and what he saw inside made him want to vomit. They had found Mirra sleeping, her long black hair spread beneath her, her smooth arms tucked under her head as a pillow. Obadiah had heard she had been sent home, a disgrace. But he was so relieved that she could not be claimed as part of Ahab's household that he did not think clearly. She had been too proud to return home.

She was partially covered with a blanket, which one man used the tip of his sword to lift, neither man talking. They saw her form, the steady rise and fall of her breath, and dismounted, circling her. Obadiah's blood stopped in his veins, a terrible frozen despair. He could not take two of Ben-hadad's men by himself.

The taller man took a length of rope from his waist, letting it fall free and straight at his feet. The other man unsheathed a dagger and bent, watching his partner for the signal. The tall man nodded and his partner grabbed her hair, yanking her head up and back as he thrust the knife against her neck. Her limbs jerked in a frenzy as she awoke and tried to move, but the knife bit into her neck and she froze, seeing the man standing over her, feeling the other who held her too firmly against himself.

The tall man laughed.

"We will not return without a prize, after all. And what man in our company has seen a woman such as this, for months?"

The man holding her shifted her against him so that he could smell her neck and look at her profile.

"Let's have her for ourselves."

The tall man considered it. Obadiah reached for the dagger at his waist. He would die, but he would give her time to run.

"No," the man said, "let's take her back to camp."

Obadiah hid behind the opening of the cave as he pulled his dagger out from his belt, careful to use his robes to keep it shielded from the sun. As he did, he saw a flicking movement out of the corner of his right eye. *No*, he thought, turning his head just slightly to be sure. A snake had coiled near his feet, its wide triangular-shaped head pointing at his right calf. It had deadly green eyes with a vertical slit, and those eyes did not change as its tongue shot out, tasting the air, tasting his fear. It slid its head further out, gliding across the air toward him. Obadiah swung his dagger in a fast movement, severing its head as the riders burst from the cave, whooping in delight. Mirra was held tight by one rider, her hands tied in front of her.

Obadiah ran after them. Tears ran down his face as he whispered her name, putting one wobbling leg in front of the other.

❧

He did not make it to the tents until nightfall. The moon illuminated the encampment so that he had to find shadows and stay in them. His cheeks were raw now from the hours of slow tears. He knew what soldiers did to unprotected women.

Ben-hadad was eating in his tent with the other kings, who were grumbling about the delay in Ahab's promise of fighting. A servant played the lyre. Most of the soldiers were sleeping, but throughout the darkness he saw several fires burning well, certain signs that someone was still awake and feeding them. He saw men huddled around some fires, talking; and some playing dice and growling over lost wages. But at the far end of the camp, he saw one fire burning high, attended by two men who blocked an entrance to their tent. The tent was set away from the others.

Obadiah moved further away into the night and circled around to the back of the tent. He stood outside and listened.

Inside the tent, a man was negotiating.

"I will pledge my support for you both as commander," he offered.

"The last man offered that and a thousand pieces of silver besides," they replied.

"No man serving Ben-hadad has that kind of money!" the first man shouted. "If you accept lies as wagers, then please, take my support and two thousand pieces of silver!"

"Excellent. You are pledged for two thousand pieces of silver and your support. Move back to your post, and we will call the lucky ones within the hour."

A woman screamed, and Obadiah knew her voice. With a swift movement, he plunged his dagger through the linen of the tent and ripped upward, pushing through the hole as the men inside scrambled for their swords. The tent flaps fluttered as the guards posted outside entered too.

Obadiah saw her, bound at ankles and wrists, her mouth bruised and bloodied, one eye swollen and purple.

He did not know where his strength came from—he had never fought for a woman, or for anything—but he drove his dagger into each man in a blinding, soundless fury. He wanted them to die, and he wanted them to hurt badly as they did. When the men lay on the ground, he drove his dagger into each of them again.

The sound of Mirra's weeping brought him out of the silent trance of his power. He knelt before her, cutting the cords that bound her hands and feet. She tried to speak, but she could only shudder and close her mouth again. He lifted her into his arms and carried her from the tent. He moved to the shadows and worked his way out of the camp. Passing the tent of Ben-hadad, Obadiah nearly stumbled as he bumped into the king. Ben-hadad was relieving himself away from his men.

The king stared at the woman in Obadiah's arms. Obadiah was grateful for once that he had been born with a face that no one ever noticed or remembered.

"A few of your men had a little accident back there," Obadiah said, walking past, keeping calm. "See to it your men are better behaved. We are particular hosts."

∼✣∽

Taking Mirra back into Samaria, Obadiah entered a modest inn built for military men without families. He paid for the room, and once inside, he laid her on the bed and covered her with his cloak. He called the innkeeper up to the room and asked for warm milk. This he fed to her in small spoonfuls, careful to avoid the raw edges where the gag had burned across her skin. When she did not speak, he brushed her hair away from her face with his hand, seeing the thin wound from the knife on her neck. Tears came and she did not wipe them away. He did that for her, the tips of his fingers gently taking each one before it marked the length of her cheek, and he shook each one away into the dust on the floor.

When she stopped crying, he wrapped his arms around her, and she slept. He breathed in the scent of her skin, the scent of perfume and salt and the resin of the wood in the room around them. She pushed her face nearer to him, inhaling deeply too. He held her through the night, feeling the rise and fall of her chest and whispering words of comfort when the bad dreams came.

Ahab

Ahab rose as the spring sun crept across the ledge of the window. He would deal with Ben-hadad today. The night air warmed and grew still, all the noisy bellies filled and returning to hidden dens to sleep before they fed again. Only Jezebel did not stir, her skin growing paler in the morning light, as if something essential fled when the sun rose to greet her. He studied her, ashamed. Her frame was so small and thin from the drought that had stolen their bread. It was not hard to confirm a pregnancy, especially one already past its halfway mark.

He ran his hand along the covering draped over her prize, her claim upon him, upon the throne.

Why would Yahweh pursue Ahab when his fate was already determined within her womb? He could never abandon his Phoenician bride if she carried an heir. It had been too late, then, when Yahweh had pushed His own claim on Ahab.

It was too late.

Jezebel smiled, her eyes still closed, and reached for his hand as it caressed her shoulder. She had won long before Ahab had understood what was at stake.

He got dressed, then went to face Ben-hadad, wondering if God would indeed save him now. Ahab had just over two hundred officers ready, about fifty commanders, plus any strong man or boy who possessed a sword to fight. About seven thousand were ready to march.

Ahab wore his royal robes and lifted the sword of Moses as he prepared to address the men from the palace steps. First light shone around the edges of the men, illuminating their armor. Beyond them, fog rolled toward Samaria from the surrounding hills, creating an eerie ring around the city, the smoke from Ben-hadad's fires making the fog thick blue. Samaria rose above it all, as if watching to see what the hills concealed.

Ahab descended the palace steps as the men parted, dividing into two rows for inspection. There were soldiers as far as his eyes could see, leading down the main road, he was sure, to the city's edges. Ahab had built the wall up, and it had gates, but it had no real splendor or power to protect. No one had wanted to build during the drought. None had had the strength. The city wall would give no protection.

The men raised their spears and began chanting. A young man, no more than twelve, took up a drum and began beating it as his companion blew the shofar. The noise and clamor was so great he felt the earth shake under his feet.

Ahab lifted his sword higher, and they went wild, screaming louder, stamping their feet until thunder boomed back at them from the surrounding walls. Ahab motioned for silence and waited.

"The Lord has given Ben-hadad and this day into our hands," he began. "My father bought this land with his own money. He established Samaria as the capital for Israel. But do you know why Omri built streets, even before he built the wall? Because there was a stronger king, with stronger men, who demanded it. Ben-hadad wanted streets so he could march on us, and observe our lives, and make easy claim on whatever he saw. Today, I tell you, the Lord will proclaim in a loud voice that Samaria does not belong to Ben-hadad! Samaria belongs to Israel! Our streets are our own! Our lives are our own! Let us march down these streets and defeat Ben-hadad in the plains!"

At this, the men dissolved into chaos, and Ahab mounted his horse, riding out. They fell in and rode too, those who had horses. Most ran on foot, some barely able to stand under the weight of their armor. The men who had once fought with Omri were too old. Even Omri stayed at the back, on an old white horse that seemed deaf to the cries of battle.

Samaria quickly disappeared into a cloud of dust stirred up by hooves and feet. He followed his guards, hands shaking from excitement and terror. Looking up, Ahab expected the Lord's fierce eyes to strike through the fog and dust, holy lightning burning his enemies.

But the sky was calm as men swirled and raged below.

The Lord was here, though. Ahab could sense Him, and he slowed his pace a little from the dread of coming any closer to this God. The Lord wanted him to come closer, he could tell, to see the battle, to see the death that follows when people trust in what is false. Ahab's heart seized, a painful skip, as his men rushed on, and he prepared to see the Lord's deadly mercy.

On the advice of the prophets, Ahab had sent the junior officers in the army ahead of the more skilled troops. He suspected the prophets' strategy would give the enemy a false confidence, and they would be lured like lambs into the real slaughter.

But the junior officers defeated Ben-hadad. A young commander, maybe no more than sixteen, returned to Ahab with Ben-hadad's flag.

"Ben-hadad's troops have retreated, and Ben-hadad fled on horseback! We have won!"

Ahab swallowed his shock and gave the signal to blow the shofar. The battle was over. Ahab felt lost, primed for a battle he wouldn't get to fight.

"The name of the Lord be praised!" a soldier called to Ahab that evening in the camp.

"Yes," Ahab replied. Though he stayed in the camp all night, no one praised his name. Ahab had hoped for a victory but had not counted on it costing him any pride.

Obadiah

It was midnight. Samaria slept below Obadiah, quiet without the men. He waited inside the city gates. Two guards stood outside; he could hear their hushed voices, but there were few men left inside the city. He held a woven cage with two doves inside. He had never been to Jerusalem or its temple, but he heard that it was good to bring an offering. Especially for a young woman seeking a new life.

The air had an edge of chill as the night grew black, and an owl perched on the wall overhead, his head turning in all directions. Obadiah watched it hunt. A small mouse crept out from a rock, drawn by the smell of bread that a soldier had dropped. The owl slid silently from its perch, never slowing, its talons falling down from its snowy white feathers as it pierced the mouse. Obadiah was alone again as the owl flew home to share the reluctant trophy.

Mirra appeared, treading so softly across the road that no dust stirred. She managed a small, uncertain smile, and he drew a deep breath.

"Did it go well?" he asked.

"My mother says you are a good man," she replied. "She blesses your name." The moon revealed shadows under her eyes that hurt his heart. He didn't want to say good-bye like this. He wanted to see her strength return, and her smile, too. To let her go now was an act of faith, and yet Obadiah knew faith was all he had ever had. It had been enough once. It would have to be enough now and forever.

"Will she tell your father when he returns from battle?" he asked.

"I don't know," she said, tears welling in her eyes. "I hope she does not tell him everything. He would be so disappointed in me."

Obadiah reached for her, knowing it would be the last time he ever touched her or looked upon her. He willed himself to remember everything: her scent, the softness of her skin and how her hair felt like water flowing across his arm.

"He will always love you," Obadiah said, the words stinging like vinegar in his throat. He spoke of her father, but he spoke also of himself, and she would never know. "You must believe that. You will always be loved."

She pulled away slightly and looked up at him. "You've been so good to me. Are you sure this is the only way?"

"Give me your outer robe," he said.

She obeyed, her brow knotting as she did. He took the robe and walked a distance away so she would not see. He killed one of the doves with his hands, those fingers stained with ink now stained with blood. He dipped her robe in the blood before throwing the dead bird out into the darkness, where scavengers would dispose of it within hours. He tore the robe and left it at the gates.

"A merchant will discover it tomorrow morning," he said. "The people will think you died, attacked by a wild beast. Only your mother will know the truth." Obadiah did not tell Mirra what a burden the truth was, and would be, for her mother. It was a weight heavier than any stone. He did not add that Mirra's mother would not have the strength to bear the burden alone; she would tell her husband. One day the entire city would know what she and Obadiah had done.

"But what of you?" she asked.

He led her to a horse from the royal stables, a fine gray one that would not be missed. Obadiah had purged it from the records. It had unfortunately died of a twisted stomach, the records said. She climbed up and held his hand tightly.

"I will keep you in my heart," she said.

He let go of her hand. "No," he replied softly. "Leave everything behind. You belong to Jerusalem now."

Jezebel

Jezebel's pains came fast in the late summer, and the hard labor was no surprise. The child had been restless from the moment of conception, refusing to be confined, impulsive and impatient.

"You have delivered a son," the Hebrew midwife said. Jezebel wept but did not speak. She did not want to invite friendship with this Yahwehist, lest she—or worse, her son—be infected with that god of condemnation.

When she heard his first raw scream in this world, she rejoiced. She needed an angry son. Jezebel stopped her tears when the midwife gave the infant his salt bath. It was a good smell, the smell of birth and sea. She would never return to the ocean. She knew that. She would birth her children in a very different world, and she would die in it, having given Israel and its god the best of her years, the best of her body. She would give her life to this nation of traitors, who had sacrificed their babies and then murdered her priests. Her son would repay them.

Ahab returned the next day from a scouting expedition with all the political officials and elders in his entourage.

Jezebel had commanded Lilith to comb her hair and set it loose around her shoulders, and to dress her in a lavender tunic with a red sash covered in gold beads. Jezebel met him on the palace steps.

She held the newborn in her arms, intending to present him to Ahab in view of all, her victory clear. But then she saw him laughing with Obadiah, at ease, content with one god and all her dead priests. She looked down at the babe sleeping in her arms and held him away from her body over the stone steps.

"I have given you a son," she called out.

Ahab was stunned to see the babe in her arms, blinking several times as if to comprehend she had given birth while he was gone.

She held the baby over the steps below. If she dropped him, threw him down, she would inflict pain on Ahab. On them all. She could give an heir and take it away just as easily. They would learn what it was like to lose.

Ahab bounded up the steps, delighted. Grabbing the baby away before she could do it, he laughed and lifted their son high in the air, turning to show his entourage and the gathering crowd. "His name," he declared, "will be Ahaziah."

The name meant Yahweh's victory.

But she didn't care. She was the one who had won the victory by giving Ahab a son, a prince, an heir. Her position was unassailable. The drought was over, and tall fringed headdresses of barley waved all around. The people were merry, shouting their congratulations and praise of their god, so merciful to forgive and grant a son, grant them the security of a continued reign. They did not understand that she rejoiced too, for no one and nothing but herself.

She spied Obadiah standing on the steps just to her right. Mirra had been killed, but she did not miss her. Yet his was a strange grief.

He ate his meals, he attended his work, like a man who wanted the distraction. Grieving men didn't want distraction; they wanted oblivion. She did not trust him.

Jezebel returned to her chamber, Lilith trotting behind, making little hints that she would love to go and feast in celebration with the court, until Jezebel dismissed her. Now that she was delivered, she could drink something strong and bitter, crawl out of this skin and sleep at last. If she wanted, she could spend eighty days doing that, the time she would be ritually unclean according to Yahwehist law. Ahab would not lie with her, especially now that he believed in the power of this god. She would be alone.

Before the eighty days were finished they would be back in Jezreel, away from this city. She could feel blood trickling down her legs. Birth was hard on any woman. A great darkness rose at the edges of the city, like a wave far out on the horizon. She watched in horror as it crested the city wall, that ineffectual wall Ahab had built, and thundered down the streets of Samaria, sweeping toward her with a roaring scream. A rainstorm was coming, again.

Jezebel picked up the edge of her robe and ran, leaving a trail of blood all the way to her bed.

Finally in the cool retreat that was Jezreel, three months after the birth of her son, Jezebel could not sleep, not even with an oil lamp beside the bed. Her only comfort was the sound of Lilith's heavy breathing. She wondered, on some nights when there was no moon, when Ahab would call her back to his chamber. Her time of cleansing was complete. She did not feel clean though. She was born dirty, a woman, and the passage of time changed nothing.

Her bleeding had stopped, however, and her strength was returning a little more every week. Her stomach had begun to regain some of its shape, but she had no routine, no schedule or order to her days. How did the Hebrew women survive this expulsion from favor?

The continuing neglect stirred her plague of anxiety. Silence stirred up her ghosts. What had really happened to her priests? Had they died by fire or sword? Had their bodies been honorably treated? At night, she heard them crawling under her bed. The Egyptians had told her that fingernails never stopped growing, even in death. She heard them scratching at her bed. When she drifted off, they climbed from under the bed, their heads twisted, eyes hollow, mouths slack, arms reaching for her. Calling her name. Carrying the children in their arms. So many children, their dark hollow mouths screaming out for the years she had stolen. They grabbed her, gnawing her flesh, craving life.

She woke, sweating, night after night. They were only dreams. The dead did not live. Guilt was a trick of the mind.

The sun became strong. She sat up toward the open window, inhaling the delicate perfume rising from Naboth's garden below. The olive trees were blooming; their blossoms had such a light fragrance, easy to miss. She ate the first fresh spinach she had had in three years, plus fennel and even apricots.

The food did not cling to her frame. She ate but was never filled. She slept without peace.

Spring promised nothing. In her dreams, she knew why.

The Lord had not finished with her yet.

Obadiah

Just three weeks after the return to Samaria, after nearly six months in Jezreel, while the royal court was holding a festival to celebrate the Feast of First Fruits, a messenger interrupted the afternoon meal. Ahab allowed the boy to whisper the news to him, and then Ahab stood. All fell silent, waiting, trying to read Ahab's face. Obadiah watched Jezebel's face and understood. The prophet's word had come to pass yet again. Her eyes had darkened. She was silent but radiated her displeasure. The prophet had proven himself and his God yet again.

"Ben-hadad has returned. He is at Aphek and plans to march against us."

The prophet entered then without looking around or noticing the guests. He looked well, not remarkably different from last year. His face was haggard from the sun and wind, but his eyes were serene and his gaze steady. It must have been a remarkable thing, Obadiah thought, to walk through the storms of the land, of this life, to be worn away and weathered, yet at peace in everything.

Ahab rose, pulling out a cushion. "Join us, my friend."

Jezebel flinched and shifted her cushions as if to make room. Obadiah knew she did not want to be touched by this man of God.

The prophet surely smelled the roasted meats, the finest grains and herbs and sweets that anyone could buy, but he shook his head to dismiss the offer and delivered the message. He spoke with the tone of confidence born of indifference to earthly power.

"Ben-hadad has said to his men, 'Ahab won the last battle because it was fought in the mountains of Samaria. Yahweh, his god, rules the mountains. Therefore we will fight again, but we will meet them on the plains of Aphek. Yahweh will not fight on the plains.' Because of Ben-hadad's arrogance, and his ignorance of the Lord your God, he will be struck down in Aphek."

It was a prophecy of victory and was met with rejoicing and words of praise for the great and merciful Lord. Obadiah finished his bowl of wine and brushed at the tears in his eyes with the back of his hand. He would be glad to see Ben-hadad dead, his head on a pole outside the city.

"May the name of the Lord be praised," Obadiah said softly. His throat burned with sorrow.

Ahab

For seven days, Ahab and his men camped on the plain of Aphek, facing the armies of Ben-hadad. Ahab emerged from his tent on the sixth evening of waiting. Though the Lord had promised victory, He must have been content to let Ahab fight the battle. Ahab was grateful, or tried to be. He had not fought a real battle since his marriage. He had been in many wars since then, but never the kind that required a sword. He flexed his arms and swung them loose, preparing for Ben-hadad to attack.

The shrill blast of the ram's horn came at dawn the next day. Ben-hadad was coming.

"Keep the lines tight," Ahab called, watching as his men stamped and pawed at the wet grass like animals. Ahab rode a horse, accompanied by two commanders, and he tried not to think of Obadiah, who was not here. Obadiah had always urged him to believe in the Lord. It was odd to fight a battle in the Lord's name and not have Obadiah here to witness it.

The land outside the city was indeed flat, dotted sparsely with trees that shook as arrows flew through them. Leaves fluttered to the ground, and limbs fell. One flew close to Ahab, who heard the stinging hiss of many arrows at once. Still, his men broke into a run, one great glorious scream roaring across the plains, engulfing their enemy.

The men ran over the soft green grasses, pounding them under the earth, and kept running until they were running over the dead bodies of Ben-hadad's men, chasing survivors. Ahab's men who had held the back lines had no men to kill. Before the evening meal, a hundred thousand of Ben-hadad's dead troops polluted Israel. The plain was an ocean of blood. Anywhere Ahab set his foot down it sank into blood all the way up to his ankle. Ben-hadad was not among the dead.

By dusk, none of Ben-hadad's infantry stood. The rest of his men fled into the town of Aphek, hiding in homes and buildings. Citizens of Aphek had stood on the walls watching the battle. When Ben-hadad's men ran for the city, the citizens struggled to close the gates to Ahab and his men, lest the battle be brought into their streets and their families killed. As the citizens pulled against the gates, heaving and shouting for the massive wooden doors to move, Ahab's horse reared up with a scream.

Lightning struck the earth, splitting it, a crack running to the wall of Aphek. The wall fell in an explosion of stone, catching the largest group of Ben-hadad's men as they entered the city. A cloud of dust rolled across the plain in all directions, evaporating on the horizon. None of Ben-hadad's troops survived, not even their horses. He was sure of that. He heard not even a moan from the men beneath the collapsed wall. They were all dead.

Ahab urged his horse forward. The horse gave him no trouble, its sudden calm demeanor unsettling Ahab more. Ahab and his commanders did not speak, but approached the city, navigating their horses through the stones stained with blood. Families stood at the entrance of their homes, silent, mothers clutching children to their breasts, watching this strange prince who marched in the name of the god of Israel. Ahab nodded as he passed, and his men moved behind, quiet. The wall's collapse had shaken them, too.

Ahab found his prize crouched beneath a pile of blankets in the inner chamber in a widow's home. She opened the door to her home widely when she saw Ahab approach, pointing one finger to the room. She braced herself against the doorframe as he entered, expecting her own walls to fall.

Ahab dragged Ben-hadad out into the streets. None of Ben-hadad's men were seen. Ben-hadad's knees were shaking, and Ahab understood.

Yahweh reduced kings to this.

Ahab reached out a hand and rested it on Ben-hadad's shoulder. "I will make the terms."

Ben-hadad nodded.

"There can be peace between us, between you and my God, but you must do as I ask. In exchange for your life, you must return all the cities you stole from my father long ago. You must swear to never again attack us, never again cost us even one life."

Ben-hadad embraced Ahab like a brother and wept for his army. Ahab left him standing in the dusty streets of Aphek to search for survivors. A messenger ran to him, pale and with stuttering speech. Ahab saw the fear in the young boy's face and remembered how death seems to the very young. He squatted down to look into the boy's eyes, not caring how such indignity reflected on him as prince.

"Do not be afraid, my son," he said. "What is your message?"

"Your ... father," the boy said, holding Ahab's gaze steady as if for strength, "he is ... dead."

Ahab

Ahab ran for the battlefield. Where was his father? Blood covered the earth in a flood unseen since the days of Noah. Wasted, blood poured through the valley, poisoning the flowers with the salted memory of life. Bodies littered the earth in all directions. Every face was covered with blood so that men of all nations looked like brothers. Death wrote the final treaty they would keep, and keep forever. As darkness fell on the land, the moon revealed the unnatural plain.

He found Omri slumped over in a chariot. The king had no wounds, and his face was slack, his eyes open. Ahab held his father in his arms and did not know if he should weep.

When he was a child of eight, his mother had died. Omri cried every day, drinking himself into a stupor at night, drinking his way through the last of their money. Omri had been a good soldier, a respected man of valor, and it was not a small sum that he drank up. But an offer came from the lord of the city of Ashdod to put down a small rebellion. Ahab's mother had been buried for two months, and Ahab had refused to leave, wanting to stay in that land to the east with her bones.

But Omri accepted the work, then drank until he passed out over his wife's grave. Ahab woke him the next day, frightened by the smell of death that rose from the ground and clung to his father. Ahab did not want to lose his father. At last, toward noon, Omri stood, scowling at his son's tears. Ahab licked them away and tasted sorrow. They left their home that evening, forever.

In Ashdod, Ahab discovered this wonder called the sea. The waves crashed and broke over sharp rocks, mesmerizing him with their relentless beauty. He found a path down to the water and followed it, and when he waded in to a quiet pool guarded by a formation of rocks, he lifted one hand to his mouth. The water was salted and bitter, stinging his throat, still raw from the dusty journey. It stunned Ahab, to think beauty could taste like tears.

Choking on the water, he was hurt by his father's laughter behind him.

"Come with me," Omri had said, grabbing Ahab and forcing him into the rough water.

Though Ahab cried, his father held him by the arms, pinning the boy in front of his own body. Waves taller than a horse swept down on them both. The waves would strike Ahab in the face, salt burning his eyes, as the brunt of the wave struck the air from his chest. He gasped between waves as his father yelled at him, "Which of us is stronger?"

At first, Ahab thought his father wanted him to be brave, to declare that Ahab the boy was stronger, but that was not so. The waves were going to kill him.

Finally, he yelled between rolling assaults, "You are! Omri is stronger than his son! Omri is stronger than them all!"

Omri released him and walked back to shore. Ahab stumbled through the surf and collapsed against a rock. Omri stood above him, not looking at his son but the horizon, nodding to himself as he repeated his son's words. "Omri is stronger than them all."

Ahab never saw his father grieve for his mother. He never saw Omri grieve or weep for anything.

And so Ahab refused to grieve for him.

Jezebel

Jezebel had Ahab's chamber supplied with fresh fruits: lemons, ripe and fragrant, bowls of them set around the chamber for perfume, and apricots for color. She had dishes prepared of spinach and meats seasoned with fennel, and wine brought in from the storehouses. She made sure the palace kitchens were ready to feed the returning troops, and feed them well, with the best dishes planned for a private meal for Ahab in his chamber. Finally, she had warned the royal nurses to be ready for Ahab's return, too. Clean clothes needed to be ready at all times and the children freshly bathed and perfumed every day until his return.

When the army was spotted on the horizon, the servants cheered for joy, everyone scampering to their tasks.

Lilith worked quickly to help Jezebel bathe and dress in a fine new linen she had imported from her father's household. Jezebel asked Lilith to braid her hair, hoping it would remind Ahab of their first days together, before the gods had fought over Israel, and before they had fought as husband and wife.

Jezebel watched from her window as the army entered the gates,

to judge their timing. She wanted to be on the steps of the palace as
he arrived, with Ahaziah and Athaliah at her side.

But it was not as she expected. The men moved slowly, a boy
marching in front, playing the tambourine and singing a dirge.
Women from the city emerged from their homes, and slowly a
loud wail rose from the streets. Death had come to Samaria.

Jezebel felt the blood drain from her heart. Searching the
gathering crowd, she saw Ahab's flag bearer. The flag rode high,
Ahab behind it. Jezebel slumped forward and exhaled. She did
not understand her relief that he was alive. Was that what it
meant to love someone, that she would fear his death? But she
had given him an heir. His death could do no harm to her now,
as long as she remembered not to love.

Ahab scowled as he rode through the wailing crowd. He
dismounted at the palace steps and went inside, without even
looking at Jezebel or his children. His face was dark and clouded,
an expression she had not seen since the drought. His men riding
in after him looked no better, though they looked more confused
than angry or afraid. The streets began to buzz with the questions. Jezebel grabbed a guard walking past, on his way to attend
Ahab.

"Who is dead?" she asked.

He sighed and hesitated before answering as if her reaction
might be unpleasant.

"King Omri," he said at last. "He died in battle, but not by
the enemy's hands. It was old age."

"You won, though, didn't you?" she asked.

"Yes," he answered and went on.

Jezebel

Ahab went straight to his chamber that evening, and Jezebel was refused entrance.

The guard was young, though, and he did not know what to do when she shoved him out of the way and entered the chamber. She was the queen now, after all.

Ahab sat on the bed, staring at the floor. Blood stained the edges of his tunic, as if he had walked through a sea of blood. His hair hung in thick tangles around his shoulders. He smelled of mud and smoke. When he shifted his weight on the bed, he groaned as if sore, as if thinking he was just a man. He was not. He was a king. Jezebel marveled that he allowed himself to feel anything but that. She had been spared so many useless emotions.

"You need to address the people," she said at last.

"I have shown mercy to my enemy, but none was given to me," he said. "We defeated Ben-hadad, just as the Lord said we would. Ben-hadad had insulted the name of our God, angered Him. That is why we were given favor. Because the Lord was angry with him. It did not mean the Lord was pleased with me." He sighed, and Jezebel waited for him to continue.

A tear ran down his cheek as he spoke again. "It was a battle deep in blood. I heard the groans of his men dying and knew they had been punished for his sin. It could have been my men dying were it not for the mercy of the Lord on me. The Lord gave me mercy, allowed me and my men to live, but that did not mean He was pleased. What more did I owe Him?"

There was no crown prepared for a queen mother of Israel. One would need to be made immediately. She had too much to do to sit with Ahab like he was a child.

Jezebel slapped him. It had no effect.

"I offered terms of peace to Ben-hadad," he said. "And while I mourned the news of my father, a prophet of Yahweh came to me and told me he had a word from the Lord for me. I was eager to know what it could be. But he said, 'Because you had mercy on the man I had marked for destruction, your life is forfeit. Your life for his life. Your people for his people.'" Ahab groaned. "Punishment. For giving mercy."

Jezebel could not speak. The shock was too great. Ahab had done wisely and acted with shrewd intent. He offered a covenant of peace with a powerful enemy, and the enemy had accepted. The Lord had promised Ahab victory and said he would strike down Ben-hadad, but Ahab had found a better way. Ahab's plan was good by any moral, human standard.

His god was insane.

Dipping a linen in the basin of water on her nightstand, she held his face in her hands and wiped away the grime. When she finished, he rested his head against her bosom. How heavy he felt, weighted by grief.

"Should I call a concubine?" she asked. She didn't want to spend her evening holding him. Those women served a purpose. But he did not seem to hear her.

At last, he released her, and she helped him into bed. That night she rested with her face against the wall, unable to bring herself to comfort Ahab any longer in his weakness. He had to break free of this god. If he did not, how could he ever rule?

Obadiah

Two days later, Obadiah stood before Ahab, holding the royal crown, a thick band of gold set with the stones of Israel's tribes. Like Ahab, Obadiah had been a boy when this crown was placed on Omri's head. How large the crown had seemed then, as if a giant could wear it. Obadiah felt the cold weight of it in his hands. It was smaller than he remembered. He placed it on Ahab's head and turned to the court, who shouted, "Long live King Ahab! May his kingdom endure to a thousand generations!"

Behind Obadiah, a steward stepped forward holding the royal warrant, a scroll containing the covenant between God, king, and people. Modeled after Solomon's oath and God's commands to him, Obadiah prepared to read it, his heart aching with anticipation. At last the words of the Mighty Lord would ring out before the people, and the court, and even Jezebel herself.

Obadiah caught himself and returned to his business, preparing to lift the tie on the scroll and read it. Ahab shook his head against it. He accepted the scroll, still bound, with a curt nod, his eyes looking straight out over the people gathered below him, just beyond the palace steps. Obadiah grieved that Jezebel long ago had requested the tombs of Omri and Ahab be moved. When she came here, they had been black gaping boxes on either side of the main entrance to the palace, built into the platform it sat on. She requested they be filled in with stone and moved. But graves would have reminded the court to put no faith in man. Faith was for sure things, like the word of the Lord. It was a bitter thought, just another truth he could not share.

Next, Obadiah held a horn with a stopper in one end, which he removed as Ahab knelt. A silence came over the people. The sun was glorious in its attendance today, and a cool breeze made all lift their faces up and close their eyes in pleasure as Obadiah began to pour the oil over Ahab's head. It dripped down his temples onto his shoulders, and Obadiah saw the change in his eyes. He was free of his father, and he was king.

Ahab turned to Jezebel then, extending his hand, as protocol would have him do. As Ahab took her hand in his, Obadiah set the new queen's crown on her head, forcing himself to focus. She had allowed craftsmen no sleep until a crown was made that exceeded even Ahab's in beauty. She had more gray in her hair than he had realized. That bed of ashes she had made had worked its way into her blood and changed her. Obadiah willed Ahab to see it too.

Ahab looked haunted. He faced the crowd as they played tambourines and danced. In the distance, the sky was white and hazy as clouds hung low over the hills, spilling toward them, concealing the distant lands.

Obadiah shuddered and wondered what might be waiting just beneath.

Jezebel

After two months, Jezebel grew impatient. The move to Jezreel had not brightened Ahab. He was still withdrawn and drank himself to sleep many nights. He had not brought his box of gods and amulets, the ones he had saved from all those past battles. If he was trying to reform himself for the Lord, she doubted he was telling the Lord much about the drinking.

She wondered what Sargon would have said. Jezebel knew what Asherah would say, and that was nothing. Asherah had not made herself known since her priests had died calling her name. Perhaps if a child were to be offered, though. A newborn would be best, but where to get one? The Israelite women didn't want to do that anymore. Jezebel couldn't offer one of her children, of course. People knew their faces. They had names.

Ahab and Jezebel had sat on the balcony overlooking Naboth's gardens, an attempt to enjoy a pleasant morning. A pink sunrise had flooded the valley with light. Ahab had stood without warning and left.

"I'm going for a walk," he said. "I want to see how Naboth's gardens have done since last year."

Jezebel retreated to her chamber for several hours, working on a letter to her father. She could no longer make sacrifices here and be assured of the gods' blessing. Perhaps her father would see that some were made in her name. Lilith entered the chamber, frowning, motioning for her to be quiet, gesturing toward the hall.

Jezebel heard Ahab's voice, a groan of abject misery escaping him.

Jezebel rolled her eyes. "Is he drunk?"

Lilith shrugged. "He went out. He came back in. Obadiah thought he was hungry, so he sent food up, but Ahab refused it."

Jezebel ran through all the possibilities in her mind. Ahab had gotten hurt or taken an embarrassing fall in front of his men. He had become ill after yesterday's ride—any number of things that a man might not want to discuss. Or maybe he was having romantic difficulties with another wife. Jezebel would not counsel him on that. But he could not live like this.

She would not allow it.

Ahab

Ahab had wandered from the palace into the gardens of Naboth. He found peace there, as if it were a fruit that Naboth grew. His father would have broken his nose for admitting this out loud, but Ahab thought nature tried to teach him.

Sometimes, when he had ridden in a chariot, the horse would take him into rough fields, and a weed, a thorny vine, would get caught up in the wheel. The horse would not slow. Ahab knew the animal didn't even notice. Not until the animal went further and further, his eye only on the destination ahead, and turn by turn, the vine worked its way through, knotting and twisting, until the wheel slowed and threw the chariot off balance. Ahab would be forced to stop and cut through layer after layer of thorns, bloodying his hands as he pried the vine free. If he had caught it early, the work would have been light and less painful. It wasn't the vine that caused such damage, but the combination of vine and distance traveled.

That was what Ahab felt, sinking regret, consternation that a simple task had turned into a painful rebuke. Nothing to be done but cut. How could he? How could he cut Jezebel loose, deny his children by her, and now another one on the way? Oh, by the Lord, if he had only said no to the marriage. If he had never kissed her and known how soft she could be.

He couldn't please the Lord without cutting away so much. He had come so far. Had the Lord ever made sense to him, ever explained why the sea must be salt and what he loved must die? God was stronger than man; why did that not satisfy Him? It had been enough for Omri.

Ahab was startled by the quiet approach of Naboth, who bore a bucket of vegetable scraps. Naboth was a short man with graying brown hair that grew thinner as it reached his shoulders. He had deep lines around his mouth and eyes, suggesting a man of great laughter. His nose was the most prominent feature of his face, too large for it seemingly, but even that just made him merry. Ahab had met him several times and knew him to be a devout man of the Lord, so he was not surprised to think of him as a happy man. Most of them laughed a great deal, for reasons Ahab never understood.

"Ahab!" Naboth called, setting the bucket down and embracing him with a brisk hug. "I was grieved to hear of your father's death."

"Thank you."

"You are well?" Naboth asked, studying Ahab's face, seeing something there. Ahab felt himself blushing, as if embarrassed, as if caught. By a gardener, no less.

"I have known trouble," Ahab confessed.

Naboth smiled, a generous and kind smile. "Well, since you are obviously not here on official business"—he gestured to make clear that no one had accompanied the king—"come and help me in the garden." He picked up his bucket and started walking toward a shady area where his herbs grew. "I need to work these scraps into the soil. Makes the soil richer."

Ahab had not moved. Naboth turned and called to him. "Come on. Soil is good medicine for troubled men."

Ahab followed, and he worked with his hands, the hands that had held a sword now wielding a small trough. Making the soil richer for new things to come. Naboth was right. It was good medicine. Ahab felt himself able to breathe deeply, as if he hadn't taken a breath, a real breath, in years.

"All this waste, it makes the next crop better?" Ahab asked.

"Stronger, I'd say," was Naboth's reply. "What we wasted yesterday prepares the soil for tomorrow. But only if you put it to work."

"I want to buy it," Ahab declared, standing up.

"What?" Naboth continued working, checking every herb bed with care, his lips moving silently as he made notes in his head.

"I want to buy your garden. All your land," Ahab said.

Naboth stopped as if he had been struck. He stood and brushed the dirt from his legs. "Come anytime you would like. I will never close the gates to my king."

"No, no, I will buy it. Sell me your vineyard, or if you prefer, I'll give you another in its place."

"My son," Naboth said, "this I cannot do. The law of the Lord is that the land belongs to one family forever. It cannot be bought or sold. To do so would be to disobey the Lord."

Ahab waited for the real reason Naboth would not sell, but Naboth said nothing else.

"You are so afraid of the Lord?" Ahab said finally, his voice harsh and mocking, but really, he trembled inside to think another man understood his fear, his total terror of this unreasonable god.

"Do you not understand?" Naboth asked. "It is not fear that compels me. It is love. I love Him so much that I could never dishonor Him."

Ahab nodded, glancing back at the path that would take him from here, back to the palace.

"Of course," Ahab said, taking his leave quickly. "Forgive me. It was only a mistake. It was all such a mistake."

Jezebel

Ahab still had not eaten and had not emerged from his chambers.

Obadiah had entered the chamber, a hand over his nose and mouth as he went straight over to open the doors leading to the portico. With fresh air moving in the chamber, he stood over Ahab, who was in bed, staring at the ceiling, blinking and sighing at odd intervals. He had not gotten up to bathe or eat. The room smelled of sweat and stale beer. His dinner from last night sat untouched on the nightstand, with the breakfast from the previous morning untouched as well on the floor beneath it.

"What can I do?" Obadiah asked.

Jezebel sat in a chair in the corner, watching it all. She had stayed with Ahab through the night, though he had never said a word.

"Get out!" she yelled. "This does not concern you!"

"Stop!" Ahab cried out. He held his head in his hands, his fingers clenching his hair.

Obadiah took his leave, slinking away like the palace rat he was.

"Why are you so sullen? Why won't you eat?" Jezebel said, moving to the bed to stare down at him.

"I tried to do something good yesterday," Ahab said. "And I've been humiliated."

"Is this how the king acts?" she asked, slapping him on the arm.

"A throne doesn't mean anything."

In that moment, Jezebel wanted him dead. She thought of holding him over the pit of fire, him instead of Temereh. Jezebel had given everything for a throne, and what she hadn't given was taken from her. Nothing was sacred, nothing mattered but a throne.

"What happened?" She sat on the bed, near defeat herself.

Ahab sat up to look at her while he talked. His eyes were bloodshot and swollen. He had been crying.

She tried not to recoil.

He began. "I know how much you like Naboth's vineyard and gardens. I decided that I would make a present to you of his land. I knew you wanted it."

He returned to that point again, she noticed, as if blaming her.

"So I made my offer. I was generous, Jezebel. More than generous. I offered him a fortune, or his selection of any other land he desired. I would have even given him both, had he asked. But he accused me of not loving the Lord."

"That makes no sense," she corrected him. He was leaving something out. She had never known him to be a liar.

"There is an old law of Yahweh. He gave each family their land, so no family can sell it. But that was generations ago."

GINGER GARRETT

"You know what troubles me about this Yahweh?" Jezebel asked Ahab. "He began with one altar, built by David, yes?"

Ahab nodded.

"Then he has a temple in Jerusalem and promises to dwell there. Then he comes to Samaria and troubles our people there. Then he follows you to Aphek and condemns you for making a covenant. Now he is in Jezreel, too? Does the whole world belong to him?"

"Yes!" Ahab said.

"In all my years listening to stories of sailors and merchants and dignitaries from every empire in this world, I have never heard of a god like this," she said, standing, pacing from exasperation. He said nothing but gave her a sullen look, like a child refusing to play.

She made a fist and pounded Ahab so hard in the stomach that he gasped. He needed to listen. "Get up and eat. I'll get you Naboth's land."

"I didn't ask you to," he said. It sounded like a declaration of his innocence, in case Yahweh was nearby and listening.

She laughed at the thought.

"No, you didn't," she told Ahab. "I can do this all by myself."

Jezebel

To host a feast, most royal courts required at least three month's preparation. The palace must be cleaned, repairs made, decorations tended to, murals added and inlays finished. Additional toilets must be constructed and tables brought in.

Jezebel loved the whirlwind she had created over the past month, the hum of activity. Every time she walked in the valley, she was met with appreciation and compliments from Ahab's men. Ahab began to recover from his melancholy as he noticed the activity and was slowly drawn in. He still had marrow in the bone.

Obadiah was the reluctant participant. Jezebel ordered him to have one hundred sheep butchered and to see to it that every dish was well seasoned. Naboth had plenty of fennel and anise growing; Obadiah could be sure to give him a fair price and see that it was done. In addition, she asked him to audition musicians. A good feast had great music, and she insisted he find quality musicians. She didn't care which instruments, only that he had plenty of musicians stationed throughout the grounds.

They would have tables all through the grounds, too, separating guests by gender, and then by rank. In the main hall of the palace, which served as an administrative center, the other tables would be set. At the far end of the hall he would place the king's table, and Ahab and Jezebel would entertain from there. Elders would flank the royal couple at their table and at the tables nearest. She made a careful point to Obadiah that she wanted Naboth seated with Ahab, in full view of everyone present. Naboth was to be given great honor.

With so much to be done, Jezebel told Obadiah, Ahab did not mind if she used his seal. He had not fully recovered from his moods, and she had to seal purchase orders for many of the larger requests, otherwise a merchant or farmer might be reluctant to send so many goods to the palace. Everyone wanted royal reassurance. And so the queen worked, sometimes late into the evening, when the birds had quieted down and the insects thrummed in the valley below. An oil lamp burned on the table before her as her own hand sealed Ahab's name to documents and contracts. One such evening, in the peace that came with the dusk, Jezebel wrote one last set of letters.

A week went by, and no one pulled her aside to whisper in her ear. No one condemned her for what she had written. Everyone understood the problem, because they all wanted something too, something the old laws would have forbade. Jezebel had always represented progress, which was why the old god hated her. The elders were on the side of progress.

And this was what she wrote in the last batch: "Proclaim a fast." A pious request that could offend no one's god.

"We will end the fast together at a royal feast." A generous offer.

"Give Naboth a place of honor." Wise.

"Find two men who will say anything for money." Not an impossible job. Drought had changed many men and loosened hard morals.

"Have these men make accusations against Naboth. Naboth has cursed both god and king." A crime punishable by stoning, a crime there was no remedy for. A merciful king might forgive slander against his own name, but Ahab had chosen to worship Yahweh. He would be forced to defend his god. The irony was not lost on Jezebel. By defending Yahweh, Ahab would be forced to break Yahweh's law. He would commit murder.

What god would want a king like that?

Jezebel would have Ahab all to herself again.

Ahab

Ahab allowed his servants to dress him in new robes. Jezebel had insisted. Today's feast was the first time some of these people had seen Ahab wear the crown. She wanted to make an impression, he knew. She cared very much about impressions.

He listened to the roar coming from the palace kitchens, carried on the breeze to his window. The sting of smoke and lure of roasting meats, the shouts of cooks commanding men to their stations, carts creaking along the paths in and out of the palace, carrying bleating animals and sweet-scented berries and cakes. So much went into one feast. Ahab smiled. Had preparations for any battle been this elaborate?

The feast began by noon, and everyone with wealth and station seemed to be in attendance, making the atmosphere stiff with pretension and polite laughs. *That is where wealth and battles differ*, Ahab thought. *The wealthy think they'll get out alive.* Soldiers rarely did. It made soldiers far better company.

Jezebel entered, and he held his breath as he took in her appearance. She wore her hair loose, falling around her shoulders, like a young bride. She wore the royal jewels from Tyre, the queen's crown of Israel, and a gown of purple linen embroidered with gold and silver beads that hung loosely over her growing abdomen. She radiated pleasure as she took in the tables and the citizens.

Servants bustled between tables, keeping their heads low, speaking in whispers to each other as the courses began. Ahab sampled a soft cheese that spread in his mouth and tasted like spring onions. He sipped the burgundy wine, and it was sharp, its tang on the back of his tongue absolutely perfect. He smiled at Jezebel, for her attention to these details had been perfect.

The afternoon wore on better than he had hoped, for not so many elders were used to drinking this early, and by the first hour a good many were drunk. They slurred their words and blushed, able to hear themselves and understand their embarrassment. The noble sitting with Amon—Ahab could not remember his name or what goods he sold—stood and asked for attention. Ahab noticed his legs sway slightly, as if on unsteady ground.

"Long live King Ahab!" the man cried out.

Ahab smiled and tipped his goblet to acknowledge him, but the man did not sit. He continued.

"You are the first son of Israel to ascend to the throne of his father. Your name means a new dawn for Israel. Your name means everything to us."

The man was drunk, Ahab thought. No man got emotional so early in the day.

"Naboth has insulted your name, my lord. He has blasphemed you and the Lord. He has called for your death!"

Ahab's stomach tightened into a knot as he dropped his knife, cracking the bowl before him. Naboth sat near him in a similar state of shock.

Murmurs rose from the tables as two other men stood and attested to the truth of the accusation. Guards took a step toward Naboth, then looked at Ahab for confirmation. Ahab picked up his goblet of wine and drained it, then poured another cup to the rim and drained that. He could feel his heart absorbing the news, swelling, the tissues stretching and thinning.

Jezebel lifted her goblet in his direction, and her smile was wide and red.

Ahab knew he would die for this.

Jezebel

Jezebel's bath the next day was a disappointment. The water cooled too fast, and Lilith shouted for more and more warmed water from the other servants. "Hurry! She is in her bath!" she yelled. Jezebel could not relax with the shouting. She rose, shivering, reaching for her linens to dry off, just as there was a burst of conversation at the chamber door. Lilith received a message and scolded the other servants for the failed bath before she closed the door and faced her queen.

Jezebel stood and waited, naked and wrinkled from the bath, livid red stretch marks across her abdomen. Her wet hair hung around her shoulders, and her face was unpainted.

"Naboth is dead," Lilith said.

"Is that what the servants were gossiping about?" Jezebel asked. She reached for her tunic.

"There are rumors you caused it."

"I did." Jezebel sat on her bathing stool and began slipping her feet into their sandals. "Naboth defied the king based on an old law. Ahab deserved that land. So I used an old law to condemn Naboth. If the people want to follow the old laws, they must be prepared to keep all of them."

"They say you paid men to lie," Lilith said. Jezebel noticed how she was backing toward the door, glancing everywhere in the room but at her. "What if Elijah hears what you've done? What if he comes back and withholds rain again?"

"He hasn't been heard of or seen by anyone, in any of the territories, for a long time. I doubt he's still alive. He was under no one's protection, and he had a talent for insulting kings."

Heavy steps coming toward them from the hallway ended the conversation. Lilith opened the door and nodded to Ahab, who entered the chamber with a heaviness in his step.

Ahab sat on the bed and motioned for Lilith's dismissal. When she left, he groaned, his head in his hands.

Jezebel rose and joined him, sitting next to him on the bed, their thighs touching.

She rested a hand on his leg and spoke to him tenderly. "You couldn't have done anything."

"Naboth loved the law," he said. "He would have wanted it upheld."

Jezebel patted his thigh. "Go on. Take possession of Naboth's land. It is forfeit to you for his crimes."

Ahab did not rise, so she grabbed him by the arm, forcing him up, pushing him toward the door.

"Bring back something wonderful, and we'll have the cooks prepare a meal tonight," she told him, her voice high and confident. "We'll celebrate a coming child and the peace of winter." She patted her womb, knowing a child was within again, her third. She hoped this would be the end: of children, and of Ahab's weakness.

By the end of their time in Jezreel, Jezebel had to walk to the dining hall with both hands under her belly to support its weight. Perhaps the child within was growing very big, or her body was growing weary. By evening she was so tired, and the weight was hard to carry. Her eyelids were heavy too. The dark sky all afternoon, the chill wind, the early shadows that fell over the valley, all these conspired to make her want nothing more than sleep. She would entertain Ahab and perhaps a few of the elders tonight at dinner but excuse herself early and return to bed.

She entered the small dining hall, which held no more than twenty, and so had not been used for the recent feast. A table was set with two oil lamps at each end, and servants worked quickly to bring out bowls and platters. The food looked no different. She groaned inwardly. Why had she labored to get Naboth out of the way if the servants didn't even know what to pick?

Several elders joined her, including one who had made an accusation at the feast. Both were cordial to her, inquiring about her health and the coming child.

Three other elders sat with them. Two of the men owned fine homes in Samaria and traveled with Ahab for the winter, presumably for relief from the weather. The other man was local to Jezreel, and a wealthy landowner himself. Jezebel looked forward to getting his opinion on her recent acquisition.

Ahab had not arrived, so Jezebel motioned for Lilith to draw near. "Find out why Ahab is delayed. Tell him his guests are seated and waiting."

She nodded and stepped away as a page entered and addressed them all.

"The king is unwell. He will not join you tonight."

Jezebel gritted her teeth and rose. She had slept in his bed every night of the winter, but he had drifted further away from her each day.

"Please excuse my husband." She addressed the men, who were still staring at the untouched food. They wanted to eat, and none dared move until she was gone. They were more concerned with offending her than with honoring their own appetites. That's what a small god reduced a man to, she thought as she left.

She found Ahab exactly as she dreaded she would. He was in their chamber, lying curled in a ball on the bed, his face turned to the wall.

"Ahab."

Her arms crossed, she waited at the door. Her abdomen was so heavy it hurt, and she hadn't eaten a thing. She had gotten rid of every enemy between her and Ahab, but she could not conquer his moods. She left him there, refusing to say even one encouraging, or inquiring, word.

She refused to fight for him even one more time. He deserved to fall into that pit and burn.

❧

Ahab remained in his chamber two days. He did not allow her to enter, and she was too weary to fight. Fighting for Ahab was pointless. His god had ruined him completely. He could have been a great king.

Two days later, she entered their chamber without knocking, motioning for the guards to step aside and remain silent. One guard's hand had flown to his sword, and he moved quickly out of her reach.

She noted the dank smell inside. His bed table had a pitcher of what smelled like stale beer, plus a loaf of uneaten bread and curds that had shriveled to stone.

She had to stop and take a deep breath. The baby tumbled inside her womb. She grabbed the blankets covering Ahab and ripped them off, letting them fall to the ground. He still did not move, but he groaned, proof he was alive.

"Get up," she said.

He did not move. She shoved one hand against his shoulder.

"Get up, king!" She sneered the word *king*, hoping to wound him. He had to fight back.

He did not move but did speak, his voice hoarse and dry. He'd been crying. "I knew. You set him up. Didn't you?"

"Do you want me to answer that? Or are you going to be a man and get out of that bed and run this kingdom?"

He sat up and turned on her, his face blotched and red and his eyes swollen. He looked like he had been in a fight, but she knew he had been alone in this chamber. He was not dressed in his royal robes but had on sackcloth, the garment of a mourner. It was a loin covering made from hair. She didn't want to look closely but judged it to be camel or goat hair. His chest was bare and smudged with ash. Ashes were in his hair, too, discoloring his face, especially along his hairline. She looked at the bed and saw it was smeared in ash.

Ashes were for the dead.

"Are you still grieving for Naboth?" she asked.

"I'm grieving for us," he replied.

She wanted to vomit. There was no end to his weakness.

"There is an old Assyrian curse," Ahab said, "perhaps you've heard it. 'May dogs tear your flesh at the city wall.' You see, when an enemy is killed, the body is desecrated and dogs allowed to eat it. The bones are carried off in different directions, even outside the city."

"The Assyrians have not crossed our borders. Even Ben-hadad is at home! Get up and take a bath. Act like a man." She grabbed his hair, pulling straight up, trying to drag him out of bed.

Ahab grabbed her wrist. "We are the dead, Jezebel."

She jerked her hand back and stood, the air in the room too cold as it entered her lungs. A coldness descended, so cold that she saw her breath as her chest heaved in and out.

Ahab shook his head, his eyes only empty darkness, staring at the black smears across his hands. He spoke in a low voice, not quite a whisper.

"I saw Elijah," he said.

The cold clench in her stomach grew tighter as the walls seemed to move away.

"He accused me of murder," Ahab said. "I murdered Naboth to get the land. That's what he said."

"How long has he been in Jezreel?" she asked. How much did he know? She thought of the letters circulating among the elders. Had Elijah read one? Or had his god whispered all this in his ear? Was Yahweh here too?

Another drought was coming. She felt the dread making her legs heavy and cold, and her head began to hurt. They had just recovered from the first one. A second one, so soon, would kill them all.

Ahab shook his head with such grief on his face, she would have thought he was wishing for that curse. He wouldn't even look at her as he spoke, and he choked on some words. Elijah's curse stuttered out in his weak and unwilling voice, the voice of a very bad child.

She pressed her hand to her mouth as he spoke, the sound of his voice unbearable, like burning oil in her ear.

"It is not a drought. He said Omri's line will end," Ahab began. "God has vowed to wipe out every male in our family line, even those of my lesser wives. And as for you, queen of the cursed, dogs will eat you by the wall of Jezreel. Any of those of our family who die in the city will be eaten by dogs. Any of our family who die in the country will be eaten by birds. No burials, no mourning, no afterlife ... We're going to die. Our children are going to die."

He tilted his head back and let out a wail that terrified her.

Then, with the slow speed of dread and resignation, he reached into a clay pot on the bed, bringing up a handful of ashes and dumping them on his head. A low gray cloud spread out from the bed and rolled to envelop her. She stepped back. She would not accept this curse or lie on a bed and wail for her throne.

She grabbed the bedside table and overturned it, food and crockery splattering the walls and the bed and her robes. She grabbed the crock of ashes from the bed and smashed it to the floor, sending a giant billowing cloud rolling across the room. The smoke rose from her feet as she pointed a finger at Ahab.

"You wanted Naboth's land. I got it for you!"

He just looked at her, his tears making fresh tracks through the grime on his cheeks.

"Your children have been threatened," she said. "Your wife, too!"

He did not move.

"Get up and fight, or I will kill you myself!" she screamed.

Ahab shook his head slowly, his gaze moving past her, over her shoulder, as if seeing something in the distance she did not. Her hands curled into fists as her body tensed, ready to hurt him, to force him from that stinking bed and out into the street to meet his accuser. Lunging forward as she raised her hand to strike his face, all strength left her. She crumpled to the floor, sobbing.

"You never loved me," she wailed.

She had given him an heir, given him security and honor, two things he could not get with his sword. Everything precious, their name and their future, was lost in these ashes. The grief of giving her name to this man who proved so unworthy of it was so great, she could not breathe. Her throat was raw and thick, and she gasped for breath between heaving sobs. She wished, with everything in her heart, that she had never married him. She wished for time to reverse, for her mother to live, for Temereh to throw her into that pit instead. Everyone would have been happier.

Finally, seeing he would not rise for her, she stood with a force she had never known. "I hope you die! The throne belongs to a man like your son. He will not be weak like you. "

Ahab stood to meet her at last, his face contorted in pain or fear. She did not know him anymore. "Could you be so blind?" Ahab yelled. "Could I have been so blind? What have I done? All these years, wasted. With you."

"That's what you never understood, Ahab. Your father never intended for you to take the throne; he didn't think you were strong enough. That's why he married you to me. I was the guarantee that you'd hang onto the throne. Your father, and my father, they knew what we were."

"Through you my kingdom was lost," Ahab said, his eyes meeting hers, cold and certain of his truth.

She stepped back and walked toward the door, the gray dust swirling around her feet as she stepped. She turned to see him easing himself back onto the bed of ashes, prepared to take up his mourning once more. She made her words clear and distinct to pierce his sullen haze.

"I made you a king, but I cannot make you a man."

Jezebel

They had peace.

Strange as it was for Jezebel to witness, peace settled over them all as the year passed. There was peace in Samaria and peace in Jezreel. They had good crops, and good weather, and good prices at the market. They traded with surrounding nations and saw their highways busy with camels and donkeys and families with children who ran ahead, laughing.

Twice a man of Yahweh had predicted utter doom for Ahab. Once he was told he had lost the kingdom, then he was told his very life was forfeit, as was hers and her children's and any male connected to Ahab.

Yet they had peace. The shadow that should have loomed over her did not. It was simply gone.

In the fall of that year, Jezebel had her second son. Ahab named him Joram, meaning his god Yahweh was exalted. Jezebel only smirked. Joram was bigger than his brother had been at birth, bigger than his sister, too. He had dark swirls of hair and dark brown eyes that peered intently into the face of anyone who held him. He did not cry much, or squirm, or protest rough handling.

She nursed him. She didn't know why, but she wanted to.

"For strength," Lilith suggested.

Jezebel glanced up. She hadn't realized she had spoken out loud. She was nursing Joram as she reclined in her bedchamber of the queen's residence in Samaria. She appreciated being back in the Samarian capital, with more space and amenities. Especially since she had no husband. He walked lightly, casting glances behind him wherever he went. He refused to sleep in their bed any longer.

"What shall I prepare for the ceremony?" Lilith asked, rising from her stool. She had been practicing her letters at the queen's desk. It was good to see her find use for her time, for these wasted hours in Israel, their wasted lives.

"The pink, with the red sash. Bright colors," Jezebel said, stroking Joram's hair.

Joram stopped nursing and drifted to sleep. He was warm, nestled against her, but this animal warmth was all the two shared. He was nothing more than a reminder that she had strengthened Ahab's claim to the throne, and Ahab was not strong enough to hold onto it. She wished she hadn't had him, but perhaps she also wished for some of her spirit to flow into his. If he was fierce, if he conversed with darkness and was not afraid, he might survive. She wanted something of her life to survive and tell her tale. If she couldn't defeat this god, if she couldn't have a real man for a husband, at least someone could warn others. Someone could tell her story.

A shadow passed over the window as a storm cloud rolled past, obscuring the light. Another storm was coming. A strong wind blew through the room, and the statue of Asherah tilted, its stone face unchanging. It toppled and fell to the floor, and Jezebel lifted her face to the moon and wept without tears.

❧

Three full years of peace and prosperity ensued. Israel renewed its covenant with Tyre, and Ahab promised Athaliah to Jehoram, son of the king in Judah. Israel would be united by marriage with the southern tribes. Israel prospered, and the children grew.

Her dreams grew bleak and strange. No longer did they frighten her with visions, but drained her in their abject silence. She dreamed of darkness without sound, without color. She was grateful to wake, chilled and her bedclothes wet with sweat, and she gasped in relief to see the sun breaking into her room.

Ahab, once so eager to love her, avoided her now. He could have been a great king with her at his side, but he lacked her strength. She had children now, though. There was still a way to make her name great, if she used them well.

She sat on the edge of her window one dawn, when the full moon was still high above. Far away, the queen of heaven was calling the tides, the waters rising and revealing the treasures they had concealed in the deep, on a shore Jezebel would never see again. Insects buzzed about, and she heard the low scrape of an olive press in the distance. One of the elders who lived nearby must have had servants up late tonight, pressing the olives, preparing for the coming winter. The drought still haunted the wealthy. Not one of them left the future to chance. Every olive was plucked and pressed, every vegetable uprooted and stored.

Steady, soft hoofbeats approached and went past. Jezebel leaned forward from between the pillars to see who went to the palace at this hour. It was a single rider bearing the colors of Tyre. He did not drive his camel hard, so she knew his business was not urgent. Standing here, in the darkness before the small statue of Asherah, she suddenly knew why he had come. A white cloud rolled in front of the moon, a shroud hung over her brightness.

Her father was dead.

She searched her heart but felt nothing like grief. He had wasted his reign.

She would not waste her own. She would not waste her children.

Obadiah

Palace business was a comfort to Obadiah, as he tended the records and oversaw the daily operations of the summer. The papyrus from Egypt was improving in quality, but he was grateful for the Phoenicians, who supplied him with better materials. Papyrus stank as it aged, even if he loved the way it soaked up his ink, compliant and thirsty, so eager for the words.

The previous evening he had finished recording the gifts sent to Tyre. Jezebel's father, now dead, had had a son by one of his concubines, and this son, Baal-azzor, took the throne in Tyre. Obadiah sent gifts of grain and gold and spices. Obadiah was slow to rise the next morning, weary from long hours bent over his desk. His shoulders hurt, and yet he pushed himself to stand and move about. He had much work to do.

Jehoshaphat, the king of Judah, was to come for an official visit. By order of King Ahab, who had specified only that he had urgent business to discuss. Jehoshaphat agreed to come, and the date was set. It had taken three messengers and fourteen pieces of papyrus to get this done.

As the hours wore on, Jehoshaphat proved his word, to the day. His entourage filled the palace to overflowing. Israel's elders gave lodging to his elders. The inns hosted his lesser attendants and servants. Once again Obadiah ordered huge quantities at the market, and the streets burst with people and animals and goods delivered to the palace. Time passed quickly, making him remember the years of turmoil, before the years of peace had lulled all to sleep.

Late in the evening, after all were settled and sleeping from the long journey, Obadiah was summoned to Ahab's chamber. The bed was tidy and the table next to it was laid with wine and fruits. Ahab had scrolls open upon his desk, with a carpet under it.

Ahab looked at Obadiah with a brief and formal nod, but his eyes did not meet Obadiah's. Ahab had trouble meeting anyone's eyes. Three years of peace, and he had felt none of it. He had grown more despondent every year, plagued by the omen hanging over his head.

"Ramoth-Gilead belongs to the northern tribes but is still in Ben-hadad's control," Ahab said.

Obadiah nodded. It was true. Ben-hadad had been spared and allowed Israel access to more markets, but he had done no more than that. He had never become a true ally—just a sleeping enemy.

"That is why I've called Jehoshaphat to us," Ahab continued. "I want him to go to war with me. Take back Ramoth-Gilead."

"Jehoshaphat does not have a powerful army," Obadiah said.

"They have the Lord," Ahab said quietly. "When I faced Ben-hadad in the past, God was with me."

Ahab sat at his desk and rested his head in his hands. Then he drew a deep breath, like a man who had thought many times of what he should say. He looked up at Obadiah with a solemn face. His eyes, though, were empty. Obadiah saw the defeat in his slumped shoulders, in the years scratching their marks into his forehead and around his eyes, how he moved as if weighed down by shackles.

"You want to be a great king," Obadiah said.

"No," he said quietly. "It is too late for that."

"Then why take Ramoth-Gilead?"

"God has waited to take my life. There is a chance I can change His mind. I can do something."

A heaviness weighted the air, making it hard to breathe. Obadiah's chest began to throb, bursting with words that demanded to be heard. It was not his place to say them.

He could not say them.

And then he did.

"It is not about you, Ahab. It is about Him. The Lord hates Jezebel because children are sacrificed to her gods. Infants, some given willingly by poor young mothers who could not feed them, some given because they are born with defects, some stolen. She calls her gods Baal and Asherah. Some call them pleasure and freedom, but they are neither. They are demons. The Lord is angry because you allowed His people to worship demons and kill the youngest children." The roof of his mouth burned as the words rushed past, saving Obadiah from the hungry dead that clung invisibly to Ahab.

Obadiah had read the truth, he had known the truth, but to speak it was a frightening new power. It was a clumsy, blunt power, but the most he had ever had. His head buzzed inside, the force of true words spoken at last making him dizzy.

Ahab's expression did not change. As if he had heard nothing, he talked of rights and cities. "Ramoth-Gilead is rightfully ours. Obadiah, you can confirm that in the records of our history. If I go out against Ben-hadad, if I can strike him down in battle, as the Lord desired, I can make it right with the Lord. Perhaps I can revoke His curse on my sons. I can face death if I know I have saved my sons."

"How many sons must die for you, Ahab, before you do what is right?" Obadiah said.

The king did not hear him.

22

Jezebel

At last, after so many years of pain, Ahab had decided to act like a king. He was going to make himself worthy of the crown he had been given. She had hated him for that more and more as the years had passed, that he had been given what she had fought for and lost, then earned on her back. She understood Omri's disdain for his son.

Tears ran down her cheeks and landed on her lap. The stain spread, its darkness growing, and she saw it widen its path, moving fast, shooting to her knees as it grew and covered her robes, the darkness reaching up over her belly, spreading up toward her neck. She watched it, transfixed. She had not seen her own tears for years.

The two kings were announced, and Jezebel stood, her knees shaking from the discovery of tears. She pressed her hand to her face, to feel them before they disappeared. They would never return. With a true king for a husband, she would never cry again.

Jehoshaphat and Ahab walked into the throne room and sat with Jezebel at the table that had been set for the first meal of the day. Each was dressed in his kingly robes, a long multicolored tunic and a shorter tunic of white linen over it, with embroidered sashes that caught the morning light. Jehoshaphat wore a purple outer robe and a sash with red workings. Ahab had his red outer robe on, and a gold sash with gold beads.

"You approve of my beloved daughter? You are pleased with the match?" Jezebel asked Jehoshaphat, handing him a bowl of grapes.

He took them from her but passed them on. "She is beautiful, like her mother."

Jezebel attempted a smile as she reached for the bowl of dates stuffed with almonds and fried in honey.

"Athaliah will be an exceptional queen someday," Jezebel said. "A strong queen in Judah, a strong queen in Israel."

Jehoshaphat choked on the milk he drank and cleared his throat, holding up one hand to keep the servants from attending him. He glanced at Ahab, and then at her, as tears from the mishap welled in his eyes. "My apologies," he said.

"Having a daughter first has always been seen as a slight from the gods, but that is wrong," she said, hearing her high, sharp voice as if someone spoke for her. "Although our work is different, we aren't afraid of a little blood. We are born rulers."

Ahab stood.

"Jehoshaphat and I have work to do," he said. With that, the men left.

Jezebel had the throne room to herself. She liked that. She stood, breathing deeply, whispering the name of the goddess. What a long road it had been, but at last the end was in sight.

Jehoshaphat's royal court entered the following night, and Ahab's followed, including Amon and her two sons. Athaliah was not present. Had she gone to Judah already? There had been more Jezebel wanted to teach her. But the boys looked well and strong, though she could not get the older one to converse with her. Little Joram was pudgy and never smiled. She thought he would make a good king.

They had been seated for an hour, waiting for the king to arrive, when Jezebel called for Obadiah.

"Have the kings not returned from the city gates?" she asked.

"They did," he responded. "They went directly to the administration rooms to prepare for battle."

"Without dinner?" It was a breach in protocol, an indignity for those who had gathered. Israel was under no threat.

Jezebel stood and lifted her goblet. "As you may know, the great kings Jehoshaphat and Ahab have assembled to discuss a plan that would benefit both empires. Though the tribes are no longer united by one king, or one god, they can be united through prosperity. Forgive my husband, your host, for not joining you tonight, as you celebrate the future."

At this, Jezebel left the banquet, leading the guards who trotted behind. Security was tighter when they had so many foreigners in the palace, but she did not wait for the guards to lead. She knew where she was going. She knew what she would find.

Obadiah had said that Jehoshaphat and Ahab were in the administration rooms. Making plans to march out on the unsuspecting Ben-hadad.

Jehoshaphat looked up, his eyebrows raised as he saw her, dread evident on his face. Ahab glanced up, and his scowl deepened.

"Go over the numbers again," he commanded. Jehoshaphat obeyed, being the lesser king with lesser treasuries.

"May I speak to my husband alone?" she asked Jehoshaphat. He nodded so quickly, she knew he was grateful to leave. Perhaps he could think more clearly without Ahab.

"I don't want you here," Ahab said. He looked at her, and she saw the familiar weak and hunted man.

"You're leaving soon?" she asked.

"Within the week. Three days, if I can push Jehoshaphat."

She nodded and took a stool next to the table, glancing over the scrolls. Everything looked in order. He was counting men and supplies and projecting what would be waiting for him in Ramoth-Gilead.

"There's been no news," she said. No news from Ben-hadad, no news from Ramoth-Gilead, no reason to push this war so fast. He had no plan except to attack. Something was driving him.

He grabbed her by the arms, lifting her from the stool, bringing her to his face. Her stomach clenched; she thought he would kiss her, but he turned her toward the door and set her firmly on her feet, pushing her in that direction.

"Get out!" he said.

Jezebel dug her feet in their sandals for a firmer grip, turning, refusing to leave. A nightmare began to unfold in her mind. "Was it Elijah? Have you seen him?"

"This is what I should have done years ago," he said.

Hairs rose along her arms as he grabbed the sword of Moses and pointed it at her heart. Hatred kindled in his eyes.

"I should have never allowed the worship of Baal and Asherah.

Your priests sacrificed children and practiced abominations. But my crime was the worst."

She took a step toward Ahab, her hands raised and fingers spread, as if she were going to leap like an animal. The tip of the sword rested against her heart. She willed him to dare it, but he did not. "You are a great deceiver, luring your people away from their god. I never strayed from my gods! I served them, and I served you, and I served the nation of Israel!"

He swung the sword with a scream, driving the blade into the doorpost. The blade reverberated, its hollow beating filling the stunned silence.

Ahab shook his head, madness making his eyes wide and dark, empty expanses of pain she could not name.

"I loved you," Ahab said, his voice flat. "God forgive me for that."

Obadiah

Obadiah recorded all the preparations for this surprise attack, his tears mixing with the ink as he wrote. A new asu, another import from Tyre, offered him a sedative after hearing his sobs from the dining hall as Jezebel hosted her growing cadre of new priests and workers.

His tears fell, and his shoulders shook as he worked, having refused the drink. Grief over the sins of others was his price to pay for having spoken truth. Maybe grief and power and truth always traveled together. In time, maybe, he would learn about this. Maybe that was why Ahab had failed as a king, because his heart had never grieved over anything but his own childhood losses.

Maybe that was why Ahab did not listen when told the truth. The prophet that had been here spoke it, Obadiah was sure. Truth had a certain sound to it.

Despite this, Ahab had marched out three days later for Ramoth-Gilead, as he had intended. He refused to let Obadiah join him, and Obadiah paced like a frantic dog as Ahab and Jehoshaphat led the men down the main street of Samaria, to the shouts of the troops waiting on the edges of the city.

"Nothing good will come from this," he cried, though no one heard him. "You heard what the prophet said!" No one listened, though it galled him. That, too, he knew, was the price of truth.

Jezebel

Two more weeks passed, and Jezebel sat, perched and tense, in the throne overlaid with ivory designs of bulls and lions, all fallen in battle, mouths open, tongues loose, with wide, vacant eyes. She had picked the design herself and should have been pleased to sit in a queen's throne at last. Instead, she felt nothing, a vast emptiness that had eaten its way through her life.

Obadiah was announced and approached, his eyes glancing back at the doors. His steps echoed across the empty hall; how lonely it seemed. Just weeks ago, this place had been the center of two empires, with soldiers staging fistfights in the streets for amusement, and songs sung late into the evening. The emptiness had taken Samaria, too.

"Ahab was angry with me before he left," she said.

Obadiah exhaled, but his eyes did not glance away.

She paused, considering that Obadiah was still a threat. He was such an enigma. All of Israel was.

"Ahab left for war without conducting an official ceremony," Jezebel said. "He did not ask a blessing of his god. He acted like a man running away in the cover of night, but he is a king going to war. Why is that? What happened to the man I once knew?"

"How would I know what is in his heart?"

Obadiah was hiding something. That was plain by the way his neck stiffened slightly before he replied. Yet he was not afraid, not of her, for he kept his gaze so steady. Could it be that he was afraid for her? This little man of words and papers, afraid he might hurt the queen mother?

"Speak, Obadiah. Do not spare me," she said flatly. She was too tired to take offense.

Obadiah complied, but he lowered his voice, and the servants in the room were prevented from hearing. "The kings decided to go to war for Ramoth-Gilead, and then Jehoshaphat asked for the prophets of the Lord to be called. He wanted to inquire of the Lord whether this decision was of Him."

"Was Elijah there?" Jezebel asked. Who else could have stirred Ahab so violently? Who else would Ahab run from?

"No. Your four new prophets spoke for your own gods. They were joined by a madman from the village, who wore horns on his head and danced for the king."

"Ahab called for my prophets?" Jezebel could not hide her surprise.

"Yes. And they prophesied victory. But Jehoshaphat was not pleased with Ahab, that Ahab had consulted those who speak for Asherah. Jehoshaphat wanted to hear from a prophet of Yahweh."

"And did he find one?" she asked. A cold impulse drove her to lean forward on her throne. "You know that I killed them. Your scrolls were a great help in knowing how many there were, and where."

His face remained like stone, unreadable, her words having no affect, like little sticks that fell after striking a bronze shield. She sat back and turned in her seat, watching him from the corner of her eye.

"One prophet remains in Samaria, his name being Micaiah," Obadiah said.

"Micaiah had a vision of God sitting on his throne, with all the armies of the Lord attending. God asked his court, 'Who will go to Ahab and convince him to attack Ramoth-Gilead, so that he will die?' Many offered to incite Ahab to go to his death, but one spirit moved forward from among them to stand before the Lord.

"'I will persuade the man,' the spirit said.

"'How will you do this?' the Lord asked. All of the court fell silent, for the spirit was the oldest among them, and the cruelest, and his name was Legion.

"'I will deceive them all. I will lie to those seekers, the prophets, and they will lie to that man, the king. I possess no greater weapon than a lie that man desperately wants to hear.'

"And so the spirit came to earth and deceived the prophets of Asherah, who deceived the king. Only Micaiah spoke the truth."

"And what was this truth that Micaiah spoke?" Jezebel asked.

"Ahab will die in Ramoth-Gilead."

Jezebel rose from the throne. "Liar!" Guards ran from the corners of the room as she lunged from her perch and grabbed Obadiah by the front of his robes. "You don't know what the truth is!"

The guards dragged Obadiah from her presence as she trembled and fought for breath, frothing spit collecting at the corners of her mouth. She heard thunder, the low roar of that distant god Yahweh. He was here in Samaria, still. He was in the throne room with her; she could feel his presence as the air grew thick with the tang of lightning and smoke. She turned to face the throne, a hair's width at a time, holding her breath, icy cold in her lungs. Though she saw nothing, he was there. He sat on the throne of Israel. A force she could not describe drove her to her knees and forced her face against the stone floor as she screamed profanities.

After the second watch of the night, when she still had not moved, the guards called for Lilith. No one had dared enter the room. The Presence did not dissipate until the third watch of the night.

Lilith ran across the floor, her feet softly, quickly padding. They sounded like camel's feet, Jezebel thought, her mind distant, thinking of turquoise oceans that had no end, a land where she had dreamed of growing up and wearing the crown. She wished to throw her crown into the turquoise waters and watch it sink into eternal darkness. But the Lord had shown her she had indeed earned her crown and would wear it forever in a land where water burned and the dead chewed and crowns were crushing vises.

Ahab

The first night they made camp, Ahab sat close to the fire, away from the company of Jehoshaphat. The sounds of men preparing for battle stayed the night with him; more troops would meet them in the morning as they rode; still more troops had arrived from Egypt. He missed Obadiah. What had he done to drive his friend away? Or was it that he had not done something? It all seemed so long ago.

"Does my king care to walk away from camp and witness the night sky?" a servant asked as he stirred the chickpeas over the fire. He threw in a handful of salt, then removed the cooking bowl and set it aside. He stood and offered Ahab his hand. He was a boy of about twelve, a little thick in the belly, with brown hair and wide green eyes. He still had the cheeks of a child, soft and full, and he was calm. This was not his first battle, Ahab could tell.

"Your father?" Ahab asked.

"With your horses," the boy replied.

Ahab stood and the boy led the way, tapping ahead of them with his staff, scaring the venomous things back into their holes at the noise. A stag stood in their path and watched them with mild interest. He did not run as they grew closer, but walked deliberately into the brush.

The boy smiled and continued picking his way to a spot elevated above them. He swept the spot bare of sharp stones and gestured for Ahab to sit. The night stars spread out before them.

"All the Lord's children," the boy whispered, pointing to the thousands of lights.

Ahab smiled. "You know of Abraham."

The boy shrugged. "I love the stories."

"Obadiah chose you to accompany me, didn't he?" Ahab asked.

The boy nodded and looked at the stars. "Obadiah loves the stories, but I think he loves you, too."

Ahab smiled and drew in the sand with the edge of a stick. What could he say to a child of twelve? Could he explain how a kingdom was lost?

Ahab smiled and patted him on the shoulder. "Tell Obadiah I wish I had loved the stories too."

Jezebel

Ahab's chariot, bearing his colors, returned on a morning a week later when white mist shrouded the fertile green fields, revealing the dusty road to be a scrape against bare pale flesh. The wheels churned and the mist swirled and the guards posted on the towers cried out in joy. Drummers, beating animal skins stretched across wooden casks, began sounding out a slow, soft heartbeat.

"The king returns!" Trumpets were blown, and Samaria exploded into activity.

Jezebel was dressed for the day, reviewing the scrolls with the palace's accounts. Hearing the trumpets, her heart leaped. Ahab had returned! He was alive, and the prophet of Yahweh proved a liar. She didn't bother rolling the scrolls, but ran from the room, eager to be first on the steps to greet the king. Lilith could not keep up.

"Get my sons. Have them join me on the palace steps," Jezebel called back to her.

Jezebel was in place within moments as elders poured from their houses and travelers moved their animals off the street to make room for the procession. She stood tall, her face lifted to the bright sun. It had eaten up every cloud in sight.

As the chariot passed through the city gates, a great cheer went up. Women lifted their hands and danced, and the elders shouted and nodded to one another, as if they had all been sure. As if they did not know what that prophet had said.

A strange murmur followed the chariot. The crowds closed in around it, eager to touch Ahab and praise his victory, but as soon as they stepped toward it, they fell back, like ones struck by an arrow. Women grabbed their children and forcibly turned them away, hiding them in their robes, their faces crinkling in fear.

Ahaziah and Joram joined Jezebel at that moment with their nursemaids, but she did not stop to greet them. Jezebel began pushing her way through the elders and servants and those assembled from the royal court. Ahaziah tried to follow.

Jezebel pushed against men who were dumbfounded and still, and against women who grabbed her and begged her not to look. She fought her way through the herd of confused, troubled Samarians, her sons on her heels, until she got to the chariot. It had come to a

stop beside a pool used in the city at the lower end, for washing and
dirty chores.

The driver looked away when he saw Jezebel approach.

Her steps slowed, as did her mind. She saw her feet as they
lifted from the dirt and arced through the air, landing again, a little
puff of dirt repulsed by each step. Jezebel looked at the chariot, with
its wooden slats tucked tightly side by side. Dark red was smeared
across the side. A hand print, clear and strong, that descended into
a smear down to the bottom. Someone had been bleeding when
they reached for the king's chariot. She stepped again until she
was at the rear of the chariot, her eyes seeing it all at once. Her
mind took in only small details: the way the boys screamed behind
her, the green color of Ahab's face, the way the dried blood on
his robes had cracked and crusted and the insects crawled around
the wounds. His eyes remained open but were flat in their sockets
and covered by a film, as if his corpse were watching Israel from a
distant place.

He was dead.

Jezebel sank to the ground. She was free of him, she knew, but
this freedom hurt. There was no pleasure in it. She looked at him
again and realized he had never been the source of her pain. How
could that be, that men had caused her to suffer, yet when she was
free of them, the suffering remained? What mystery was this?

She stood and kissed him on the mouth, wondering if he could
still feel it, if his spirit hovered near. As she raised back up, Ahaziah
cried loudly. She tasted Ahab's blood on her lips.

Obadiah fell to his knees, weeping. He was on the other side of
the chariot, closer to Ahab's body. He was always closer, she thought.

She heard his wail change into a chanted word. "No," he wept over and again. "No."

"Your god was right," Jezebel said to Obadiah. He stopped his moans and looked at her, like he was seeing a stranger for the first time.

"Your god was right," Jezebel said. "Be happy."

Obadiah gathered his strength and faced the body. He placed his hands under Ahab's legs and torso and lifted the king from his chariot. Obadiah carried the fallen king through the streets of Samaria, refusing to let anyone touch him or help. Jezebel followed behind. Obadiah carried Ahab up the steps of the palace, the palace that Jezebel had brought to life. The ivory and gold winked at her as it swallowed Ahab inside.

Behind her, a woman whispered, "Which is to be the king?"

Jezebel realized she was speaking of Ahab's sons.

"Your king is Ahab!" Jezebel shouted, turning to the crowd, searching for the woman who dared say such a stupid thing. "Have you already forgotten that? Ahab is your king! And you never loved him! None of you!"

Jezebel gritted her teeth until she could not breathe. She steadied herself before walking on, but as she did, something began to form in her mind, like a child struggling to create his letters. She waited as the words assembled.

"No," she whispered. Yahweh's prophecy crept over her like a spider walking across her neck.

I will bring disaster on you. I will cut off your name and kill every male connected with you.

God was always right. Jezebel grabbed for Ahaziah's hand. Where could she run? She turned round and round, the sun too bright, mocking, blinding her as she searched for refuge. She could not face the throne or stay in the streets. The Lord was here. And he was going to strike her sons. He would strike her, and dogs would lick her blood.

But a rasping sound comforted her, the sound of a serpent moving in the streets. She looked into doorways and between the feet all around her, but she could not see it. But a serpent moved here, too.

She wiped her mouth, and her hand came away red. The Lord would strike her, yes.

But not yet.

... a little more ...

When a delightful concert comes to an end,

the orchestra might offer an encore.

When a fine meal comes to an end,

it's always nice to savor a bit of dessert.

When a great story comes to an end,

we think you may want to linger.

And so, we offer ...

AfterWords—just a little something more after you

have finished a David C Cook novel.

We invite you to stay awhile in the story.

Thanks for reading!

Turn the page for ...

- **Letter to Readers**
- **Resources**
- **Acknowledgments**

LETTER TO READERS

Jezebel reigned in Israel for about sixty years, dying an old woman in her seventies or eighties. Incorrectly painted as a seductress, Jezebel relied most often on raw courage and intellect. However, her real legacy may be one of mass child sacrifice.

A *tophet* was discovered a few years ago in the ancient city of Carthage, a city that Jezebel's people founded. This tophet, which is a Hebrew term for "the place of burning," is believed to date back to the Phoenicians and contains the burned remains of more than twenty thousand infants.

Child sacrifice was not an uncommon practice among the ancients, but this evidence suggests that the Phoenicians engaged in these sacrifices in unprecedented numbers. Of course, no modern country wants to be associated with such a gruesome history. More than one government has ruled against any further excavations to see what else can be uncovered from Jezebel's days as Israel's most infamous queen.

Modern readers will likely not know much about her, although one piece of text exists that might hold a real surprise. In the scene when Jezebel is led into Samaria for the first time, a song is sung in her honor. You may know it better as Psalm 45. Scholars believe Psalm 45 may have been written as a wedding poem for Jezebel and Ahab. The words that faithful Christians use to worship our God may be the same words that were once sung to please Jezebel.

In another strange twist, Jezebel has become an unlikely folk hero to a new breed of feminists, who praise her ferocious strength in a time when men seemed to wield all the power. Although her seal was discovered in a dig in Israel—a ring bearing her name and ancient symbols—the secrets of her reign may forever lie buried.

Until we meet,

Ginger Garrett

RESOURCES

There were several volumes I relied on heavily and would recommend to your library:

Chronological and Background Charts of the Old Testament and The IVP Bible Background Commentary: Old Testament by John H. Walton.

I also liked the Holman Bible Atlas and the Holman Book of Biblical Charts, Maps, and Reconstructions.

Of course, many details were inspired by works published by the Biblical Archaeology Society's magazine, Biblical Archaeology Review. Seeing the objects and artifacts that link us to these stories gives shape to the times and makes the characters more accessible. Biblical texts have been taken or adapted from the New International Version and THE MESSAGE.

ACKNOWLEDGMENTS

I am so grateful to the many good people who have helped make this book a reality.

Writing is a delicate balance between following my vision and submitting to the wisdom of those around me. I am blessed to have such a strong and wise team.

First, to Mitch, for never letting me give up. Second to Nicci Hubert, a gifted and patient editor, who never let me give up either. Both can attest that this was an odd book to work on, plagued by strange events and setbacks. What normally would take me six months took almost two years. At times, I would just lay my head on my desk and wish to be anywhere else. I thank God for you both, Mitch and Nicci!

I also wish to thank the bookstore owners and sales staff who have helped readers discover my work. I appreciate your every effort.

I owe another debt to my readers, many of whom I've had the pleasure of meeting at signings or through my website, www.gingergarrett.com. Nothing has made me happier as a writer than to hear from my diverse base of readers. My favorite comment is always, "I liked your book so much I went back to read the Bible's version and see what really happened." You all get it.

I want to thank Terry Behimer for being so gracious despite the setbacks and my fumbles and foibles. And Marilyn Largent for introducing me to so many stores. And Ingrid Beck, for having every answer I possibly need. A huge debt is owed to Caitlyn Carlson, too, for her work as the finest copyeditor I've ever known.

A writer's work is done in seclusion and privacy, but I am never alone. Writing a novel is rarely easy, and I fight laziness, exhaustion, and distraction every day, but as the days go by I begin to see the beauty of a disciplined effort to follow Another's lead. My wishes are for each one of you who has had a hand in bringing this book to fruition. May your efforts be repaid in blessings ten times over.

EXCITING, DRAMATIC
THE STORY OF ESTHER
FROM GINGER GARRETT

The first in the LOST LOVES series—the story of a girl
unsparingly plunged into heartache and chaos, a girl who
would save a nation ... a girl who would be queen.

THREE WOMEN LOVED HIM.

TWO BETRAYED HIM. ONE FULFILLED HIS DESTINY.

Meet the biblical strong man Sampson through
the voices of three strong women who loved him—his mother,
his wife, and the famous Delilah.

a tale of darkness, deceit, and deliverance

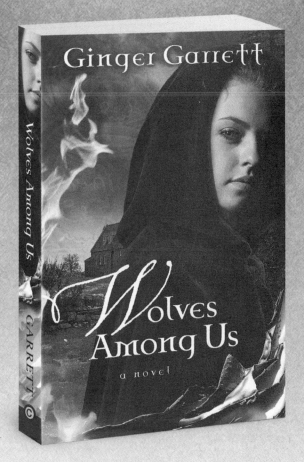

Sometimes a savior can bring destruction.
Sometimes a doubter can save a town.

David C Cook

transforming lives together